Innocent Escape

by

Toby Limbach

authorHOUSE®

AuthorHouse™ UK Ltd.
500 Avebury Boulevard
Central Milton Keynes, MK9 2BE
www.authorhouse.co.uk
Phone: 08001974150

First published by AuthorHouse   12/5/2007

ISBN: 978-1-4343-4554-7 (sc)

Printed in the United States of America
Bloomington, Indiana

This book is printed on acid-free paper.

Prologue: USSR 1986

Vladimir Beschak paused, exhausted and dripping with sweat, and adjusted his heavy pack. It was well past midnight and, having been unable to find suitable ground for a campsite, his survey of the lonesome Ukrainian mountain was slowly becoming more than he could handle. A stocky body and coal-black eyes were his downfall: comments about Inuit descent were probably the reason he was given the arduous Job.

"We need to get out of the wind," Karl growled from behind him.

Vladimir turned to find his companion, a dark-skinned man with burly shoulders silhouetted against the faint sheen of moonlight. His cartwheel-sized hands were clasped at the broken buckle on his belt, forfeiting the ability to whisk the long matted hair out of his eyes.

"We'll go down to the bottom," Vladimir shouted back, raising his voice to hear himself as the fierce breeze pounded back from the rocks in a high-pitched echo.

They stumbled down a small crag: the moss-strewn boulders resembling crude stairs to entice the traveller onwards. The ravine seemed almost peaceful in the dim light, and daylight would enshrine it as a blanketed jumble of rocks, the odd flower trying gallantly to reach the sun.

Vladimir caught himself on a branch and cursed. Too much food and years without exercise had weakened his lung capacity, despite the outward appearance of toughness. He felt for blood and wrapped a crude bandage around the wound to protect it.

He blamed the Russians for his misadventures. Having counted on hospitality near the power station he had left his heavy-duty gear behind. The Chernobyl security staff had blocked all access to the surrounding areas, leaving Vladimir and Karl stranded on the mountain without the hope of a helicopter ride back.

"Curse Russian funding," he bellowed.

Karl put a hand on his friend and pulled out some vodka. There was no sense in panic. Vladimir handed it back empty a mouthful later.

"Nearly there," Karl soothed, although he wasn't sure how far the bottom was.

Vladimir grumbled, too low for Karl to hear, and carried on along the mountain pass. Faint markings were now visible on the trail, and Vladimir's scientific mind automatically analysed them. An acute man, his mental capacities easily compensated for his physical age. He stopped suddenly, eyes curiously wide in unbelief.

"What is it now?" Karl asked hesitantly. Throughout the trip his friend had acted oddly at sporadic intervals, but something in the Russian's eyes told him this was different. He unholstered his pack and crouched down to where Vladimir was pointing, slowly rubbing his back. A print, etched in a rare patch of dried mud, compressed a single blade of grass. "A goat footprint," he said, unimpressed.

Vladimir shook his head, still in a state of shock. Almost with a sacrificial reverence, he bent down and eased the mud out of a tuft of grass, just off the main path. "An early bison print," he whispered. He was a book archaeologist in his spare time, and could estimate the weight of an elephant from a single footprint.

Karl glanced at him, not recognizing the significance.

"Bison have been extinct in Ukraine for a long time," Vladimir explained excitedly. "And this is one of the early types. See this fourth toe?" It was a stump compared to the other three, but still clearly defined. "They evolved and eventually lost this toe," Vladimir continued. "This print is millions of years old."

"How has it survived?" Karl asked enquiringly, furrowing his brow.

"Mystery," Vladimir admitted, but the excitement of the find overcame any doubts. "Let's follow the trail."

Karl muttered expletives under his breath, annoyed at the disruption. The last thing that he wanted to do was hunt for ancient relics, but Vladimir was adamant, and he grumblingly stayed on his knees.

Vladimir yelled again. "Tracks," he shouted. He scurried off into the bushes without waiting for Karl, the night's exhaustion suddenly forgotten in eager anticipation.

Vladimir searched furiously in the undergrowth, passing back stones and other evidence to Karl, who grudgingly took photographs and blinded himself with the flash.

The trail began to thicken, and soon Vladimir didn't even have to look properly before announcing it as a find. He wondered why no one else had found them before, but quickly realised how far off the beaten path they were. Mud was squelching uncomfortably underfoot, and the track often led them through, if not over, shrubbery and coarse vegetation.

Eventually the brief marshland stopped, invaded by a tall wall of trees that clung to the rock face and impressively dared the marshes to encroach. It could have been his imagination or the return of his eyes after the bright glare of camera flash, but Vladimir sensed he could see better here. A faint red glow, only just visible in the darkness, flowed from the branches.

Karl turned to look where his friend was pointing, not sure what to expect: only the pale glow being visible through the trees. Curiosity awakened despite the weariness, they set off towards the source, not daring to hope it was light from another camp.

Vladimir led the way through the jungle. The thicket cut off the rest of the moonlight and progress was slow, but the trunk wall was thin and easily navigable. The ground was hard and firmly held together by the roots, and relinquished the tiresome need to trounce further on the surrounding sopping marshland.

The reddish glow grew brighter as they neared, revealing a huge cliff that extended to the top levels of the mountain. The light seemed to emanate from a small crevasse, cut almost deliberately in the smooth expanse of sleek, hard, rock.

Karl barely disguised his relief as he realised it was a cave. "We can spend the night here," he announced, hurrying past Vladimir into the gap.

Vladimir followed, wanting to be cautious about the cave but knowing from experience nothing dangerous lurked in the sparse landscape. He shook off the uneasiness and entered to find Karl gazing at a pile of bones. The remains were easily identifiable as bison – the intact scapula above the spine made it straightforward – and lay undisturbed by the elements in the protection of the cave.

"Let's get a fire going," Karl ventured, seeing that the floor was dry.

Vladimir nodded. It would give welcome warmth and enable him to properly study the remains of the bison. He waved Karl out to collect firewood and turned back in awe to the skeleton in front of him.

Karl returned ten minutes later to a horrifying sight. Vladimir was lying on the floor, his black hair lying in a jagged halo around his head. Pockmarks and burns covered his scalp. Not recognising the fatal signs of radiation exposure, Vladimir hurriedly built up the fire, thinking his friend had fainted from the cold. He fumbled for the matches and snapped several before his stiff fingers managed to get a fire going. Blowing into the flames to speed up the reaction, a cloud of red particles swirled into the air and descended on the fire on a mass pilgrimage of death.

Karl never found out what had happened to Vladimir. They were both vaporised as the first particle wormed its way into a white flame. The mountain erupted in a toxic fireball, sending shockwaves throughout the surrounding area as it destroyed itself against the power of the mountain. The power station at Chernobyl caught the front of the blast and imploded, destroying its reactor shield and unleashing the power of the atom in a horrendous explosion.

The worst nuclear accident of the 20th Century would leave thousands dead in a wind of radioactive smoke.

Chapter 1

There was absolutely nothing wrong with the plan. It was perfectly formulated down to the last hidden detail. The men had spent hours scrounging through libraries in search of ways of how to disable the alarms, and then bought equipment from various stores around the country to avoid suspicion. One of them had even enrolled at university to get access to the wealth of knowledge that could be extracted from professors. The hitch, the one thing they hadn't planned on, the one thing they didn't expect, was half a mile distant, running at a steady pace towards them.

The target was a beautiful Georgian house, the lovingly restored brickwork that poked through a wall of twining creeper reflecting on the cars that dozed on the gravel. It was the place Dr Wright called home, a retreat away from the hustle and bustle that surrounded his position as a military research scientist.

The sun was shining as the four men approached the hedge circling the grounds. A figure was spotted crossing one of the fields that made up the Essex countryside, but they ignored him. The churned rows of soil that stretched to the horizon proved to be a mixed blessing; there was no cover, but it also meant that no one would be around to see them.

One of the men studied the guy leaping across ditches, and shook his head in disgust. "Go ahead lads," he said. "It's a kid."

The kid paused one field away from the house and made his way back to the road. He loved summer. The warmth flowed through his body and he soaked up the sun. The smell of grass and trees filled his nostrils and he inhaled, breathing in the soft fragrances that he had grown up in.

Humming happily to himself, he continued his way along the road, occasionally wiping a bead of sweat from his neck as it threatened to invade the cooler space beneath his shirt. He was wearing shorts and running shoes as well as the loose top, keeping a measure of temperature in his body.

The boy passed the gates of the long sweeping driveway and sat down on the bank, looking over the fields. His breathing slowed, and he turned his attention to a sharp noise behind him. Spinning, he peered through a gap in the hedge, searching for the maker, but found only silence. He was about to give up and turn away when he caught a flash of silver coming from an upstairs window. Focusing on the new target, the boy strained to discern features on the shadow his eyes found, but the glare and reflection of the sun was too bright.

A crunch told him he was not alone. He swivelled and found a man, not much older than himself, frozen in mid-step, silently cursing the small stones that gave away his position.

The boy looked uncertainly at the axe the man clenched, startled. The blade gleamed in the light, and by the tense look on the holder's face it was obvious he wasn't felling trees. The quiet movement in the house flickered back across the boy's mind, and he suddenly realised he'd walked into the middle of a robbery.

The man flew at the boy; surprise was no longer an issue. The axe was raised menacingly above his head, and a banshee like wail pierced the silence.

The boy threw himself sideways and then scrambled to his feet as the axe glanced off his arm, the resonance still sounding minutes later after the swing missed his ear by inches.

Blood splattered onto his shirt and trickled to the floor: a visual explanation of the pain that shot up his arm. He gasped, although the shock of being attacked kept him from crying out. His mind went into overdrive and he was overcome by fear. Someone had tried to kill him. Why? Who was this man and why had he tried to stick an axe in his brain? What were they trying to steal that was worth his death?

He looked from his arm to the man sprawled on the floor, his foot having caught him as he had leapt sideways to avoid the axe. A feeling of cold anger steadily began to replace his fear, and he kicked out at his attacker, watching with a slight satisfaction as the man tumbled sideways away from the axe.

The thug tried to reverse his roll and reach out for the weapon, but feet suddenly blocked his way. A hard elbow thud in his back told him resistance was useless, and he sagged limply to the grass.

The boy stopped. He was breathing hard. He'd never attacked anyone in his life. The odd punch had been thrown, but never a serious fight. The past moments overwhelmed him, but surprisingly his mind was clear. He picked up the axe and snapped the end off, holding the stick.

"Who are you?" he said harshly.

The man turned and looked up at the long hard handle of the axe held in the muscular arms of a teenager, no longer the kid he had dismissed earlier. The face was strong and silent, framed by wavy strands of dark-blonde hair, and intelligent eyes flickered briefly as they recovered from the shock. "You'd better run," he spat viciously. "The others are inside. They'll come out in a minute."

The boy dropped one hand and brought the axe handle swinging down, stopping centimetres from the mans neck. Now he could see his opponent properly he knew he was in control: his strength and wit being far superior.

The man flinched, and the teenager knew his adversary wasn't accustomed to being on the losing side. Probably a bully with no social life and hard on drugs, the teen thought. "How old are you?"

"Twenty," the man replied with the look of loathing. "You?"

"Sixteen," the teen said calmly, "The names Hayden. Why were you trying to kill me?" He spoke as if he were ordering an ice cream, retreating just out of the mans reach.

"Because you're scum."

Hayden looked at him with distaste. "Why are you here?"

"Are you deaf man?" he asked mockingly. "My friends will come out in a minute, and then you won't have a chance."

"Whatever," Hayden said indifferently. "If they fight anything like you, I'd be more worried if they aim for the hedge."

The mans face contorted with hate, and he began to rise when a voice rang out from the driveway.

"Adam," the voice yelled.

Hayden peered through the hedge at the three men, two of whom were holding massive suitcases and grinning like dogs. The third man was dressed in dark trousers and a blue shirt, and stood with two more suitcases by his side. A handful of notes were clenched in his fist and a look of dark triumph was etched on his face.

"Thieves," Hayden muttered.

The man behind him got to his feet and sprinted round the corner.

Hayden turned and leapt down the bank, but gave the man up as he realised the gates to the house were over 200 meters away. Instead, he lightly tossed the axe handle over the five-foot hedge and jumped up to an overhanging tree that hung a few feet above. He caught it on his third attempt and hauled his legs up; thankful for the times he had suspended himself up-side down in his local village park. Quietly and efficiently Hayden swivelled on the branch and crawled over the unseen air boundary that separated the road from private land. He knew he shouldn't be doing this; getting involved would be dangerous and probably stupid. He had no idea what he was getting himself into, having never fought before. He assumed he'd have to fight. The whole idea was incredulous. He would have called the police, but he didn't have his phone.

But then again, if he didn't, who would? There was no one in miles, and the way the men were acting, they knew it. There was no way out.

He realised he was breathing hard and stopped, taking deep breaths to calm himself down. A quick glance towards the house gave him the confidence he needed. Suddenly incensed, he dropped down.

There were two hedges surrounding Dr Wright's sanctuary. The outer hedge of the compound was primarily for keeping people out, and beauty took an undignified second place. The spiralling mass of branches and hidden thorns did not create a nice garden, but were blocked from view by another line of more aesthetic defence. Hayden landed in between the two, slightly catching his foot on a root.

Looking around for the axe handle, he manoeuvred along behind the inner hedge, a soft-leaved fir, and reached the outside wall of the house. Hayden was now behind the criminals, and he took full advantage of it. Hayden reached up and plucked an apple, still small and unripe, but that made it easier to throw. Edging carefully out onto the path that followed the strict contour of the house, he ducked down beside one of the unharmed vehicles: a dirt covered quad bike. It wasn't as high as he'd like, but it was close enough.

Hayden snatched a glimpse through the handlebars, and then, satisfied the two men were facing away from him looking around, raised his head and sent the apple flying through the air.

The apple missed the nearest man, a burly fat man with ripped clothes, but just as Hayden began to feel disappointed, the man's bald comrade moved into the line of fire, feeling the fruit cannon into his head.

The man jumped back and threw his hands up to his face while his friend spun around, a look of surprise on his face. He blinked before grabbing the stick he had dropped, and stared at the apple on the floor.

"Ah, there's Adam" the lead man said, oblivious to the confusion behind him.

"Jay, that guy stole the axe," Adam gasped, having just sprinted all the way up the drive.

An apple sailed over their heads, striking with a clunk on a bonnet.

Hayden stepped out from behind his quad bike and fixed the men with a deathly stare. Three more apples flew through the air, two striking their targets, before Hayden stooped, grasped the axe, which he had found to have 'Greta' emblazoned on the side, and planted his feet one behind the other.

The four men, Adam, Jay, and Shaven Haven and McDonalds: names conveniently invented by an adrenaline rushed Hayden, looked at each other before an understanding came between them, and started towards him.

"Now you've had it," cackled Adam.

Hayden grinned mischievously, but remained silent. There was a dark seriousness smouldering in his eyes, and he carefully sized up his opponents.

Shaven Haven rounded the car and approached, still furious about the apple. Hayden blinked, not fully realising that this was life or death. Panic began to creep into his mind, but he brushed it aside. Just smack him, he thought.

Raising Greta, he deflected the knife Shaven Haven had produced and brought the axe handle round, using the other end in a swift stabbing motion. Not pausing for thought, Hayden quickly delivered a solid blow to the head, feeling the thud vibrate up his arms. The man tumbled backwards, landing with a sickening crunch on the gravel.

McDonalds gazed coldly at Shaven Haven lying motionless on the ground, and threw his own knife.

It missed, but Hayden knew the man wasn't bothered. McDonalds was coming at him with his hands. Two big fists reached out in front of his body, making it impossible to connect Greta with the massive hulk. Every time Hayden moved McDonalds moved with him, blocking off the exits, forcing him into a corner. Greta simply bounced off the muscles.

He felt his back hit the wall, and knew he was running out of options. Desperation filled his brain, and he lashed out before turning to leap onto the trellis, feeling rather than hearing the crack which wrenched Greta from his grasp.

McDonalds looked down at his hands, seeing blood seep out from between the knuckles, and hesitated. Hayden twisted out of his range and jumped onto the wall, climbing blindly. His fingers scraped the concrete as he wrapped them round the creeper, hurriedly sticking his hands forward to grab anything and pull himself up. He crossed over a window before the roots gave way, and he tumbled awkwardly to the ground.

"Come on then," Hayden yelled. He picked Greta up and whacked McDonalds in the back, sending him to the floor.

Jay simply smiled, pulling a gun from his back pocket. Hayden froze, but then eased slightly as Jay threw the weapon to Adam. "If he wins, shoot him," he ordered, picking up a wrench from the floor.

Adam grinned softly.

Jay advanced slowly on his nemesis, balancing the heavy wrench in his hand.

"Don't toy with your prey," Hayden rebuked in a mutter. He swung Greta around his head and jabbed forward, intent on making the first strike. The shaft narrowly missed Jay's thigh, but it got his attention. That's better, Hayden thought. It had turned into a game of skill.

Jay focused on the axe handle, eying the sharp spikes where the blade had been snapped off.

Hayden grinned slowly and drew Greta out to the side, allowing Jay time to think.

He turned his gaze to Hayden, locking eyes. Hayden smiled back, knowing Jay had made up his mind. He would have used that tactic himself, looking the opponent in the eye to disarm him while preparing to strike. He lowered his left leg slightly, transferring body weight.

Jay pounced, bringing the wrench to his left and watched as Greta snapped cleanly in two. Elation rose throughout his body, but he barely had time to notice before a sharp blow landed on his chest.

Hayden launched a foot into Jay's stomach, knocking him breathless. He'd enticed him into attacking Greta, leaving Jay's body wide open. He followed up with two thrusts in the chest and watched as he fell to the floor.

Chapter 2

Adam gulped in disbelief as Jay crashed to the ground, but before he could raise the gun a fifth man appeared from the garden. He was carrying a shotgun under one arm and a sword under the other.

Hayden's face turned grave as victory slipped from his grasp. He'd gambled and lost, and the consequences were grim. He glanced down at his bloodstained shirt and raised his hands, wincing as the cut on his arm contracted. He caught sight of Adam in the window reflection and was surprised to see him scared, the gun abandoned on the floor. He turned back to the shotgun with renewed interest, noticing the man's gaunt face and thinning white hair. The crinkles lining his face reminded Hayden of an avocado, a Mexican fruit that had never enlightened his taste buds.

Avocado surveyed the driveway, gripping the shotgun. There were now five men instead of the three that had locked him in the basement. Three were injured, and two of those were on the floor.

Hayden spoke up. "Sir, who are you?"

"What do you mean who am I?" Avocado replied harshly. "I live here."

There was nothing Hayden could say, so he muttered, "sorry to disturb you sir."

"What do you mean sorry," the old man queried in almost a scream. "You break into my house, vandalise up my car and then act as if nothing happened."

"I didn't," Hayden began, but Avocado cut across him.

"That's right, blame it on the others," he sneered derisively, his eyes nearly popping out of his face. "You can tell the police when they get here."

"Fine," Hayden retorted. "Have it your way. Check the cameras, and you'll find that if I hadn't been here, these men would have gone, and you'd probably be dead."

The man stared obsessively back. "I'll have you know," he screeched. "That if you'd spoken to me like that back in my day, you'd have been whipped." He ended with a small flourish of the sword, quite adamant that that was the way it was to be, and no other.

Hayden could see that the man was mad and clearly out of his mind, but the gun made him uneasy. It was impossible to fight against. There was too much distance between them. "The police might be a while," he ventured. "Do you mind if I sit down?"

The old man pondered this for a moment, and then said, "oh yes please do," as if his outburst a minute before had been forgotten.

"What are you going to do if those men wake up," Hayden asked, gesturing. He knew McDonalds was unable to fight, broken knuckles attested to that, but Jay and Shaven Haven could come round at any time.

Avocado chose not to answer this. Instead, he turned his wrinkled head towards the road where Dr Wright had just walked in, back from the nearby village.

Dr Wright stopped, his eyes widening at the scene, and then pulled a miniature pistol out of his pocket and picked up the wrench. He was a small man, dressed comfortably in shorts and a straw hat with wisps of brown hair poking out from under the rim. His face was tight and drawn, and dark circles under the eyes showed signs of stress. Hayden's first impression was that of a man out of his depth in a country house: the modern features of a London flat would have clothed his personality better. The aura of power that seemed to demand attention would have blended perfectly with many high-powered lawyers and politicians, and the country appeared to make his movements look awkward and confined.

"Dr Wright," said Hayden tentatively. He knew the man was connected in some way to the military and possessed political clout. The article in yesterday's newspaper had declared him responsible for the increase in army budgets, and Hayden didn't want to mess with him, especially when he found himself staring down the business end of a gun.

"What?" Dr Wright snapped. The destruction of his cars angered him, and his face turned the colour of beetroot.

"There's been a mistake."

"You mean you got the wrong house?" Dr Wright growled. "Who are you and what are you doing here?"

"My name is Hayden," he replied defensively. "I'm staying at the hotel with my friend. He's involved with an army exercise, so I went out for a walk. I just passed the house when this guy," indicating Adam as he spoke, "came at me with an axe."

Dr Wright looked at Adam and noticed the bruises and limp way he held himself, and then faced the two men playing dead on the gravel. "And then?" he asked, now intrigued.

"I saw these other guys smashing up the cars, so I jumped over the hedge and asked them what they were doing. They came at me with knives so I, well." Hayden stopped, suddenly unsure.

"How, may I ask, did you 'jump' over the hedge?" Dr Wright said scornfully, gesturing at the impassable wall of vegetation. It was a tactic the army used: laughing at their story to see their reaction.

"I climbed the tree," Hayden explained, not buckling.

"You may want to know that we have cameras covering the drive," he said briskly, becoming business-like.

Hayden noticed the man cagily keeping his eye fixed on him while pretending to examine Shaven Haven.

He glared back. "Check them."

"Oh, I will," Dr Wright assured him. "But I don't trust you. You may have done as you said, but then again you may not. Consider yourself guilty until proven innocent."

"Thought it was the other way round," Hayden muttered.

"I don't take chances."

"I see."

Dr Wright paused. The boy clearly wasn't the type to be involved in a robbery, and the offhand attitude unsettled him slightly. "Tell you what," he said. "I can't do it myself if you are with this lot, because I'll be a sitting duck, but you can." He grinned and threw Hayden a piece of rope. "Tie them up, and Harris will get the tapes."

Hayden obliged, firmly securing Jay's hands and feet before laying him against a statue and wrapping the remaining rope around him, preventing any escape. He did the same for Shaven Haven, but only bothered with the legs of McDonalds – his hands were inoperable and he wasn't going anywhere.

Dr Wright examined the work carefully while keeping the gun solidly staring into Adam's forehead. "I'm impressed," he said. The lines were tightly wound and triple tied at the ends. He could see no slack from where he was standing. Harris appeared, this time with a walking stick, and confirmed Hayden's status as responsible for the capture.

"Well I suppose I ought to thank you," Dr Wright said, apologizing for his earlier ferocious manner. "Why don't you come in and have a drink?"

Hayden looked at his cut and felt the perspiration sticking to his face. "Thank you," he said weakly. "I'd be glad of some patching up."

Harris led the way inside, instantly blending in with the upmarket décor if not for the dust marks on his jacket. A cold marble floor covered the entrance with statues that matched the stately home for charm. Hayden could see that this home was immaculately preserved, with magnificent detail on the chandelier that hung easily from the painted ceiling. French doors opposite led the way to a wide lawn with barely any shrubs, which surprised him, as flowers were often the main attraction for country mansions. The grass was in need of a cut, and he got the impression that Wright cared more for his cars than the flowerbeds.

Wright paused, his brown eyes warmly echoing the dark wood, and murmured waspishly at the scratch marks on the floor. Hayden followed through a small door set almost invisibly in the wall, taking in the modern furnishings that replaced the 18th Century grandeur. Metal, leather and glass replaced wood, although he noted that the windows were unchanged and still single-paned.

"I want to thank you for what you did," Wright said serenely, settling himself on the sofa. "As you might know, I work with the military and understand the value of bravery."

"It was my own skin I was saving at first," Hayden said, still standing up while a man more medically minded than Harris bandaged his wound.

"Nevertheless, thank you. Now, you may also have noticed that I'm rather rich," Wright carried on bluntly. "So if there is anything I can do in return…" He trailed off, leaving Hayden to lead his mind on.

Hayden contemplated, but knew there was nothing he really wanted. "I'm fine."

"No really," Dr Wright insisted seriously. "Extremely valuable family heirlooms from my past generations were nearly lost today, and I would consider it an honour to reward you."

Hayden paused, but decided not to question. "I could do with a new bike," he said lamely.

"Consider it done," Dr Wright smiled. "In fact, my brother runs a fitness resort off the coast of Italy. He's just modernized the place and it's got just about everything, including a massive cycling section. How about a month there? You and your friend can both stay and test drive some bikes, then take your pick. Am I right in thinking that he finishes with the army this afternoon? If he's accepted, he'll start in August, so you'll have enough time."

"Sure." Hayden couldn't quite believe or understand it. He'd come out for a walk and found himself with a ticket to Italian sunshine and an exotic resort.

"Excellent," declared Dr Wright. He turned to Harris. "Book the next flight to Sicily for two," he ordered. "Pick them up at the airport," he told Hayden after Harris produced a slip of paper with the details on. "I'll book the tickets under the name of *Swaron Anthris*."

"Thank you very much," Hayden replied, stuttering somewhat.

Dr Wright smiled. "Now then, about that drink I offered you. Harris, could you rustle up some snacks, and ask Lucio to come in?"

Harris clicked his heels. "I'll go and look for him sir."

"He could still be locked up somewhere," Wright explained angrily, still testy about the robbery.

Hayden nodded and turned his attention to a crunch of gravel that floated in through the open window. Two military jeeps were turning round on the drive, while a company of marines herded the suitcases into the back.

Harris returned before Hayden could enquire. "I can't find Lucio sir, and he seems to have cleared out his locker."

Dr Wright looked baffled. He turned to Hayden. "I'll have to owe you that drink. I'm afraid I'm missing a member of staff."

Hayden took the hint. "I'd better be getting back," he said. The old man seemed pleasant enough, but there was something about him that didn't quite add up. Army security for family heirlooms? And then there was the missing security man. He was glad to be out of the house, running swiftly back across the fields, and decided to find out all he could about Dr Wright. He was so focused on the elusive answers that he didn't notice a motorbike roar down the lane, its overweight rider talking furiously into a mobile phone.

After Hayden had gone, Dr Wright sat back in his chair and swivelled cognac around his glass. There was something strange about that boy. It was something he couldn't place, not even a man with his experience. He half suspected that Hayden had not let on his whole character, and found the attitude disconcerting. He could fight, and fight well. The video cameras had caught him in full view. Dr Wright couldn't believe the boy had never fought before; he understood the rules more than most recruits in the army.

He looked placidly at the suitcases being piled into the jeeps, an idea coming into his head. He picked up his phone and dialled a number.

"We've found another diversion," he said, when the call had been connected. "Get some copied suitcase covers to the airport by Tuesday. The codeword is *Swaron Anthris*."

Chapter 3

Hayden lay sprawled on a chair inside the crowded lobby of the Swallow Hotel. Several frantic holiday-makers kept surrounding him as they tried to organise their departure: made all the more difficult by their mischievous offspring, who seemed intent on disappearing. Hayden watched with a bemused interest, and couldn't help but chuckle when an unsuspecting waitress tripped over a pile of bags.

He wandered over and offered the woman his arm, staring down into soft violet eyes, delicately framed. They showed signs of embarrassment, and Hayden could see stress hiding what would otherwise have been a very attractive woman. "Watch your step," Hayden said lightly. Then he manoeuvred his own way past the jumble of luggage and vanished up the stairs to his room.

"She's a bit old for you," Joey said, his face lined with mirth as he stepped out behind Hayden on the second floor.

Hayden stopped, annoyed, and turned to face his friend. "Where did you come from?" he spluttered, bewildered. There was nowhere to hide on the stairs; they had found that out the previous night when executing a raid on some university junkies.

Joey arched his thick shoulders in a shrug, and grinned mischievously. "I'm just lucky," he said.

Hayden ignored the jibe. Joey had managed to escape from the pillow fight after the university team began to fight back, and left him cornered on the stairs. He could still feel the bruises. "How did you get in?" he asked. He had been watching the lobby carefully.

"Drainpipe," Joey said indifferently.

Hayden rolled his eyes. "Trust you to break in while the front door's open."

"You need to know the escape routes," Joey replied knowledgably. "The army do it all the time."

"What exactly is it that you do there?" Hayden asked curiously.

"Training regimes," Joey answered. "Most are dull fitness tasks, but we get to shoot each other at the end."

Hayden raised his eyebrows. "I'm assuming that's in a simulator."

Joey shook his head. "We use light beams and trounce around a field."

"Let me guess, you won?"

Joey grinned. Hayden was referring to the times they had gone bird shooting, and he was well practised in hitting small targets. "Nearly."

Hayden opened the door to their room and flopped onto the springy bed. "What do you know about Dr Wright?" he said casually.

Joey looked puzzled.

"Small man, military scientist," Hayden probed.

"Lives near here?"

Hayden nodded.

"He's a genius in military circles," Joey said, suddenly enlightened. "I don't know much about him, but he's heavily influential. Why?"

"We had a little confrontation this morning," Hayden replied, crossing over to the window and gazing upon the small garden that lay below. A stagnant pond lay by the edge of a few tufts of grass, and the earth looked hard and rough. "He was robbed."

"Not by you, I hope," Joey joked.

"Never, but I caught the slime that did." Hayden recounted the tale, including his suspicions about Dr Wright.

Joey looked stunned. "You mean that two military jeeps came and carted the suitcases off afterwards?"

Hayden nodded.

"Well that makes it easy," Joey said, lounging on the windowsill. "The army won't take custody of personal heirlooms. He's lying."

"But what for? A cover up?"

"No idea," Joey replied. "Seems to be, but I doubt it's worth finding out about." He stared up at the wallpapered ceiling, digesting the conversation. "How are things with Alice?"

Hayden closed his eyes and pretended not to hear. He had ended their relationship ages ago, and she had lately taken to stalking him.

Joey threw a cushion at him.

Hayden flexed and yawned. "She got lost," he muttered, giving in. "Literally."

"What did you do?" Joey asked, suddenly interested.

Hayden let a small grin crawl across his face. "She spotted me shopping in Norwich and tailed me for an hour, so I went out towards Cringleford and jumped off the bridge over the A47."

Joey raised his eyebrows. The A47 was a notoriously busy road, the closest thing Norfolk had to a motorway.

"I grazed my arm on the barrier," Hayden added, "but I landed safe between the barriers down the middle of the road."

"You actually jumped onto the A47?" Joey couldn't believe it. His friend was more likely to slap the girl than attempt a possible suicide jump to get away. The drop was over 20 feet.

Hayden shifted uncomfortably, but couldn't help grinning. "It wasn't exactly a jump," he admitted. "There's a lamppost just over a meter away from the side of the bridge so I used it as a fireman's pole."

Joey burst out laughing. "Typical," he said. "I would have loved to see her face when you dropped over the side of the bridge."

"She was furious," Hayden said brightly. "I don't think she knew that I'd seen her, so I just walked to the side and hopped over."

"Where did you go then?"

"I sat on the barrier and conned the first driver I saw into thinking I had a broken leg. He took me back into Norwich."

Joey shook his head in amazement. "Unbelievable," he muttered.

"That's not as bad as when you pelted eggs at that gang of bikers last year," Hayden retorted. It had been Halloween, and Joey's neighbourhood was known for trouble-makers. Joey had gone out, watched them shake up cans of spray paint outside the school, and caused such a commotion with a set of fireworks that the police turned up in riot gear.

"One of them nearly got me," Joey chuckled. He peered at his forearm. "I can still feel the scratches from when I jumped through that bramble hedge."

"Lucky for you they had an aversion to being spiked," Hayden teased.

"I'd have trussed him up so bad his own mother wouldn't have recognised him from a turkey," Joey scoffed.

Hayden smiled. "Shall we go down for tea?" he asked pleasantly.

Joey slapped his stomach and heaved himself out of the chair. "Ready when you are."

The hotel restaurant was small but cosy: a brisk log fire prevented the evening heat from fading as a slight breeze chilled the air. Candles and shaded lamps surrounded the dozen tables, creating a warm glow with pale shadows dancing across the cream walls. Heavy red curtains defended the room, and a birch counter with polished metal posed as the serving hatch.

Hayden walked over to the most secluded table next to a window, and sat down. Almost immediately a waitress appeared with a menu.

"Thank you," Hayden said, flashing a wide smile as he recognised the woman as the one he had helped earlier.

Joey rolled his eyes at his napkin, and picked out roast lamb from the options. "The port wine sauce sounds good," he said, sneaking a glance at his friend, who was underage.

Hayden pulled a face. "Are you sure you're not feeling tipsy?" he enquired, peering in mock-drunkenness across the table.

"Just so long as you don't need a bib," Joey retorted.

The waitress watched the contest with rapt fascination. She stared blankly as Hayden's face conformed into a grin and calmly ordered a steak with mushrooms. Despite the outward charades, Hayden and Joey had been strong friends since childhood.

The waitress gathered her composure and disappeared into the kitchen.

"So what do you make of this holiday Dr Wright proposed?" Joey asked, staring past the dull car park onto wide grasslands.

Hayden shrugged. "He seemed incredibly relieved that I'd been there. I presume it's some kind of reward to make him seem more natural; make him feel better about what had happened.

"It'd stop us asking questions as well," Joey added. "Attempted armed robbery would tempt people to go to the press."

"He can definitely keep an eye on us in Italy," Hayden said, deep in thought. "It didn't seem important, but Wrights brother owns the resort."

Joey raised his eyebrows. "Interesting," he mused. "We'll have to keep an eye out while we're there."

"Do you have enough holiday time?"

"Sure, we finish a week before."

They were interrupted by the food: large, steaming plates of homemade delicacy complemented with dry cranberry-flavoured water. Joey stared impressively at his giant-sized lamb before tucking in with large mouthfuls.

Hayden suppressed a smile at Joeys eating habits and winked at the waitress before picking up his own fork.

After the food had been digested with a quick swirl of wine – Joey's order, Hayden walked out to the back of the hotel and glanced appreciatively at the silhouetted landscape. The sun was sending its last rays over the horizon as it awoke a new dawn to the other side of the world. Hayden pulled out his phone and dialled a number.

"Hello."

"Good evening," Hayden replied pleasantly.

There was a pause. "How did you get this number," Dr Wright asked, curious yet slightly irritated at the teenager.

"Lucky guess," Hayden said easily, not giving an inch. He'd rung his mobile from Wright's phone and saved the number on his handset. "I was just speculating what your security man looked like."

Dr Wright ignored the question with well practiced charm. "Don't start getting paranoid," he said smoothly. "The heirlooms are under military protection and we found Lucio trapped behind the basement cupboard."

Hayden lowered his own voice to a serious undertone. "Then he isn't 176cm tall, 84 kilograms, with light grey hair and slight red patches below both eyes?"

"I stand corrected," Wright replied indifferently. "What's it to you?"

"I've seen him four times since I left your house, and the posse normally surrounding a biker on holiday is missing from his armament."

"Where is he now?" Wright demanded. There was a slight strain in his voice, and Hayden detected a not of urgency.

"He isn't staying at our hotel, so I don't know."

Dr Wright cursed.

"Anything wrong?" Hayden asked.

"Nothing much," Wright expressed irritably, though it was clear he was lying.

"I've been thinking about the resort in Italy," Hayden pressed. "And I was wondering whether we could move the timetable up. The weather is better this time of year."

"That should be fine," Wright replied, still thinking about Lucio. "My brother is never fully booked. Not that it reflects on the resort," he laughed. "But it's a large island and only the rich can afford it."

"Sounds good."

"How does tomorrow sound? Ten o'clock flight?"

"Great, we'll be at the airport for eight."

Hayden hung up and puffed a long, slow breath into the sky. The heirlooms are under military protection. He thought back to what Joey had said. The military would never do that, and with Wright's security man potentially following them, it was clear that things weren't as straight as they seemed. Maybe it was time to get out. Hayden rang home to inform his parents where they were going, and then walked slowly back up to his room to pack.

Chapter 4

The airport was packed, and Hayden and Joey manoeuvred carefully round the laden trolleys that stood motionless in the entrance. There had been some sort of security scare, the taxi driver had said.

They checked in with a middle-aged man, his hair turning slightly grey at the temples. The password was given, and the man paused at his screen. "Please wait a moment," he said, and disappeared through a door. He returned with two metal suitcases under each arm. "Please can you put your cases into these," he panted, pushing the metal boxes over the counter.

Hayden and Joey exchanged glances, but did as requested.

"Dr Wright asked if you could use them," the man explained, snapping shut the complicated locking system. "Boarding is from gate 4. Have a nice flight."

"If someone does that to me again," Joey muttered as a man pushed roughly past. They both immediately checked their pockets. Satisfied they hadn't been pickpocketed; the pair passed the metal detector and walked up the long gangway to the plane. Someone had already been to their seats to lay out the packet of nuts that Hayden found amusing.

They were the last pair to board, and they had barely taken their seats when the plane began moving, taxiing to the start of the stretched runway. A paused moment obtaining clearance from the control tower and they were off, hurtling along the ground before lifting gently into air.

Casually watching the airport shrink into miniature as they rose higher, the teenagers discussed the unusual events that had dominated their holidays. Joey had been accepted into the army, and now held an official rank. Hayden preferred to take his talents into the academic world. It was a matter of choice: both being able to fill the others shoes if the roles reversed. They had been together since primary school, and although Joey was two years older, remained friends throughout high school and played in the same band.

Their conversation had just turned to army training regimes when the overhead speaker burst into life.

"All attendants report to cabin 1. Urgent."

Hayden and Joey exchanged looks. "Let's go see what it is," Hayden said cheekily. He got to his feet and entered the cubicle nearest the huddle of flight attendants.

The chief steward was a tall, dark-haired man, hiding smoothly contoured muscles beneath his immaculate uniform. "Heathrow just radioed," he said. The sound of the in-flight entertainment covered his voice, but the words travelled easily to the half open door of Hayden's cubicle. "A security guard was found dead ten minutes ago. There's a big uproar over there, and there'll be an extra check when we get to Sicily."

Hayden flushed the toilet and stepped out, pretending to be extremely interested in his hand as the steward glanced suspiciously in his direction. He walked quickly back to his seat and sat down.

"What was it?" Joey whispered.

"A security guard has been killed," Hayden whispered back. "The Brits are going nuts. There'll be extra checks at the airport."

"I don't envy the men trying to catch the guy that did it," Joey said. "Heathrow security is good. The man's either crazy, or he knows exactly what he's doing."

The intercom chimes interrupted him. "We have turbulence ahead, please return to your seats and strap yourself in." The pilot's voice was deep but cheerful, and

Hayden pictured him as a jolly man with a thick curly mop of brown hair.

The man behind him stood up and reached for his bag. The nearby flight attendant, a smiling Italian woman, asked him to take his seat, but he pushed her aside. She stumbled and fell into a young boy in the seat next to the aisle.

The man ignored them and strode towards the front of the plane. The next officer blocked his way, but soon retreated after a gun was thrust in his throat. Gasps rose throughout the plane. A moment later the attendant was on the floor with a bullet in his hip, while the man pulled open the door and entered the cockpit.

A thousand questions flew through Hayden's head. He recognised the man as the one who had pushed past them at the airport, but how did he get a gun through customs?

Joey answered the problem. "The gun is a Heckler and Koch mp5," he whispered. He must have killed the security guard and nicked it off him once he was past the metal detector."

Hayden marvelled at his friend's powers of observation, but then again he was in the army, and he noticed guns. "What's he going to do?" he murmured. The question felt stupid, as if it came from a two year old. Terrorists were in the news, but to actually be involved with a hijack. It was beyond acceptation, to be on a plane faced by a man with a gun. It seemed surreal, and he had to pinch himself to make sure he was still there.

He was, and as the plane began to veer sideways, he knew he and everyone else were in real danger. "Come on," he muttered.

Joey jumped across to the other aisle, excusing himself to the passengers, and took a quick stock of the planes occupants. He read honest fear on all but one face, and he quickly approached the sleeping man.

He tapped him on the shoulder and waited for a response. It didn't come, so Joey tapped harder. Still no answer. Joey was sure that no one would have slept through the screams of the hijack, and suspicion grew in his mind. No man works alone. He grabbed the man's bag and emptied it.

A fist landed in his stomach as the owner miraculously woke. Joey grunted and grabbed the man's hair.

Hayden flew across the aisle, knocking a cup of water over a frightened toddler, and grappled with the hijacker's hands. He threw himself into a seat behind the fight, wrapping his arms round the neck in a headlock. The man went limp, and Hayden eased the pressure slightly.

Joey kicked through the contents of the bag that were lying on the floor, finding a second gun. He ejected the bullets and span it round his finger. "Is anyone any good at knots?" he asked quickly.

A slightly-built pensioner came forward, obviously a fisherman even without a rod, and trussed the suspect up with seatbelts.

"The cabin," Hayden said quietly, secure in the fisherman's skill.

Joey nodded seriously, keeping the empty gun and running towards the front of the plane.

They reached the door, almost daring it to open. Hayden pulled the handle, but it was locked. "We'll have to force it," he said.

Joey bent down and peered through the keyhole: a shape was visible, presumably the man with the gun. He hesitated, but Hayden nodded, and they attacked the door with a well-practised shoulder charge.

The hijacker spun round, gun ready, but he was too late. The door crashed into him, crushing him against a bulkhead.

The gun went off, punching a hole in Hayden's trousers but miraculously missing the skin, and the blast reverberated throughout the screaming plane.

Joey swung sideways and delivered a crashing blow to the skull, feeling the man cease the struggle as he pushed him against the cabin wall. Hayden retrieved the gun and searched him, finding nothing except a bag of syringes.

The pilot turned round at the bang, unaware of the disturbance because of his headphones, and stared at two teenage kids, the unknown hijacker between them, both casually leaning against a broken door.

"What the…" he began, but fell silent.

Age was against them. It might have been different if they were grown men, but at 16 and 18 they weren't taken too seriously. Joey was six foot three compared to Hayden's six; yet their faces discerned them as younger than they were. The pilot was more shocked than anything, but he managed a grin and said in his customer announcement voice, "boy are you guys in time."

"How far have we gone off course?" asked Hayden.

"About forty miles. The French went crazy when we started going east. Nearly sent fighter bombers after us." He pointed to the still flashing radio. "Who are you guys anyway?"

"Just tourists," Hayden smiled. "We decided we'd rather see Italy before we died."

The pilot laughed. "Good job too."

Joey and Hayden left the clearing up back to the airline company, and returned to their seats.

"Famous at last," Joey smiled, amid the choruses of clapping that accompanied them, but Hayden was more weary. Two attempts on his life in three days made him feel uneasy. He relayed this back to Joey, but his friend airily brushed it off. "With Dr Wright you were just in the wrong place at the wrong time," he reasoned.

Hayden knew he was probably right, but couldn't shake off the feeling that someone was watching him. Eventually, he took out one of the syringes he had secreted past the attendants. He didn't have a clue what was in it, but the pale yellow liquid didn't look like an ordinary shot of growth hormone.

The rest of the journey was uneventful: Joey slept through the clouds whilst Hayden's thoughts turned to what Dr Wright's brother was like. He had been told that the island resort was superb, although that could have been a spot of advertising on behalf of his relative. Either way, he was looking forward to a peaceful holiday.

The pilot's voice was again released into the plane, notifying the passengers that they were beginning to descend. The unknown man had woken up, finding himself locked to a chair by a pair of handcuffs, generously lent by an excited ex-policeman, who had thought it was a much better idea than giving them to his Italian nephew as a present.

Hayden knew there were going to be questions asked at the airport, but he didn't want them. Let someone else take the limelight, he thought. He imagined lots of boys would have dreamt about saving an aeroplane from terrorists, as the newspapers would blare, but he would be held by investigators while everyone else carried on with their holiday. He didn't mind the reporters; British Airways had agreed to withhold their names and the story would be lining tomorrow's bins, but the police investigation would take time he didn't want to give. He'd rather disappear quietly and leave the world to do what it wanted to do.

He pressed the button above his head and summoned an attendant. Viola came down the aisle, smiling as usual despite the still-obvious shock.

"Is there any chance we could get into Italy without passing customs," he asked.

"I'm afraid not," she replied. "The police want to talk to you."

"And if we forced our way past you?" Hayden enquired slyly.

"You wouldn't be able to get out of the airport."

Hayden turned over and poked Joey. "It looks like we're going to get lost in bureaucratic tape," he said morosely.

Joey sighed. "And I was looking forward to meeting some nice Italian girls."

"I'm sorry guys," Viola said, trying to figure out whether he was being serious or not.

"What a shame," Hayden said pitifully. "We'll just have to pull our disappearing act."

"Remind me how that goes again," Joey muttered, yawning.

"We make it up," Hayden replied sombrely. "And run when we get the chance."

The plane was descending swiftly through the clouds, breaking out into the glorious Italian sunshine. The horizon stretched out before them, and the city below them spanned out like an intricate web. Hayden and Joey were less interested in the view; their attention was focussed on the row of security vehicles that had lined up just off the runway.

"Looks like we're joining the party," said Joey, as the plane touched down and then taxied to the waiting posse.

"Sounds like a hot reception," Hayden replied, eyeing a mounted gun fixed on top of one of the buildings. "The press are going to love this."

"Let's make it count," Joey said. "I wonder what we'll wrangle out of it."

"Nothing, we're kids remember." Hayden paused. "It doesn't matter what we do or don't want, all we'll get is a press article and a load of hassle."

"True," Joey accepted, "I just hope they don't get a picture. My hair's a mess."

Hayden laughed. "Typical. We probably saved our lives and all you care about is your hair."

"Every man for himself," Joey said, trying to make a comeback, but then turned serious. "If the police get us, I'm going to demand we find out what that man's motive was."

"We won't have long," Hayden replied, indicating the shadows in the open doorway. Words were spoken with the attendants, and then Viola gestured to the pair.

Hayden got up and stretched, Joey yawned loudly, and the pair stumbled towards the front.

A few people clapped, and 'speech' was shouted from the back. Hayden was already at the door, but Joey turned and announced, "If you'd like to make a donation, please send them to Molly's Flying Circus," before he too was ushered out into a waiting car.

Chapter 5

Aldo Benyafield paused in thought, his eyebrows twitching as he scanned the sheet of paper in front of him. His small nose was often the first thing people noticed when they met him: it pointed strangely to the left, spiriting any attention away the pale skin that was the colour of dishwater. His height was average, but bulging forearms suggested heavy labour in the past, and the cold, focused eyes had the warmth and humour of charcoal. A scratching pencil could be heard from one of his companions seated around the teak conference table.

Aldo looked carefully around the group before turning back to the paper. He had before him men with abundant wealth, and not just in terms of money, he mused. As head of the Anti Globalisation Network, he had the privilege of combining all the forces granted to him in a terrible army of power. Ironically, his undertaking the battle to fight globalisation included men from all four corners of the planet: China, Russia, Saudi Arabia, America, and Brazil were among the nationalities joining his lair.

A balding man with oriental features put down his own sheet and turned to Aldo. "Is this true?" he asked with interest.

Aldo smiled as every head in the room suddenly looked round at him. The effect was that of nails scraped across a chalkboard, and only the most cold-hearted of men could sit unnerved through Aldo's smile. His appearance was nothing special, but he nonetheless dominated attention and revelled with a captivated audience. "This information is from a security guard who has recently left his post guarding a senior military advisor," he said. "My sources insist that this is genuine."

"Then you mean that we finally have a means of achieving our goal?"

Aldo stood up. "Albrecht Larsson was a man far ahead of his time," he lectured, repeating the tale each man already knew by heart. "Even in the late 19th Century he recognised the problems we would face when global powers began to consume everything this planet has to offer. Little did he know those days were less than 100 years from his death." He paused, drinking in the history that was the cause for his every act. "Larsson prophesised the downfall of the free citizen: a time when people are forced into actions they would not normally do. I'm talking about the worst times that will ever be experienced on earth. Famine, poverty and disease are nothing compared to what Larsson predicted."

"So many dominated by so few," quoted the Chinese man.

"Exactly," pounced Aldo, gloating at his spin of Churchill's phrase. "We all know how people can be influenced by the media and government. Let us imagine them joining forces. They would have unimaginable power. Any propaganda thought up by governments would be gulped down and swallowed by their public. Protests wouldn't have enough press coverage to gain momentum, opposing parties would be continually hammered by newspapers and reporters, and anything that the government wanted would be pushed through. We would be facing censorship like North Korea, a country where life is controlled by their self-loving leaders."

"It still beats me how this could happen in the western world," one man piped up. He was new to the group, and quickly fell silent under the glare Aldo directed at him.

"It's no mystery," Aldo said sternly. "The World Bank together with the London, New York, and Tokyo Stock Exchanges easily have the power to combine these forces. Their economic power is too strong even for the British and American governments to tackle."

"It is clear they already dominate the world," added another man. He was a Russian oil tycoon amassing millions a day, but like most rich men, he would never have enough. He detested the manipulative governments that robbed him with taxes. "Most people have no idea of the stranglehold the World Bank is slowly winding round their necks. By the time they realise it will be too late."

"Which brings us back to this," Aldo added, brandishing the sheet of paper. "Our aim, to break the power-hungry governments and World Bank associations, giving control to those who can govern without lust and ambition, is nonetheless ambitious. But with this, we can achieve it."

"Are we justifying the loss of life?" asked the Chinese man.

Aldo shrugged off the comment. "It is few compared to the billions slaughtered by world powers," he replied. "Plus," he added genially. "A smaller population will mean fewer emissions for global warming."

The comment was followed by raucous laughter from around the table.

"The British Military will be a tough nut to crack," the Russian mused. "Not that we can't succeed," he added quickly, realising he was thinking out loud. "But we should at least be prepared for other approaches. This is mainly a scientific breakthrough. We might look into copying their methods for our own advantage."

"Philip Morel?"

Aldo thought for a moment, scratching his chin with short, blackened fingernails. "Yes," he smiled. "Philip Morel will do perfectly. Arrange transport to the French Alps. I will talk to him myself."

Joey and Hayden were whisked away deep into the airport. It felt strange to be escorted by armed men through the crowds, but they soon left the tourists and headed through a maze of administrative offices. A small elevator juddered and squeaked its way underground as their escort drove them into a secure bay.

A grim-faced man was waiting for them, suited in dark grey and peering carefully over rimless glasses. He was seated behind a desk cluttered with telephones and various files. There was no nametag on his lapel, but the air of authority exposed him as head of airport security.

There followed a narrative in Italian that Hayden and Joey could only wonder at, but resulted in them being moved into a side room.

Hayden rolled his eyes upon moving through the door. None of them had been there before, yet it looked strangely familiar. The non-existent furniture apart from the central table, dark décor, and large mirror on one wall; almost an exact copy of interrogation rooms shown on TV.

Joey echoed Hayden's thoughts. "Recognise anything?" he said calmly.

"I guess they'll have an interpreter," Hayden replied humorously, then grinned. "I wonder if they'll understand slang."

Any further conversation was cut short as the officers left the room, leaving them in the company of another official.

"Good morning," Hayden said pleasantly, addressing the fair-haired man. He casually observed the person, who looked out of place in his tight fitting uniform. He envisioned him as a methodical man, never late for work; one who did what he was told.

The man moved suddenly, proving Hayden wrong. The quietness was a façade to measure anyone who came through the door, note their reactions and work out the best way to grill them.

Joey caught on and quickly became impassive, although he suspected he'd already been sussed. "We're not here to be interrogated." It was more a statement than a question, correctly figuring the man's game.

"No," the man replied bluntly, pulling his chair up to the table and gesturing for the pair to do the same. "I want you to tell me what happened."

Joey told him. Shortly, without bothering to elaborate, he spilled out the facts. Hayden remained silent.

After he had finished, the official looked up. "Ok," he said before continuing. "Firstly, what you did was extremely dangerous. I would not have advised it. You could easily have been killed without knowing what that man was going to do." He spoke simply, as if explaining to a wide-eyed 6 year old.

Joey exchanged dark glances with Hayden. "What about a mans right to protect themselves?" he asked incredulously. He couldn't believe he'd been through an attempted hijack only to listen to an office worker lecture him on health and safety.

The man looked distastefully at him before ignoring the question. "As it is, you will have to stay here for the time being. I'm sure you understand the situation."

"We're due to be at Insel Weiss," Hayden interjected, referring to the island. "We've told you all that we know."

The official adjusted his glasses. "I'm afraid that's impossible," he said apologetically. "The government are demanding a high level enquiry. We're going to have to hold you for a few days."

"Are we allowed to use a phone?" Joey asked.

The man smiled briefly, pausing at the door on his way out. "You'll have to be monitored, but that shouldn't be a problem."

"Do you get the feeling we're being used," Hayden whispered, now alone in the room.

"I don't know how the police work, so I wouldn't know," Joey muttered back. "But I would like to see your disappearing trick sometime."

Hayden grinned. "So when are you going to take me to see Molly's Flying Circus?"

"All in good time," Joey replied gloomily.

Two days later, Hayden and Joey were still underground. They had been shown to a room; whitewashed and spotless, with a metal bunk bed and two old but comfortable bed sheets.

The door swung open, and an officer entered, carrying a tray of food. Hayden pounced on him.

"We want to see someone from the embassy," he demanded. "You can't keep us here indefinitely." He doubted whether the man could speak English, but it was worth a try.

The policeman left.

"I intend to find out what's going on up there," Joey murmured. "They haven't even given us a newspaper."

It was true, Hayden thought, as he glanced around the bare room. They had been completely isolated. It was more a prison sentence than a retention bay for further questioning. "The only trouble is," Hayden stabbed moodily at a potato, "is that I don't know any of the rules. They could keep us here for months under some weird terrorism act, and we wouldn't be able to do anything about it."

"Don't give them ideas," Joey replied. "I get the feeling they enjoy having us here."

"I'm not hungry," Hayden announced suddenly. "Besides, if we keep up our ridiculous inventions about how Italian police are out to get us, the roast chicken has got hiccup potion in it."

Joey snorted.

Later that evening, another policeman arrived. He gestured for the pair to follow him and led them down an old-fashioned passageway with fading posters on the walls. Its tiles and long, dusty strip-lights eerily reminded Hayden of Second World War bomb shelters. Upon leaving the ghosts and re-entering what resembled part of the modern world, they were again shepherded into the questioning room.

"Hello again," Hayden said, recognising the fair-haired official.

"This isn't a laughing matter," was the reply. The tone was dark, as if he was about to proclaim there was an outbreak of Black Death. Hayden shrugged and sat down, staring defiantly at the official. He wasn't in the mood for another lecture, especially after the suspected unlawful detainment.

The man took a sip of coffee before entering his main speech. "Our case is now closed," he said, quietly watching their reactions. "You are free to go. But I must warn you," his voice rose sharply. "This is not to go public. You are to sign an Act which forbids you to divulge any information you have on the subject."

"Two days," Hayden said sceptically. "I may not know much about the police, but international terrorism has wide repercussions. The English will need a complete revision of their security, the press will scream for war, and the CIA will probably get involved. You can't clear this up in two days. The politicians are the people who will decide what happens next."

"You're very shrewd," the official replied carefully. "But as far as you are concerned, the case is over. We have handed our complete report over to the relevant sources, and we will now step aside and act as a consulting body on whatever the government deems necessary."

Hayden didn't bother to argue: all that mattered was that they were getting out.

"Who was it?" Joey asked.

"I'm afraid I can't answer that."

"I want to know."

"I can't tell you."

"I think you can."

There was a long silence.

"Sorry." The man took another sip of coffee. "It doesn't concern you. It wouldn't make any difference to you if you knew."

"It doesn't concern us?" Hayden raised his eyebrows. "I think you're mistaken. We're the ones who got you out of this mess. I think we deserve to be told who tried to kill us."

The man paused. "The name is irrelevant. The only thing I will tell you is the motive, which is no secret anyway because the press seem to have guessed. They don't know that it's the truth, but the Home Secretary, who was on the plane, was the target."

"Since when did the Home Secretary travel on public planes?" Joey asked disbelievingly.

"His government plane reported technical difficulties just before take-off," the man replied icily. "No doubt obvious as sabotage, but as the Home Secretary was due at a very important meeting, he decided to risk a commercial flight."

Joey accepted this. "One more question," he said. "Why do you have your headquarters underground?"

The man looked puzzled, but gave the answer anyway. "During the War our admin block was separate from the terminal, so we demolished it. It was too easy a target to hit. When we extended the terminal at the same time, we dug underground to protect us from attack, and disguised the earth moving from satellites by transporting it in trucks that were used to build the new terminal. Its not very big, but it'll do."

Joey seemed to have satisfied his curiosity. "I guess we can go then," he said to Hayden. "Unless you want a guided tour of the Italian underground."

"I'm fine," Hayden replied.

"I hope I don't see you again," the official said, pushing a hidden button under the table that stopped the tape recorder. "Because it'll mean you're in trouble," he grinned, looking at the confused faces.

Hayden and Joey stood up and walked through the door into the main office section. The chief had disappeared on business, so Joey borrowed his pen and wrote a sarcastic thank-you note on a scrap piece of paper. He placed it on the desk, but couldn't help noticing several photographs among the clutter. The bright images stood out from the piles of typed paper like candles in the dark. Strange, he thought. Why would the chief of police have pictures of their suitcases on his desk? Probably to do with the bomb scare the terrorist had managed to instigate, he reasoned, and then went into the elevator.

Chapter 6

High in the French Alps, two people were talking.

"My source claims they have just been released from the Italian police. We have the information we need," Aldo stated.

"Wait," the second commanded. Despite being 34 years younger than his friend, he was already the same height with a bit more plump around the middle. He was dressed in a silk dressing gown as befitted the early hour. "I do not rashly commit my forces. Follow them, find out if they have it, and then I will give the order to attack."

"What would you do if you were them?" the first man asked, pretending to step down his authority level. Though Aldo was in control of his partner, the younger man was impatient and often spoke above his station. The only reason Aldo put up with him was his undeniable brilliance. The highly-trained former marines at his command were a bonus.

"I wouldn't imagine Dr Wright has told them everything. If I were them I'd want to find out more. Such as why they have no protection."

"How do we know that?"

"We followed every single person from the plane. Everyone checked in to where they were supposed to be or went at least 50 miles away from the airport."

"So our tactics now?"

"Confuse them and make them delay. They'll want to find out about Dr Wright – and we should let them." He grinned. "Well, we should definitely give them *some* information."

"Insel Weiss is a tourist resort; they'll only be able to find out about Dr Wright on the internet."

"So we shut their computers down?"

Aldo's partner shook his head. "I'll arrange for it to be changed."

Once again among the hustle and bustle of tourists, Hayden and Joey hailed a cab, and gave the directions to the harbour. A boat would take them across to the island.

They sat back in their seats and watched urban turn to rural, relaxing as the wind blew in through the window, keeping perspiration at bay.

The cab turned off the main road, weaving its way down a small country lane that looked as though it led to nowhere, but signs of life kept appearing; a small family of ducks, and then a group of walkers flashed past the glass. Suddenly the road opened up, and the narrow hedgerows that flanked the lane disappeared, leaving a vast expanse of farmland with the sea glittering in the distance.

Joey, not usually one to be surprised, drank in the view with earnest, but Hayden kept only a modest eye on the surroundings, too busy trying to check they weren't being followed.

They homed in on their destination, passing crowds of locals, most eating ice cream from a smiling barman, and reached the dock.

A short female, dressed in immaculate uniform despite the heat, greeted them in English, paid the driver, and directed them into a waiting boat. A stout but pleasurable-looking craft, the *Predator* was far from what its namesake suggested. The woman, whose tanned skin would have looked equally at home lounging on a beach, smiled briefly upon noticing Hayden's casual inspection. She flicked the ignition and set a leisurely course out into the bay.

"Beats English weather," said Hayden as they skimmed over the sea. The blue water was crystal clear and in shallower spots the bottom was visible, sitting serenely under the waves. No fish appeared, doubtless hiding away from the boat; forewarned by the noise that, although little, was amplified underwater.

Yet no matter how peaceful the water seemed, Hayden knew he would never quite feel at home above the depths. Respect and awe at the power and relentlessness of the ocean were easy: it dominated almost ominously the thoughts of countless men that had crossed its surface, but the sea had been unwilling to offer him a more intimate bond. It was something he couldn't quite fathom, but he had always avoided the sea since he was younger. Like being afraid of dogs, he had often mused. You grow out of it, but can never feel a safe connection.

Still, he could swim a fair way; swimming pools being one of the options he never turned down. Biking was another hobby, having saved up for a year to get his first racing bike. He couldn't work out how he did it, and felt sure he wouldn't be able to do it again. Fondly remembering his dad first teaching him to ride, he knew his life would never retire into a reliable office worker who tended his garden every Sunday morning. The cold winds with hard muscles pumping to stay on the road, the rush of air on the downhill flats, and the sweat of pushing the boundaries had embedded themselves in him. The bike had become his friend, overcoming all that weather and tiredness could throw at him, ever ready for the next corner, the next road.

Gradually, he realised, the more time he spent on the saddle the more natural it became, and he regularly used it as an excuse to escape. In a world where pressure and time was everything, it offered a way out where he could think, the extra oxygen his heart was pumping round giving his brain a more focused approach. Many of his best ideas had come from the road, struck by sudden inspiration as he dove down hills.

Brought back to the present, a small wooden platform rose up to meet them, jutting out into the sea. The boat eased up to the side, where a deckhand was waiting to secure it to a small red bollard that sat on the planks.

A path led onto the beach where it disappeared for a few moments in the golden sand, before it retook its outline, leading through a grove of luscious palm trees. Nice design, thought Hayden, admiring the impressive landscape.

The building that awaited them was simple but effective. It was a white stone structure with no fancy loops or patterns, but retained a simple elegance that was usually missed by tourists in the mainland Italian architecture. "The streets are normally too crowded to notice," explained the woman, who had since introduced herself as Nicola.

The inside was cool, protected from the heat by a powerful air conditioning system. Potted plants were spaced periodically around the room, surrounding the designer chairs and reception table.

Another woman was behind the desk, this one looking resplendent in a more hotel-based uniform, and watched them sign in.

"Your room is over on the other side of the island. Nicola will show you where to go," she said in perfect English. "If you have any problems just ring 123 from your phone. I hope you enjoy your stay."

"It amazes me," Joey muttered once out of earshot of the desk. "How all these hotel people can keep the same enthusiasm for every guest."

"They're paid for it," Hayden responded.

"True," Joey admitted, as they approached the second base. This one was slightly more modern than the first; a long glass structure that curved round in a loop, offering wide views to the beach. Elegant benches and a carved signpost lay by the main doors, thoughtfully providing rest and navigation for the heat-stricken guest.

A man, who could only be described as a porter, met them and took their bags, while Nicola took them to meet Dr Wright's brother, who took his wife's name of Bose.

They found him in the shade, dressed in casual shorts and an open shirt, lazing peacefully in a deckchair with a glass of lemonade beside him.

"Greetings lads," he said, visibly pleased to see them. He rose and extended a hand.

Joey took it, feeling the firm grip. "Mr Bose."

"Call me Alfred," he said airily. "I hear you've done a few things for my old brother," he continued with almost a rueful smile.

"We get around," Hayden replied, not sure whether to say anything.

"That's ok," the man replied, casually brushing past the subject with a wave of the hand. "I suspect you're tired after all you've been through. Do you want to start your schedule tomorrow?"

After two days of inactivity in an underground cell, the last thing they wanted to do was rest, but they accepted and found their way to their room. It was set apart from the other suites, the layout familiar to anyone who kept glossy holiday brochures.

The cabin was wooden but classically so, and was fitted as a five star hotel should be. To the front, a stilted veranda extended towards the sea, lying on pillars that rose out of sloping sand, moulded comfortably to the landscape.

Once inside, Hayden dropped his bags and explored, surveying the interior with newfound respect.

Joey followed him, throwing his duffel sack onto the sofa. He wolf whistled. "I thought you said we'd get treated like kids, not VIPs," he teased.

Hayden looked at him. "It feels better when you've cheated death," he retorted.

"So if you're playing secret spy, aren't you going to search for hidden microphones?"

"Spies are superstitious. Only banana-throwing monkeys give the right luck for microphone hunting."

Joey shook his head in bafflement then grinned. "There's a monkey up there," he said, pointing to the wall.

"What am I supposed to do?" Hayden enquired exasperatedly, locking eyes on the pale brown creature that embossed a rectangular painting. "And anyway, he's not throwing bananas."

Joey slowly took out a pencil. "We can soon alter that," he smiled.

"Don't I need to check it isn't a bomb before you ruin it," Hayden asked. He crossed over to the painting and carefully examined the frame.

"Nothing," he announced.

"And the back," Joey insisted mockingly, now lounging on the sofa. "It's my life we're talking about here."

"I know," Hayden laughed, but turned the painting over anyway, running his hands over the surface.

"I think I've found it," he said earnestly, fiddling with a loose screw. "They changed the frame for a bomb but we came before they could put the last screw in."

Joey shook his head. "I am seriously indebted to you for saving my life," he laughed. He closed his eyes, only to be reawakened by a sliding noise above him.

Hayden was standing still, looking in amazement at a hole in the ceiling. They caught each other's eyes and burst out laughing.

"You really have got it in for me," Joey said, staring amused at the bent screw that served as an activation leaver in Hayden's hand.

Only one question went through Hayden's inquisitive mind. "You or me?" he grinned.

They hastily assembled their suitcases in a tower and stood on them, balancing carefully while peering into the gloom. The light from below only pierced a short way into the attic, yet it was enough to give a brief glimpse.

Hayden reached up, grabbed the ledge and pulled himself up, expertly lifting his body through the gap. Joey followed, and they crouched in the dim light.

"Light switch?" Joey whispered.

Hayden groped the air and found one. He flicked the button, casting a glow around the space. It illuminated a normal attic; a few dust covered boxes and a Christmas tree, but there were no skylights. Instead, a few spots on the walls were painted green, and a handle lay beneath them.

Joey pushed one, letting a cool breeze penetrate as the wooden lifted up. "Not bad place this," he muttered.

Hayden looked up, a box half open. "Let's go on the roof," he said.

The windows were small from top to bottom, but Joey found a screwdriver and loosened the catch.

Once out into the air, they found the roof to be stable. The central ridge wasn't sharp, and the timber gave ample grip.

They sat at the front, where the design provided a ledge, and stared out at the open sea. The sun was still beating down, but this spot was shaded; a forest of trees being the benefactor.

"I fancy a milkshake," Joey said.

Hayden sighed. "You have to wait until we're on the roof before you want one."

"A natural trouble maker," Joey agreed.

"Anyway, we need to unpack."

Back on ground floor, Joey snubbed the unpacking after watching Hayden wrestle his bag into a wardrobe, and flopped on a chair.

"Now will you let me have a milkshake?" he called.

Hayden laughed. "Make me one as well. And the porter," he added, noticing a uniformed figure approaching the cabin.

"An invitation from Mr Bose," said the porter, presenting himself with a small bow. He handed over a white envelope and was about to leave, when Joey appeared with the milkshakes.

"Do you want one?" he asked.

"No thank you." The porter made another small bow and turned to depart, but Joey advanced.

"Come on," he cajoled. "We would like to ask you some questions."

Surprisingly, the porter turned and rejoined them.

"It's quite hot out here," Hayden said.

"Yes," the porter replied, grateful for the cold drink.

"How long has this place been around?"

"About two years."

"Your English is very good," complimented Joey.

His comment earned a smile. "I studied for seven years."

"What would you recommend we wear tonight? Smart or casual?"

"Smart, but not formal. No ties, and no jackets, but a good shirt would be suitable."

"Bring any of that Joey?" asked Hayden.

"Not a lot," replied his friend, "but I'm sure we'll get by."

"I can arrange," the porter offered, but Joey declined.

"We don't want the trouble. By the way, how many other guests are there?"

"We're half full. About twenty in the fitness complex, and a further hundred in the hotel."

"That's not too bad. Do you get good reviews?"

"Oh yes." The porter was in his element, obviously proud of the levels of service. "Thank you for the drink. I have to return to work."

"Come again when you want some more," Hayden said as the man left.

"That was fun," said Joey, wandering onto the white-hot beach and laying out his towel. "I wonder how many people we can get sacked if we carry on like this."

Hayden joined him and closed his eyes. "We'll just get charged for using up all their strawberries," he grinned.

Chapter 7

Joey and Hayden left their cabin as the first midgets appeared for the night. Dusk was an hour away and the sun still dominated the sky, although its fading light was slowly relinquishing power to the lamps situated round the island. They followed the path back towards the heart of the island, and noise gradually began to drift through to their ears as they approached.

A servant was there to direct them inside the glass building, and onto the inner courtyard. The walls were different from the within; glass gave way to wooden elegance, framing windows that provided cursory glances into the indoor passages.

The jazz band, producing the melancholy music Hayden had first heard, was in the corner, surrounded by tall-leaved fronds. Waiters stood in their traditional white and black, ever ready with trays of refreshment, and a short buffet table waited patiently for its lids to be removed.

"Don't say we have to mingle and speak small talk," Hayden groaned, carefully deciphering the accents around him. "The English here look like they own half of Bristol."

He was right. The three English couples were standing 10 feet away examining the decorative carvings, occasionally shaking a wrist that seemed to be made out of gold. Joey took one glance and turned away in disgust.

"I'd hate to know their insurance bill," he muttered, wondering if one man could fit any more bracelets on his arm.

They were about to retreat and disappear inside, but were spotted by Alfred, who seemed to bound out of the doors like a joke-man on stage. In any normal crowd, heads would have turned upon entry; he was a man who controlled the moods of a room, but among the rich he looked small and insignificant.

He searched around the court, darting in and out with a smooth grace that looked for someone to pounce on. Aware that everyone had someone to talk to, he settled on the uncomfortable-looking English pair, and briskly motioned for a waiter.

"Glad to see you could join us," he said, holding his glass of champagne. "Take a drink."

Joey would have loved to get alcohol into his system in front of an under-age Hayden, but decided to keep his head clear. "No thanks," he said. "I'll have some water."

Alfred looked slightly disappointed, but carried on in his jovial demeanour by suggesting a tour of the facilities.

"You're obviously proud of your establishment," Hayden noted, accepting the offer.

"Built it from scratch. My brother paid for most of the island, but after that it was easy."

"Its probably a silly question, but do you have the Internet here?"

Alfred nodded. "In the library. If you're still here in an hour, I'll show you, but I have to mingle with the guests. I'm as much a host as a manager." He pulled a face; obviously this was part of the job he detested. "I'll see you later."

"He looks too cheerful to be a manager," Hayden said, watching the man bounce round the courtyard. "But I suppose he can't help it with the Italian sun all day."

Joey nodded. "Let's go find the library."

They set off in the direction of two doors they had not yet been through. One led back to the foyer, and the other presented itself as toilets.

"Next," they said in unison after entering to find urinals.

"Ever wanted to speak Italian?" Joey asked as the accents rose around them. He crossed over to another door, Hayden slightly behind him.

"Not really," Hayden replied. "Apart from German, all incidents with language have ended in disaster." He was referring to high school French, an unwanted burden he had been forced to bear for three years.

They re-entered the building and made their way left, aware that all signs were Italian.

"Nope, that's the dining room," Hayden said, as Joey was about to push through some doors.

"How do you know?" Joey replied, poking his head through the door to check.

Hayden rolled his eyes, pointing at the sign next to the door where some pieces of cutlery were drawn.

"Oh yeah," Joey said, suddenly enlightened. "How's this one?"

This time the doors gave way to a modern room, sofas taking up the centre area while the walls covered themselves with bookcases. A stairwell led up to a room above, which looked over the library. Computers could be seen; sitting silently on their desks waiting for unknown users to access them.

Hayden checked them: they were on, so he touched the mouse, watching as the screen blinked to life. "Internet

Explorer," he muttered, clicking on the icon. "What do you suggest?"

"There won't be anything on Google," Joey replied. "Or any other search engine."

"Great. We don't know what we're looking for, and we can't ask jeeves."

"Try it."

Hayden typed in the address, and waited until the smiling cartoon came up. It appeared instantly, looking his usual electronic self.

Hayden spoke as he typed. "Can you give us what we are looking for?" He pressed the enter button and sat back, looking incredulously at the advert for Mexican hats that popped up. "Maybe not."

Joey reached over, entered 'The Telegraph' in the URL, and followed up with 'Wright' in the website search. He looked carefully at the items that came up before selecting the top one. "Go to the printer," he said, clicking the print button.

A whirring noise told Hayden the machine was in the corner, and he returned with a biography of Dr Wright. "Not too much paper," he asked, looking at the wedge in his hand.

"It'll keep us going tonight," Joey yawned. "We can take it apart and check up on anything we find."

Hayden paused. "And when was the last time you used your analysis skills?"

"Geography coursework, two years ago," Joey replied briefly, not avoiding the issue. He grinned. "I bet I can still beat you."

"You're on."

In the French Alps, a team of website designers breathed a sigh of relief. Redesigning pages of text while their target roamed the Internet at will was exhausting work. Their job was done for the moment, and they could relax until the target returned. The request had been strange, but the €10,000 they would receive had squashed any doubts. Pots of coffee were brought in and any who needed were escorted to the toilets. Perhaps it was normal for industrialists to act over sensitive, one man thought. Especially when they were skirting the edge of the law.

Hayden and Joey spent the evening pouring over the report. It took a few hours, but at the end they had a list of facts to check up on.

"Naturally they're writing this in favour of the man," Hayden said, "but they're not too careful about his dad."

"What's that?" Joey replied, not looking up.

"Dr Wright senior is described as controversial, despite the fact he was knighted. I'll check it."

"Seems innocent enough, but no harm in trying."

"Anything that gives us the edge, I'll take," Hayden muttered, attempting to unravel the confusing mass of intricately typed script. "What have you got?"

"Nothing yet."

They swapped over their piles of paper and re-searched them to see if there was anything else they could glean.

"You missed a bit," Joey said loftily. "Seems you're not as good as you thought." He had complete confidence in his friend's ability, but the relaxed competition kept them on edge.

Hayden ignored the jibe. "What is it?"

"One of his promotions in the army."

"Sounded logical to me," Hayden defended.

"How many promotions did he have again?" Joey teased.

"Seven," Hayden replied comfortably.

"Check his sixth." He tossed the paper over and watched while Hayden studied the text.

Hayden glanced back up at Joey, his face quizzical.

"It seems quite strange that his biggest promotion has virtually no information on it. The others have plenty," Joey said.

"Why was his sixth promotion the biggest?"

"The biggest jump in rank. The seventh promotion to Chief Military Scientist came after the previous guy died. He was second in command by that point so was the obvious choice."

"I'll check it. How did the other guy die?"

"Doesn't say. You want that as well?" He wrote the points down on the back of one of the pages, and resumed his scan.

"Too bad old friend. You've missed one as well." Hayden was examining the later stages of Dr Wright's life. "There was a scandal with The Sun. He sued them for making up a story about his private life."

"What's wrong with that?"

"One, he probably has something to hide, and two, I don't imagine The Sun will be too pleased. If we turn up blank we can ask them."

"What about the Data Protection Act."

Hayden shrugged. "A mere technicality."

"Scam them?" Joey asked, reading Hayden's thoughts.

"If it comes to it." Hayden paused. "You've missed another gem."

"The supposed cover up from the government?"

"Yep. It says Dr Wright was accused of working for some foreign company. It then goes on to say that he was feted around the country for developing a banana bomb."

"A banana bomb?" Joey asked sceptically. Shaking his head at the name, he continued. "Why was he feted for making a bomb?"

"It replaced the nuke," Hayden explained. "It has the same power, but no radiation. Britain started nuclear disarmament."

"When was this?"

"About 7 years ago. Why?"

"Logical," Joey muttered, deep in thought.

Hayden waited patiently, not sure where this was leading.

"2001. Election year. Labour beat the Conservatives four years before that," Joey said slowly. "And if I remember correctly, that was when they were in deep trouble. The odds were deeply stacked against them to retain power."

"Labour haven't lost power since then," Hayden said.

"No, but nuclear disarmament is a pretty good argument for keeping office. We'll have to look that one up. When was the big celebration?"

"The day after the tabloids went mental."

"Interesting. If he was working for a dodgy company the war heroics would have put anyone off. People would have voted him PM if he'd stood."

"There was a government enquiry," commented Hayden, re-reading the opening paragraph. "But it was broken up in just over two hours."

Joey frowned. "When exactly did Dr Wright complete his fruit salad of destruction?"

"It doesn't say, but it would have been a few days if not weeks before the public knew. Why?"

"Funny how the enquiry ended when the government realised he was a political lifeline."

"This could get tricky."

Joey nodded. "Up for a challenge?"

"You bet."

"I'll race you there." Joey leapt off the sofa, landing with a thud on the thick carpet, and sprinted out of the door. Hayden was close behind, and they tore neck-and-neck back towards the party.

Joey won by a few feet, and startled a napping bird that was resting on a signpost. He stepped inside, skipping quickly out of view of Alfred Bose, who had suddenly materialised, and headed back to the library.

"Apart from America, who does the army work with?" Hayden asked, settling himself behind a computer.

"Joey?" Hayden repeated, seeing his friend flicking through a book.

"France," he said, and then returned to the pictures depicting the Vietnam War.

"As long as they write in English, they'll do for starters."

Hayden opened Google and searched for French newspapers. Scrolling down the list, he picked a half-broadsheet, half-tabloid paper, and went onto their site. A proper broadsheet would be careful around foreign army matters, but tabloids were often unreliable.

Once on the website, Hayden clicked on the archives section and scanned the toolbar. All newspapers have site searches. He found it and tried 'Wright', in the month of January 2001.

Nothing came up, so Hayden reversed his steps and tried another. Still nothing. Slightly annoyed, Hayden typed in the exact date of Wrights promotion and checked the headlines. Mad Cow Disease was the main story, and the rest was full of French idioms and crosswords.

"What about Sky?"

"I doubt they'd meddle in these affairs," Hayden replied, but checked the website anyway. Still nothing appeared, but the headlines gave him an idea. "2001 was the year we kicked up a big fuss about Iraq. What's their national paper called?"

"No idea."

Hayden shook his head. A Vietnam War fanatic, Joey could remember the date the first Vietnam newspaper came out and was able recite the entire front page, but he couldn't remember an Iraqi paper that was still in circulation. He searched for it and soon found what he was looking for.

"Al-Jazeera," he said to himself. "Of course."

Accessing their website, he once again typed in Dr Wright's name. Joey put down his book and came across.

"Be careful. Your mum would never forgive you if you were killed trying to hack for Iraqi military secrets," Joey teased.

"It's a newspaper, not Naval Intelligence," Hayden muttered. "Aha."

A picture flashed up on the screen. "ID confirmed," Hayden said.

"The titles not too nice considering he just got promoted," Joey commented, reading the text.

Hayden looked like he stumbled on a gold mine filled with skeletons. He swiftly copied the document and sent it to the printer. "Get it," he said quickly, before closing Microsoft Word. "Anything we get has to be wiped off the hard drive."

"How do you do that? Computers remember everything. It'll be on internet records for months."

"Watch this," Hayden replied, grinning slightly. He gleaned the site for any further data, sent Joey to collect it, and then went back to the homepage. He held down the control key, and then hit H. A menu flashed up at the side displaying all the sites they had been on.

"It's as easy as that?" Joey said sceptically, watching as Hayden deleted them.

"Not quite." Hayden typed another URL into the Internet and pulled up a program before minimizing and accessing the computers hard drive. He was blocked by a password, but Joey switched back to his Internet site and set it hacking through the code. Once in control of the hard drive, he accessed the Internet files and deleted those as well. "That's all. Let's go."

They climbed out of an open window and landed on the emergency balcony. Swiftly dropping through the levels and disappearing over a flowerbed staying clear of the spotlights, the pair headed back to their cabin.

Unbeknown to them, an error was flashing in the main control room, warning the staff that an alien user was in the network. Hurriedly, the network manager was called and Mr Bose was alerted, afraid it might be a hacker. But, as soon as Hayden and Joey left the room, the message stopped. All systems returned to normal, and a confused electronics wizard remained, puzzling over the apparent lapse in security. He started scanning the entire mainframe, but it was two days before he found the virus.

In France, the team of hackers flexed their fingers after furious typing, and relaxed. They had seen the system warning alert and were slightly disappointed at being detected, but the virus would delete their actions. Eagerly each man stood to receive their payment, and were then ushered out to waiting helicopters.

Chapter 8

The next morning Hayden began the arduous task of sifting through the Al-Jazeera information he had lifted. Of course, being an Iraqi newspaper, it was bound to be biased against the English, but it probably had the dare and tenacity to probe into holes the Telegraph kept well clear of. Political issues they dealt with, but there were laws about Army press coverage.

Joey sat in the kitchen, talking on the phone to one of his mates back home, so Hayden was left on his own.

Tirelessly scanning and re-scanning the document, he rubbed his eyes and lay on the sofa, letting his gaze wander out onto the beach. It wasn't yet ten o'clock, but already the sun was blazing above. Typical hot day, Hayden thought, before returning to the creased paper.

There was plenty of trouble in the report, but it was near impossible to tell whether it was true or simply speculation. He needed an expert.

Yet what was he thinking? He was just 16, and was slowly dragging himself into a world of danger and espionage, where every negative comment seemed to judge the person it concerned. Anyone could be a villain, and so an impossible game of hide and seek began, forever running from superstition and fright: the constant thought of an unknown enemy nagging at your mind. Get a grip, Hayden told himself angrily. Any top army job is going to be surrounded by speculation. It's a coincidence that one of the other applicants was killed in a car crash.

But no matter how many times he tried to drill this into his brain, a niggling suspicion kept forcing its way to the fore. What if?

Hayden kicked angrily at the floor, unable to get his head round the words. The writing was there, but there was nothing between the lines: no hint as to anything of use. He needed a drink. He was sure he had missed something, something important, but whenever he tried to put a finger on it, it escaped.

Joey walked into the room with a tall glass of water.

"You like to rub it in don't you?" Hayden said exasperatedly.

Joey paused and took a long sip from the straw, pulling another glass from behind his back. "What have you got?" he said, handing over the tumbler.

"His promotion was jinked, he works for Lapcon Industries as well as the army, and he sold half of England's weapon programmes to Iran."

"The last one's a load of rubbish."

Hayden tore the sheet up.

"Who are Lapcon?"

"They make electronic equipment. Everything from computers to neodymium magnets. Based in Berlin."

"They should be ok if they're in Berlin. German law people aren't known to be slack"

"Doesn't leave us much."

"What are you going to do?"

Hayden looked at the clock. Alfred had promised them to try out the bikes before lunch, and they'd start their expedition in the afternoon. "Not much we can do. We'll go see Bose, and sort this mess out later."

Joey looked suspicious. "What happened to the gung-ho beat-everyone-up attitude?"

"Bad day at the office," Hayden explained dryly, neatly folding the paper into a bundle. He held it up. "What shall we do with this?"

"Destruction I can do," Joey grinned, jumping down the steps. He landed on the hot sand, and dragged a foot through the grains until he had created a small bowl.

"Welcome to the Majestic Dumping Sphere," he said grandly, admiring the misshapen hole. "Give me the paper."

Hayden shook his head in amazement. "You're not going to bury it?" he asked, but his friend merely grinned and produced a bottle of whiskey. "Nice time for a toast," Hayden commented, still at odds as to the plan.

Joey returned the look with an easy one of his own and stuffed the paper into the whiskey. A cloth followed, the edge just floating on the liquid to connect the chain, and then he sat back and pulled a lighter out of his pocket.

Hayden groaned. "Surely there are less extreme ways," he said despairingly, recognising the Molotov cocktail.

"You paid for the delivery man, and a delivery man you'll get."

"Fire away solider."

Joey embedded sand around the bottle to contain the flying glass, and wrapped a towel round the neck. "Members of the audience, beware!"

The cloth was lit, and fire was slowly kindled. It stuttered and paused, edging cautiously up the material, before taking hold and erupting into a ball of flame. The bottle exploded, sending rivets of sand soaring into the air. A muffled roar echoed from the airborne particles, but the flash of fire was gone, all but extinguished in the short but violent alcohol flame span.

Hayden and Joey sat a short distance away, staring at the stifled exploit. "That was fun," Joey gasped, choking some of the dust out of his mouth.

Hayden retrieved a sieve and rescued the broken glass. "Beats eating the paper," he said, recollecting the World War Two spies. "Let's go see Alfred."

They found Mr Bose in his hammock, a trait they were told was habitual, but he presented no ill feeling at being disturbed. Instead, he leaped out onto the patio and motioned for drinks.

"Hello boys," he said jovially. "How's your day so far?"

"I think it measured pretty high on the Richter scale," Joey said, allowing a smile to cross his face.

"Good. I'll show you the sports rooms." He led the way through a network of passages until they came back outside. Doors opened to a wide open space, where a well-worn path split the grass. Another building, this one more conservative in design, stood tall amidst a flurry of tress.

"By the way, did you find the library?" Bose asked, moving into the sunlight.

"We went last night," Hayden said, trying to sound casual.

"Good." Bose showed no signs of setting verbal traps, but Hayden wasn't taking any chances. "We had a problem with them this morning, and we've had to take them off-line for a while."

"You've got a good set-up," Joey complimented, hastily trying to open the way for a possible distraction.

Bose nodded in agreement. "It seems our security isn't up to scratch though. A virus got in. My computer manager thinks it was a hacker, because although we know someone was working on them, we can't find much trace of what they did."

Hayden's mind went into a whirlwind. Someone had hacked into the computers when they were on the Internet? His trick had only cleared the websites off the hard-drive: there was plenty more information on their web access.

Their entrance into the gym pushed all thoughts from his mind. Modern décor fenced a spacious room, rows of gleaming equipment stacked neatly by the sides. Powerful air-conditioning vents spaced themselves in the ceiling to refresh the air, the infectious atmosphere was one of sparkling health. Hayden almost felt fitter just by being there.

"This way," Alfred said, showing them a smaller room that held two mounted bikes. A screen covered an entire wall, and hidden speakers pulsed quietly in the background. "I'll leave you to it," Alfred said. "There's an outdoor track that weaves through the forest, but I'd stay inside with this heat. The monitors on the handlebars record distance, there's energy bars and water in the fridge, and if you need anything, press this button. Have fun." A customary smile and he was gone, presumably back to his hammock.

Hayden stood for a minute, admiring the bikes. "That's £5000 worth of candy," he said softly, jumping on a blue one.

Joey, less energetically climbing onto the black version, was more interested in the remote control. "Pick a video," he said, scanning the drop down menu that appeared.

"Put a gig on," Hayden said, testing the gears. "I could use some music."

Joey selected a music channel from the internet and downloaded it – entertainment ran off a different network to the library and was unaffected by the virus – and was soon enjoying the smooth feel of guitar melody and rocking drums.

He turned his attention to the bike under his feet. "Hey that's cheating," he exclaimed, noticing Hayden had already done half a mile. He gritted his teeth and pushed his legs down. "Bring it on," he muttered.

Two hours and thirty miles later, they stopped for lunch.

"Not as hard as I expected," said Joey.

"You wait till we get to a hundred," replied Hayden. "Your legs will go like jelly."

"They'd better not," Joey remarked darkly. "We've got a party to go to tonight."

"Which one's that?" Hayden said lightly, wondering what hair-brained scheme his friend was cooking up now.

"Those girls we passed earlier. My Spanish is good enough to know they're planning a good bash tonight."

Hayden rolled his eyes. "Trust you to chat up the women at the first chance you get. And where did you learn Spanish?"

Joey winked. "One of my many hidden talents," he said.

"So after we get kicked out for crashing a party, what then?"

"We sneak in round the back and slip some vodka in the punch."

Hayden laughed. "We'll definitely get kicked out if we make everyone drunk. I'm going to the toilet."

He exited the room and made his way back round the corridors, locating the correct sign in the entrance hall. A group of thick-muscled men had just come out of the main gym area and were talking to the attendant. Wouldn't like to meet them in an alleyway, Hayden thought, entering the toilets.

He returned, noticing the men were gone, as well as the attendant. He wasn't sure why, but something unsettled him. It could have been the drawn curtains behind the front desk, covering the admin area, or the complete lack of people.

A click came from behind the admin door. Hayden started walking, not sure why his heart was beating so fast. He went into a jog, realising his brain was screaming for him to run, but forced himself to slow back to a walk. He was sweating over a missing member of staff and the clink of a coffee cup.

He broke open the door and found Joey sitting on the sofa, smiling through a cheese sandwich. "You look like you've seen a ghost," he said conversationally.

"A posse of weightlifters," Hayden said, regaining his footing. He went over to the bikes and examined the mounts. Mechanical workings fascinated him, and although he'd never pursue it as a career, he imagined he'd take it up as a hobby, maybe working at a local tip on Sunday mornings.

A central bar jacked the back wheel off the ground, and was joined to a secure network of minimalist pipes. "Keeps the bike stable and still," he said, tapping the casing. "And it's easy to take off." There were two levers that disconnected the bar, allowing you to pull it out and set the bike on the floor.

Joey threw a packaged sandwich at him. "You can take it apart when it gets cool. I'm not biking in that heat."

An alarm sounded through the building.

"Do it or die," Hayden shouted suddenly, pulling the levers clean off the mount in an abrupt burst of strength. He yanked the bars and threw them across the room, grabbing a helmet in the same move. "I smell trouble, and I darn well aren't walking into a trap."

A small side door gave way to a grassy garden lying next to the outdoor track. Joey put one hand on his bike, jerked it off the ground and wrenched the door handle. A sharp clatter rose out of the distance and a window disintegrated above them, proving Hayden's suspicions.

"Machine guns," Joey yelled, backing into the room amid a shower of glass. "I'm going down the corridors!" He didn't have a clue what was going on, but he trusted his friend's instincts implicitly.

Spinning the bike in a smooth 180 degree turn, Hayden kicked out at the other door and wheeled his racer into the corridor. Jumping onto the saddle, he shoved his foot down as hard as it would go, and sliced down the passage. Turning right and then left, Hayden had no idea where he was going, but pressed on away from their room.

The 23mm tyres offered little purchase on the carpet and required nerves of steel to round the corners. Hayden, who had a racing bike at home, was concentrating more on avoiding people that seemed to swarm out of everywhere. Joey only had to follow him, the way being carved open of people by his friend, but found the tires hard to handle. The designated emergency area was the front entrance, so to the frightened holidaymakers, the two men looked like they were on a suicide mission.

Dropping the left foot, Hayden spun left and braced himself for the obstacles that loomed up ahead. "Steps," he yelled, but the rush of wind kept the words from Joey's ears.

Joey fell down, bumping uncontrollably, but managed to stay on his bike. Regaining his breath at the bottom, he followed Hayden through a set of doors and into the sunlight.

"Let's go," Hayden roared, turning to face the track.

Chapter 9

Alfred Bose, up in the control room overseeing the exercise sector, looked pale and frightened. He was bound to a chair with tape stretched across his face. The ears, pert as ever, were twitching rapidly. His eyes were glued to a television portraying the outdoor track.

"Who do those two think they are?" The words came from a thickset man, tall and well built. A mass of stubble covered his chin, and the fair hair was parted at one side.

Alfred gave a muffled reply. The man laughed and hit him.

"You talk when I say so," he hissed, pushing his face close to Alfred's.

"Campos?" One of the other guys spoke up.

"Yes." The man called Campos spoke pleasantly enough, and but for the situation and over-worked muscle, he could have been mistaken for an ordinary man who walked his children to school. In reality he was an assassin, adept at blending in and moving unnoticed.

"Do we send people after him or wait for them to come round?"

"Both. You three," he barked. "Get after them and flush them out. Use tranquilizers."

The three men instantly disappeared, running to hijack their own bikes. Former army veterans, their mental toughness was marred by recent physical inactivity, but they still possessed the power for a chase.

"Two men here with me to check progress," Campos organized. "A further guard at the end of the corridor, and one in the communications room. The rest on the track."

His remaining team of eight split and departed. "Advise on positions," his sub-command requested, once he had reached the track. With the benefit of the cameras Campos had a better idea of the layout. Maps could be memorised, but no one had counted on people running onto the track.

"Trip wire the road, and position yourselves behind it." The orders were sent out via headsets, enabling long-range communication.

"Received." The sub-commander quickly set up his troops. He had three men with him; only one less than the teams he had worked with in the army, and he organised them with a well-practised hard efficiency. The area chosen was a wide section of tarmac, designed race-like for a sprint finish. Raised plant boxes and trees stood at the edge, creating a semi-covered terrain with the road in the middle.

"You go forward and wait in the trees," he said, pointing to his left hand man. "Make sure they come this way."

"Yes sir." The man left his cover and made his way up the track, stopping past the final corner to find a tree.

"Situation secure?" Campos asked, watching the proceedings.

"Yes sir."

"Bikers, what's your position?"

The sound of heavy breathing came over the microphone. "One mile in, no sign of them yet."

"Keep going." Campos idly checked his watch before addressing Bose. "Are there any incoming shipments today? You can nod or shake your head."

A barely perceptible shake was made, Alfred's fearful body trying to crumple for a smaller target.

"How long is the track? Head right for higher, left for lower. 10 miles."

The head went left.

"Nine?"

Still left.

"Eight."

This time a nod.

"Thank you. I reassure you that we will not harm you or any of the guests. We simply want to talk to Hayden and Joey and then we'll be on out way."

Alfred's eyes fixed themselves on a gun held by one of the men.

"Our devices and apparent hostage are simply to make sure that we are not opposed," Campos explained. "We do not care for ransom of you or your island. In our game, consider yourself the unfortunate victim of a bigger power." He returned to the screens, noting his men had gone a further half-mile.

Unbeknown to their pursuers, Hayden and Joey had gone flat out for two minutes before the roadside turned to quiet forest scenery, broken only by the grey streak that disturbed the otherwise thick foliage. Here they stopped and retreated into the undergrowth, pulling their bikes with them.

"You're not going to tell me that was a machine gun," Hayden panted.

"Heckler and Koch," Joey replied sombrely. "What do we do now?"

"Seeing as we have no weapons and are out of whiskey, I suggest we get help."

"You want us to find a telephone in a building with murderers in?"

"You got a better idea?" Hayden asked. He leant his bike against a tree and stared around the forest.

"We don't know their motive. They could have what they want and be gone in an hour. We might not need to risk ourselves."

"A Heckler and Koch would make most people see sense," Hayden agreed. "But I'm not hiding in the bushes waiting to be found. I vote we do your army creepy-crawly thing and check out the buildings."

"You realise what you're saying? They have guns, and know we're here. It's not some pimp with a handgun who thinks he can rob the White House. These guys mean business."

"I thought the army were never afraid," said Hayden cheekily. "Besides, we've got cover up till 50 meters. We need to scope the place out."

Joey nodded. "And if we get shot?"

Hayden grinned. "It's your fault for not taking out holiday insurance."

"I signed a consent form," Joey grinned back. "You got any rope?"

"Rope?"

"Yeah. We can't leave them for our attackers to find."

"Hide them in the bushes."

"That's for petty robbers," Joey scoffed. "Molly's Flying Circus can do better than that. Pass me that bike tool and get up that tree."

Hayden obeyed, retrieving the set of instruments and swinging up onto the first branch. Joey pulled out a wire cutter and snipped the brake wires, lashing them together until he had a rope.

"Catch," he said, tossing one end up into the sky. Hayden caught it and dropped it over the other side, becoming aware of the plan.

Joey tied his end onto the bike frame and grabbed the loose end. "Pull," he smiled, and hoisted the bike into the air.

Hayden secured it, untied the rope, and lodged the bike a few branches up. "They'll probably find these in ten years time," he laughed, readying himself for the next load.

The second bike joined the first, and Hayden dropped lightly to the ground.

"Ruddy wire," Joey grumbled, rubbing his hands. Though he had wrapped his shirt round them to soften the stress, lines could still be seen where the thinness had cut into him.

"Keep it," Hayden said, retrieving it from where Joey had thrown it. "We may need it."

Joey set a finger to his lips, standing frozen in mid-step, his head turning slowly to catch the sound.

Hayden heard it too. "We've been followed," he whispered, as the thin whine of racing tyres started to fade. "Looks like they do care about us."

"We'd better get going," Joey said, setting off though the trees. "If they want us, we should get them before they find out we know."

"Plus they're men down. If we have a chance, its now."

Back in the control room, Campos was getting increasingly frustrated. His men were five miles round, and there was no sign of the two boys. His earphone crackled.

"We've been had." It was the team on the track.

"What makes you certain?" he snapped. Though he trusted his force implicitly, the lack of success was beginning to get to him.

"A water hose burst and soaked the road. There are no tire marks after the spill."

"Any way they could have avoided the puddle?"

"None."

Campos swore. There was over three square miles of forest to explore, and the slow start had cost him dearly.

"Reception unit 1. Objective has disappeared into the jungle. Prepare to search."

"Sir, we can't reach Hodge." This came from the sub-commander.

"What do you mean?" Campos snapped. "Where is he?"

"His headset isn't working. We sent him down the track to make sure they came through our trap, but we haven't heard from him since."

"Check it."

"One man already searching sir. He arrived in position twenty seconds ago."

Campos overrode his sub-commander and spoke directly to the man conducting the search. "What do you have?"

Mullit was one of Campos' most professional soldiers, but there was no mistaking the shock in his voice. "I've found him sir. He's unconscious."

"Knocked out?"

"Yes sir. There's a mark around his neck sir. Looks like chicken wire."

"Where's his weapon?" Campos sounded urgent now.

"Gone."

"Get out of there," Campos snapped. What had begun as a simple kidnapping had broken into a deathly situation, and he wasn't going to take any more chances. "We attack and search the forest in two minutes."

Hayden and Joey crept silently along the floor, pausing occasionally to check the surroundings. Joey knew the routine well, having completed it to apply for the army, and took the lead.

"Remember when we used to do this at home?" Hayden whispered, equally at home sneaking among the shadows.

Joey stifled a laugh. "When we pretended the school was on fire and had to rescue the safe?"

"That's the one. I've never been near a bonfire since," Hayden said, recalling the foul taste of the smoke they had hidden themselves in after discovering it wafting over from next doors garden.

"Nearing the edge," whispered Joey, recognising the unusually shaped plants that were grown near the buildings.

Moving slowly across the ground, sometimes taking a whole minute to cover ten meters, they approached the path. The foliage was still quite thick, and ample cover compensated for the slow progress.

Hand signals were now being used to communicate; such was the level of secrecy that they intended to keep. There was no room for error where life was concerned.

Joey's hand leapt up, silently flattening out in a stop sign. Hayden froze, noticing the man at the same time.

Half hidden behind a tree trunk, the pair caught sight of him from behind: a small patch of black that moved against the brown.

Hayden pulled the wire from his arm, well aware of the gun holstered by the assassin.

Joey melted back a few meters, crouching behind a large shrub. "We don't know how many there are," he mouthed.

"I'll check him," Hayden whispered back.

Carefully approaching the guard and seeing no one, Hayden was about to return to Joey when the headset burst into life.

"Sub-command calling Hodge."

"Confirm," the man replied in a barely audible voice, adjusting the mouthpiece.

"Your position?"

"Ready and waiting."

"Good. When they appear, don't shoot but follow them round the bend and come up from behind. Stay on the right hand side so we don't get caught in any crossfire."

"Acknowledged."

Hayden backed off to find Joey scanning the surrounding trees. "He's a loner," he gestured. "He's there to force us round the bend into some sort of trap."

"I wasn't brought into this world to die in a stupid plan like that," Joey said brazenly. "You or me?"

"You had the bottle," Hayden grinned. "It's my turn." He turned back towards the man sent to kill him and swallowed. The outward game of charades was the only thing that prevented him panicking. Deep down, he was scared.

Joey picked up a few stones. "I've got your back."

"So long my friend."

"So long," Joey replied solemnly.

Hayden returned to his now well-worn spot behind the guard. Edging forward, the soft earth gave no noise, and he was able to get within a few feet without being seen.

Safe behind the second row of trees, a scant trunk was all that stood between him and possible death. Hayden tried to slow his breathing, aware that any sound would have him dead. In front of him, the guard shook his leg to ease cramp, and leaned on the tree. Behind him, Joey, who had a clear view of the guards back, stuck his thumb up.

Hayden gripped the wire and stepped out from the trunk, wrapping the cables around the mans neck.

The guard jumped, more from shock than anything, and but for the sharpness of the wire, his army reflexes would have turned the attacker into a corpse.

Joey followed up with a hail of stones, causing concussion as a lack of oxygen threw the man into darkness.

Chapter 10

"How do we find two men in three square miles of landscape?" Campos sounded more thoughtful than desperate, his methodical brain sifting through answers while trying to keep time out of the equation. It wasn't really of essence, but the longer they stayed the more likely it was that something would go wrong.

"Attacking the unknown is dangerous," the other man replied philosophically. He was perched on the edge of a chair, mentally sharp but showing signs of anxiousness. He was the only man in the team who hadn't served in some war or another, and the tension was starting to get to him.

"Any ideas?" Campos asked. Though his unit of villains could hardly be called civilised, he didn't like to dictate and welcomed opposite opinions. It cleared his mind and made sure he covered all the bases.

"Brutality?" the man suggested. "Westerners always fall for that."

"As long as they haven't disappeared by now, it should work." A satanic look fell on his normally calm face. "Get two of the prisoners. Two girls."

His mate smirked back at him and turned to his radio. He sent out the orders, and then turned back to Campos. "Do we kill them?"

"Make sure they can see, then kill one and threaten the other," he replied with no hesitation. "And keep the three bikers in reserve. When ready, tell them to come in from behind."

"Yes sir."

"Do you copy?" Campos spoke this time to his sub-commander, who would have followed the narrative on his headset.

"Copy that. We'll move in once we have the girls. Three men down the centre. One on either side in the trees."

"Cameras show we have the hostages. Ready when you are."

The sub-command turned to face the oncoming escort: a pair of fairly attractive females hustled in between two reinforcements. Facing the tarmac once more, he forced the women down the track at gunpoint, keeping a steady 5 paces behind.

"Either of you two stop, we shoot," he hissed in Italian.

They proceeded down the road, shifting their eyes over every inch of forest. Any sign of movement and there would be one dead girl on the ground. The two trackers kept wide, not wanting to be discovered, and moved with a stealthy quietness.

"One hundred meters in," the sub-commander whispered.

"Copy," Campos returned. He re-scanned the map that lay exposed on the centre table. There was a wide area to cover, but he was betting on them staying near the track.

"Sir, I think we have them." The guard pointed to a camera screen, whose source was just past the final checkpoint.

"Nice to see your visitors get their privacy," Campos muttered to Bose, staring at the figures on the screen. "Give the back-up team the co-ordinates."

"Proceeding," his sub-command verified.

They marched straight up to the checkpoint; illuminated by two red pillars on either side, both containing a device to capture the time done by a rider.

"Freeze," the sub-commander shouted, pointing his weapon into the trees. "Any hostile action will be returned by killing a hostage. We have men in the forest, and back up coming in from behind you. You cannot escape." He paused, waiting for the full extent of his words to sink in.

In the foliage, Hayden and Joey looked at each other.

"Looks like the game is up," Hayden said simply.

Joey shrugged. "A mere technicality. What about your disappearing act?"

"It's still a prototype." He turned serious. "What do we do now?"

"There's nothing we can do. They may not even know we're here. I'll bet you they'll move on in a minute."

"You're on."

A shot erupted in the silence.

Joey went deathly silent. "What was that?"

Hayden strained his eyes, peering through the gap. "They just shot one of them," he whispered, horrified.

"I hope you realise how serious we are," the sub-command shouted. "We don't play jokes. Show yourself within 15 seconds and we will leave the other girl unharmed."

"Split up," Hayden said in an urgent undertone. "If we shout they'll home in on us like bees to a honey pot. You've got ten seconds."

Joey took one look at the seriousness in his eyes and was away, slipping through the undergrowth to take up a retreated position.

Hayden faced the direction of the road, just visible through the leaves, and shouted back. "Who are you?"

He was right. By a pre-arranged signal one of the men coughed, bringing the reserve into play. All the unit had to do was play for time and wait for the other members to sneak up from behind.

"You don't know?" Mullit said quietly.

"I don't generally associate myself with murderers."

"Think of us as the cleaning squad."

"I thought communist bin men were extinct a long time age."

Mullit smirked. "You may be interested to know that our employer is a westerner. He doesn't particularly like word games, so if I were you I'd watch your step."

"Luckily for me I can. Your gunman's aim was so pathetic I'd be more worried if he were aiming for Belgium."

The sub-command's face reddened slightly in annoyance. "You have until the count of five to come out here, or we'll blow the whole forest. You already have one life on your hands. I don't advise you to take another." The hostage was forced onto her knees, a barrel tip placed crudely on her head.

Hayden bit his teeth in frustration. There was nothing he could do. He threw his weapon at the floor and stepped out onto the road.

"Glad to see you." Mullit cracked an evil grin, obviously pleased with his catch.

"How about a close inspection of my fist," Hayden muttered.

Mullit ignored him. "Where's the other guy?"

"Here." Joey walked out from the bushes, his weapon also discarded.

Hayden looked at him and groaned. "Why can't you ever learn to not get involved?"

"Sorry mate," Joey replied casually. "The stakes were too big to resist." He pointed back to where he had come out of the wood, highlighting the back-up squad emerging from their den.

"Let the hostage go," the sub-command ordered. "You two, any attempt at escape will end in a futile death. Do you understand?"

"I think I get the drift," Joey replied dully.

"Good." They set off, running at a brisk pace back towards the fitness centre, making no effort to conceal themselves.

"I take it you have the place under your caring control," Hayden asked, daring to stretch his stride to level Mullit's.

The response was a sharp jab in the back, the pistol trained squarely at his upper torso.

They rounded the main building, knowing the camera's would have informed Campos, and made a bee-line for the helicopter pad. Swiftly hurdling flower beds and lawns, they moved across the casually paved path that led to the waiting chopper. Here the tall trees blocked the sunlight, giving a cool shade for the sweating men. But the pace never decreased: the sub-commander driving his men ruthlessly towards their escape. The longer they spent on the island the more chance there was of discovery.

"Shame we don't have breadcrumbs," panted Hayden, spotting the chopper a little way off.

"Or heroin. The new police dogs can smell that a mile off."

They approached an eager Campos standing by the helicopter. "Get them aboard lads," he yelled, the pre-flight checks already complete. "We're going home."

Hayden and Joey were bundled into the rear cargo compartment, the slammed door reverberating in their ears. A quick scan told them all controls had been rendered inoperable by means of welded boxes over the buttons, and it lacked the toolbox Joey insisted that all helicopters had.

"You got a watch," Hayden asked.

"12.35," Joey replied.

"That's digital?"

"Yeah."

"That makes it slightly harder, but I can work with that." He picked up a scrap of paper from the floor and rubbed his finger in the dust. "I can't do analogue GPS, but I can make a compass." He carefully drew a circle on the paper and added numbers.

"A clock," said Joey sceptically.

"You should know this," Hayden replied disappointedly. "Clocks can use the sun as a compass. We have the time, so we can make our own."

"I remember, "Joey said excitedly. "We're in the northern hemisphere, so we point the hour hand at the sun and south will be halfway between that and the 12."

"Get timing. We need to know how fast we're going, and for how long."

Joey grinned. "My digital watch hasn't failed after all then."

"I suppose so. Lets ask Muggins how long the journey is." He banged on the door a few times until a voice shouted back.

"Five hours," said Hayden, returning to Joey, who was finishing the clock. "At least we'll be finished by night. I don't do star-gazing."

"Ok, you can take the first watch." He propped himself up against a support, and promptly dozed off.

Four and a half hours later, Joey awoke to find Hayden himself had taken a nap; the sky had turned a deep, pastel-covered cobalt in the approaching sunset. He checked the bearings Hayden had written down, noting he had only just fallen asleep. According to the now-smudged clock, they were still heading north, but the scenery flashing underneath had turned to land.

Joey gazed down towards the earth, feeling the thin metal flooring that held them in the air. He dreaded touching down, knowing that wherever he landed wouldn't be his choice of accommodation, yet deep down, he was ready to face it. Funny how time goes so slowly when you're a hostage, he thought, remembering the quote from one of his army lectures.

A muffled clink punctured his thoughts. The key turning in the lock, Joey softly kicked Hayden awake.

A head poked its head around the door. "Hungry?" He grinned. He'd obviously been enjoying a few of the in-flight comforts, and held up a bottle to prove it.

"Depends what's on the menu," Hayden yawned.

"Flesh," was the evil reply. "When one of you dies, the other gets to eat him." He cackled and slammed the door shut again.

Hayden and Joey looked at each other. "I'm vegetarian," they said in unison, and burst out laughing.

"Amazing how we can still laugh at times like this," Hayden said, wiping his eyes, but then turned serious. "Where do you think we are?"

"Somewhere in the middle of France, Spain, Austria, Germany, Switzerland, or possibly Luxembourg."

"Great," Hayden exclaimed sarcastically, rolling his eyes. "Because I don't suppose they'll give us a map to escape."

"Escape?"

"What else do we do? It may seem stupid, but if we're dead men, we might as well go out fighting."

"Won't it be expected?"

"Probably."

Joey shrugged. "We don't even know who they are yet."

"I'd prefer it to stay that way. The sooner we get out the better."

"You've got to know what you're up against in order to fight back," Joey replied warningly.

Hayden's answer was cut short by a sudden banking of the helicopter. Swinging left, Hayden hastily adjusted the compass to get a bearing, but Joey peered out of the window.

"We've arrived," he said shortly.

Hayden abandoned the paper and looked down at the illuminated helipad. It was surrounded by tall forest, dark and foreboding, which swayed ominously in the light breeze. It circled the light, keeping it hidden from the valley below.

"Infra-red laser beams," Joey muttered, catching sight of one out of the corner of his eye. "This place is pretty hushed up."

"Don't tell me we don't have flying lights on," Hayden asked.

"Looks like we're being sneaked in," Joey agreed. "If they've fitted an escull on the engine this bird wouldn't be heard 100 meters up."

"There's still enough light for a visual," Hayden reminded him.

"Yeah, but we've been way higher than I've ever been in a chopper. If we can't distinguish individual houses they won't be able to see us from the ground."

"Territory is all right though," remarked Hayden, looking at the landscape. The valley they were entering was one of many that spread out before them in a twisting chessboard. The peaks were crowned with trees that extended towards open valley beneath the contours, and the occasional village could be seen nestled quietly by the meandering river.

"Remote," commented Joey. "If we get out of wherever we're taken, it'll take us at least two days to get to any substantial settlement. The villages will have to

be ignored, because that'll be the first place they look."
He spoke as if discussing the weather, instead of his dire
survival hopes.

"So we head where?"

"If it comes to it," said Joey wearily, "we head west.
Oh, and watch the landing," he added. "Helicopters come
down with a judder."

True to his word, the landing was not as smooth as
most people tend to think. The vibrations deceased as the
engine was shut down, and the light dimmed to let the
people on board get off.

"Time to go," a hoarse voice shouted, and the cargo
doors were pulled open. Hayden and Joey were scrambled
out into a waiting golf cart, and stared wistfully at the
helicopter: the closest memory they had of the once-
perfect Italian holiday.

The air was still warm to the skin, but lacked the
humid heat of the Mediterranean. The wind soon began
to bite at the thinly-clad teenagers, who started to wonder
how long the journey would last.

A moment later, another clearing emerged in the
forest, and the lights of the golf cart were drowned by
bright spotlights that encompassed a huge garden.

"French?" muttered Joey, staring at the back end of
a house that resembled a royal palace. "It definitely isn't
Spanish," he continued, referring to the architecture. A

gunpoint silenced any further discussion as the golf cart herded its occupants round the side of the house.

The cart stopped, and Hayden and Joey were ushered through a side door into the building. They stopped in the darkness while one man searched for the light switch, throwing life into the kitchen. Fancy show-off, Joey thought, looking at the immaculate 18th Century kitchen. Burnished pots and bronze pans clung to the walls next to a magnificent industrial-sized oven, and the stone-flagged floor looked like it had never been stepped on.

"This way." A chiselled man spoke from the corner. He limped heavily into the middle of the room and pointed at the two teens.

"Are you the owner of this hotel?" Hayden asked politely, easily meeting the fierce stare directed at him.

The man glared at him with dark, almost inhuman eyes. "Head of Security," he said gruffly. "When you're here you obey the rules, or you face the consequences."

"That's a nice offer. How about one of ours?" Hayden said sarcastically.

"I don't advise you to play games," the man growled, again raising his fingers towards Hayden's face. "We've been ordered," he spat, clearly not liking the taste of the word, "not to harm you. But there are several techniques that will leave no trace." He dropped his voice down to a whisper. "If I were you, I'd be very, very careful."

Chapter 11

A sandstorm can be a dangerous freak of nature. Springing up from almost nothing to a blizzard, many a traveller has been lost in the fury of the desert. Shelter is nearly impossible to find, with the biting sand flying against every part of exposed body. This particular sandstorm deep in the heart of Iran was no different. Three brothers simply disappeared, poorly equipped with little protection. Further south, a local Shepard herding cattle across the plains went missing for different reasons: his head severed and buried in the sand.

A campsite he had been unfortunate enough to see had appealed to him, and he went towards it for supplies. Upon entering, he was unceremoniously shot and his goats taken.

Two men, having found the reason for the unexpected gun blast, resumed talking. They were sitting inside a large tent, sown decoratively with silk and braids beneath the tough camel skin hide. Within a few meters, two hundred men were at their command, with thousands more elsewhere.

"We have the fugitives," Aldo began. He was visiting one of his contacts with news of the past weeks events. The Arabian controlled the greatest force of men that Aldo could wield, and it paid well to visit him in person.

"That is indeed fortunate," the darker-skinned man replied.

"We tracked them to Sicily where they went to a separate resort island. We booked as soon as possible, and Philip Morel sent a helicopter in once our men were in position."

"They were killed?"

"Not yet. Philip took them to France to make sure of a few things. No doubt he'll order their deaths he's finished with them."

"The suitcases are in our possession then," the second man said greedily.

"One of our men in England reported a nest of military activity," replied Aldo. "It strains me to think of it, but I believe we have been outfoxed. Philip will confirm when he finds out how to open the cases. Our thought of the commercial flight via Italy was too smart: the two men were merely a distraction while the army transport the boxes straight to America on a military plane."

A cloud of sudden hatred darkened the Arab's face. "What about the safety feature Lucio mentioned? Does he still have it?"

"The scandium?"

"Yes. Even if we don't succeed in our dream, the British will pay dearly for it."

Aldo paused for a moment. "I'll find Lucio and get the scandium. Then give him a fake passport and let him think he's done a good deal."

"What about the two diversion suspects?"

Aldo looked thoughtful for a minute, and then grinned. "I'll let Philip have some fun with them, and then they will be disposed of."

"We will meet again when there is more to discuss," the second man replied. He preferred desert life to the dirty city streets. "I wish you luck with your mission."

"What do you think?" Joey asked. It had gone midnight by now, but they were still up, leaning against the metal bed they'd been given in their cell.

Hayden turned and yawned slightly. "Me thinks we're screwed."

"No thoughts for escape?"

"If we get the chance, but I doubt it. We're going to have to bluff through this with our lives at stake."

"I'd go for the sympathy vote," ventured Joey.

Hayden shook his head. "Not with that dead girl in Italy. If we could pull that off we'd know by now. These guys are serious. We either try and match them punch for punch, or sit here and play deaf."

"I wonder where this place is," wondered Joey aloud, changing the subject. "I'm still going for French architecture, but France is one huge spit of land. We could be anywhere."

"The Alps?" Hayden offered, remembering the contours they had seen from the chopper.

"Possibly, but it won't do us any good. Impassable hills are good for hiding in, but I doubt we'll find a McDonalds."

They sat there in silence, feeling the dampness spreading through the stone floor. Darkness had prevented a thorough tour of the premises – the light switch having been thoughtfully smashed – but the feint glow from Joeys watch revealed a windowless room somewhere under the main building.

"That's reminds me," said Hayden, the light flickering as the digits changed. "How did you smuggle that in here? They took my pencil and emptied my pocketful of dust. Not even a fly could have got through their searching method."

Joey grinned, just visible in the gloom. "I hid the strap in the chopper and put the head under my tongue."

"Remind me to send your mother a bunch of flowers. I always thought waterproof watches were for nutters who couldn't wash their hands properly."

"Twelve red roses," Joey agreed dully.

"Your watch won't force me into romance," Hayden chuckled. "I imagine daffodils will do."

"As long as they aren't lilies," Joey replied. "Do you think we'd better get some sleep?"

"I don't see why not. These beds aren't full of maggots are they?"

"Only the best worn blankets I'm afraid," Joey said, tossing a couple over to his friend. "Don't leave without me."

"Depends how loudly you snore," Hayden muttered, already half asleep.

There was no sunrise to welcome them when they woke. Instead, a cruel bang shook them from an uncomfortable sleep. Joey pushed himself from his bed and turned to face the incomer, standing a scant few inches from the ceiling.

"Could you make less noise please," he said weakly. "You're disturbing the peace."

The intruder, a multi-coloured mass of oiled hair sleek on a hollow face, clutched a rifle in his right hand, and a hammer in his left.

"Sorry about that," he grinned, a slight accent distributed across his words. He banged the hammer again, gong-like on the door. "But I like disturbing the peace. The boss wants to see you."

"What's the time?"

"Tuesday. Now out," he barked.

"Some hospitality," muttered Hayden, rising with a disgruntled stare at the hammer. He turned his face to the man. "I would dearly love to cut off your shiny mob of worms, but the mess would be terrible."

The man stopped and stared murderously at his prisoner. His English wasn't perfect, but he fully grasped Hayden's intention. He stuck out his gun and walked forward until they were almost touching. Hayden held his ground, worn, dishevelled, an acting war-hero, lowering his gaze to meet the smaller man.

"You touch me, and I will impale you on that foul hammer of your," Hayden said calmly, noticing Joey moving slowly into position. "I suggest you take us to your boss."

The man pushed the rifle into Hayden's stomach. "Before you even think about ordering me about," he hissed, his lower lip quivering furiously. "I'll have you fed to the dogs." He turned his head slightly and whistled. Another man entered, pistol in hand, and motioned for Joey to follow him.

Hayden took the opportunity to thrust the muzzle sideways and pushed past the guard, knocking into his shoulder as he did so. He stepped behind Joey and the second man, who was still covering both of them with his pistol.

"Out," he said, but the first man crashed into Hayden, swinging the rifle butt into his back.

"That's the last time you ever stand up to me," he shouted, fury etched in his face.

Hayden felt the flash of pain and grimaced, but stayed silent.

"Up," the man continued, pointing sharply with his weapon.

Trudging through the corridors in a complex underground network, they met no one except cameras, aimed at strategic spots along the solid concrete walls. The passages were long and straight, and doors in the structure were few and far between, making it easy to block in the event of a prisoner escape.

At last they came to a set of stairs, leading upwards to an iron door. A camera on the wall detected movement and switched to active, showing the party clearly defined on a screen the other side of the door. Automatically the computer blinked blue, and the security staff manning the door checked the image and pressed in the code.

Entrance from the prison cells opened into a small room: no bigger than a large cupboard, the access of which was covered by a tapestry in the kitchen.

"I'm guessing the authorities don't know about this," muttered Joey as they were led through another set of doors, these leading to what resembled the modern equivalent of a drawing room. Expansive windows spanned the two outer walls, but tinted shutters cruelly blocked the sunlight shining on the interior. Glass and leather furniture decorated the polished floor, complimented by a full wall painting at the far end. Two further doors were set into the wall; each looked after by passive guards.

Joey walked over to one of the chairs and flicked an imaginary speck of dust from the armrest.

"Very funny." The voice came from a figure sitting behind the desk, swathed in shadows.

"Bonjour," Hayden replied, turning around from a bookcase. He stopped mid-sentence, unsure of what his eyes were telling him.

The shape leaned forward from the shadows, revealing a round young face with dark blue eyes. The skin was pale and waxen, surrounded by short, black hair that failed to hide the malice hidden beneath the surface. He couldn't have been older than 14.

"Not expecting a kid," whispered the boy. "Not many people do."

Joey looked startled, but slowly broke into an amused smile. "Does that mean we got the French part right?" he said brightly, quickly overcoming the barrier. Guards with guns may be intimidating, but there was no way he was going to be bullied by someone younger than him.

The boy narrowed his eyes. "I frown upon sarcasm," he said. "Sit down."

Hayden and Joey sat down at opposite ends of the room, making the boy turn his head whenever he was speaking.

"Just because I am young does not mean I am less clever than any of you," the boy replied, catching on to the ploy. "I can speak five languages, have three inventions under my name, and discovered the Huldon Vortex. No doubt," he smiled, "you don't know what that is." He seemed to take great pleasure in other people's lack of knowledge, and even if he had not held them at gunpoint, Hayden would have immediately classed him as a first-grade idiot.

"I daresay it's absolutely essential to human survival," Joey yawned.

The boy was about to launch a scathing reply, but Hayden interrupted: flowing conversation could be important.

"I always wanted to be clever," he said wistfully, ignoring Joey's amused glance. He had in fact got near-perfect results in his GCSEs. "I mean, you could do whatever you wanted. You wouldn't have to revise for exams for a start; I suppose you could get whatever job you needed. Philosophy, entrepreneur, government think-tanks, scientist? You could even become a politician and dazzle the world with your brilliance," he finished, with only a hint of sarcasm.

"Western politics has nothing to give me," the boy barked coldly. He tensed and seemed angry, and the fingers were taut and stiff. "The arrogant politicians, who think they know everything," he spat. "Never. I will conduct my service to the world from here."

"How nice," Joey muttered sarcastically.

"Not a bad idea though," Hayden replied mildly. "You could solve world poverty just by selling this house."

The boy turned. "There are many reasons for keeping the rich people rich," he said slowly.

Joey spluttered into laughter. "What sort of person are you?" he asked incredulously. "Just because you think you're clever doesn't mean you can take control over people's lives."

A faint smile crossed the youth's face. "You're wrong," he said quietly. "I do have power over life and death. That is the blessing which comes with money."

"Well aren't we revealing everything today," Hayden exclaimed. "Why don't you rewrite the Human Rights

Act? Rule number one:" he said, miming reading from a script in an overly-important loud voice. "You shall have no other God apart from a sadistic French kidnapper."

The boy froze. He had never been spoken down to before, and it used all his patience to prevent him ordering the captives shot. He snapped his fingers instead, and two guards came forward with rope, ruthlessly tying the teenagers back-to-back and pressing them to the floor.

"Money is an art," Philip whispered icily, staring down at the inert pair struggling on the floor. "It advances technology, dominates people's lives, enables technical wonders and structural masterpieces to be built, and can make people feel either security or despair. To observe its use is an advantage when living in this world."

"It's more the age at which you flaunt it," Hayden replied distastefully, spitting out part of the carpet. You can't substitute maturity, which you will only grasp when you have passed through the turbulent life of a teenager."

The boy grew angry again. "What do you know?" he thundered. "Youth is innocence. My age is what gives me strength." He pressed his face towards Hayden's. "There have been examples of youth brilliance throughout history. Chinese Emperors were often younger than twenty. Cleopatra saved Egypt when she was only seventeen. Even England has had its moments: King Edward was nine when he inherited the throne. I aim to show the world that it is still possible."

Hayden paused in thought, wondering how to reply. He was well aware of the guns clenched by his kidnappers, and one wrong comment could all too quickly spell the end. "There's a chink in your armour," he replied slowly. "How deeply did you research these people?"

"I know their entire histories," the boy returned maliciously.

"Then you'll know that King Edward was hidden away by his advisers, got the country into a mess, and then lost the Peasants Revolt," Hayden grinned, bracing himself as the boy stood on his hand.

"Cleopatra wasn't exactly as golden-edged as you claim either," Joey added brightly, watching for the effect. "She only seduced Caesar and Mark Anthony because of her body, and when Rome had a little trouble, she killed herself."

"That is of little consequence," the boy replied coldly, clearly taken aback by the sudden pressure of conflicting arguments. "Where they have failed I will succeed."

"Are you the Chinese Emperor then?" Joey asked cheekily. "Because when their Empire was at its greatest, they had a massive army and were up against uncultured rabble who barely scratched a living."

"I don't have to listen while you procrastinate yourselves to death," he hissed.

"You brought us here," Joey muttered in protest, but decided not to push, noticing the drawn batons held comfortably by the guards. He lay still, staring at the floor.

The boy noted Joey's sudden submission and felt eager to be in control again. "Have you had breakfast?"

"No," Hayden replied, not giving him the satisfaction of hiding.

"Good," the boy continued somewhat pleasantly. "Because you will not get any. You will soon learn that good behaviour will be rewarded with sustaining your life."

"Screw you," Hayden smiled. "You could learn a lot from us."

The boy never wavered. "Seeing as you're eating my carpet, that's not much of a bluff."

"It wasn't one."

His interrogator looked up and stared directly at his captive. "What can I learn from you?" he said mockingly. He motioned for the guards to haul Hayden and Joey to their feet, then walked briskly out of a side door and down a set of stairs. A concrete room greeted them, with an impenetrable metal gate in the corner.

He opened it and marched through. Hayden, bound between two guards, followed, eyes widening as he found himself surrounded by a maze of equipment. Huge robots with intricate claws and laser-controlled arms stood to attention either side of a steel operating table, and a conveyor belt snaked round the outside of the room. Dozens of instrument panels, detection hardware and test tubes were piled on benches, and a large electron microscope sat in one corner. A first rate scientific lab, Hayden thought.

"What's your project," he asked lamely.

"Nothing that concerns you," the boy replied smugly.

"I suppose you think I won't understand," Hayden said, yawning. He pointed to some metal containers that resembled heavy-duty thermos flasks. "Does it involve coffee?"

The boy clearly didn't find it funny. "They are…"

"Magnetic trapping devices," Hayden interrupted. "Used to increase the efficiency of laser cooling by suspending atoms in mid-air through a carefully controlled magnetic field." He paused. "They can also be used for hitting people," he added brightly.

"Otherwise called evaporative cooling," the boy said, ignoring the jibe. "Laser cooling uses photon waves to reduce movement among atoms, but the photon kick, while freezing nucleon vibration, will continue to disturb the electron orbital. In other words, it will freeze an atom for dissection."

"So you're into atomic research," Joey said, acting impressed.

The boy wasn't fooled. He turned and watched Joey struggle against the rope. "You were saying what you could teach me?" he said scornfully. "I'm interested."

"Oh yeah," Hayden said, casually flicking his hair. "The one lesson you can't learn from a book. Humanity."

The word sparked a tension in the air: the boy stood upright, his body frozen. Only the eyelashes moved, framing cold, piercing eyes. White hands clenched by his side.

Hayden remained relaxed and leant against the wall, holding the stare with a warm glow from his own. "You don't understand me?" he asked softly.

They boy snapped out of his trance. "How dare you," he whispered menacingly.

"It's quite simple," Hayden replied, easily brushing aside the malice directed at him. He'd had enough of the games, and he faced the boy with an unyielding defiance. "I dare, because quite frankly I think you're a sadistic and self-obsessed jerk, and I don't care what you do to me."

Chapter 12

Hayden and Joey exchanged glances as they were escorted back to their room.

"What do you make of that?" Joey whispered once the door had been slammed shut.

Hayden, too busy pulling faces at the door, took a while to respond. "Lets call that one Viper," he said, indicating the hook-nosed guard, before he turned back to Joey's question. "Apart from a delusional kid acting like he's conquered the sun, the moon and everything in between, not much."

"He could be a front," Joey suggested.

Hayden shook his head. "He's genuine. There's no actor that age that could pull that off. Besides, they'd have to speak at least two languages fluently."

"Why would he bother to see us?"

"I don't know. There's no obvious motive, except possible revenge."

"The plane?"

"Your guess is as good as mine."

"But what's he got to do with it?"

Hayden shrugged. "That's what we have to find out."

"I'd be interested to know the guy's set-up. How on earth he got hold of a mansion like this at his age I will never understand."

"Family heirloom?"

"If we get out of this alive I'm coming back here with the marines," Joey said resolutely.

"Remind me to buy a ticket," said Hayden gloomily. "Seriously though, it'll be nigh on impossible to break out. They don't have any reason to take us out of here unless he wants to talk to us, which isn't very likely, and then we'll be accompanied by armed guards. They won't take us for a nice walk in the forest so we can knock them out."

Joey spread his hands out in irate helplessness. "Looks like little Philip can do with as he pleases then."

"Little Philip?"

"Philip Morel. That was the name on the document on his desk."

"Suits him," Hayden muttered dryly.

Joey glanced over at Hayden's dejected features. "That's objective one complete," he offered. "We know who he is."

"That's not going to help us." There was a short pause, both men contemplating whether they would survive the next few days. Fanatics with armed guards cared little for the lives of others.

"Here, you always liked taking things apart," Joey said, changing the subject. He kicked the bed. "See if you can make anything out of this junk."

"Too bad, they're welded together," Hayden replied, but checked under the bed anyway. He reappeared a few seconds later, his face no longer sceptical.

"We're in," he grinned, and dove back under the bed. A few metallic scrapes later, a dust covered object rolled out and stopped next to Joey's foot.

"What's this?"

"Bed springs," Hayden said eagerly, adrenaline surging through him as he retrieved another coil, hope rekindled. "Totally useless, but the wire holding them in place packs a mean punch."

He straightened up, holding a thick piece of wire. The ends were blunted, but Joey spotted a hairline crack at one end: enough for a splinter.

"Pick the bed up," Hayden ordered, placing the shaft in a spring. The other springs were attached perpendicularly, letting him keep hold of the shaft without getting his hands in the way.

Joey manoeuvred the bed into position and waited for the signal. Hayden took his t-shirt off and wrapped it round his hands to soften the shock, then nodded.

Joey dropped the bed onto the upright spring, splitting the shaft nearly in two before it veered off and pounded the earth.

Hayden coughed and found the largest part of the wire; the rounded end was intact, but the piece where the bed had contacted it had snapped, leaving a sharp point.

"Weapon number 1," he said cheerfully, holding it aloft.

"Are we putting the springs back in?" Joey asked. "Or do we annoy them and take them all out?"

The decision was made for them as the door was opened and Viper stepped in.

"Unlucky mate," he grinned nastily, obviously pleased with himself. He pointed to a grill set in the roof. "You've been caught on camera. Now out." He gestured into the corridor with his gun.

Hayden felt as if he was dead already. It was bad enough being kidnapped, but to let your kidnappers know that you were intending to attack them was beyond repair. Now that the bullet lay in the chamber, Hayden was scared.

He tensed his body for the shot, assuming his death. Instead, a sharp pain shot through his head, and he fell into darkness.

Hayden awoke to an empty room. Sorely rubbing his head, he realised Viper must have hit him when he had his back turned. He groaned and waited for his head to clear, and then stood up. He banged on the door a few times and sat down, staring at the grill.

"What do you want?" A gruff voice came through the door, seemingly not too pleased at the intrusion.

"Where's Joey?" Hayden complained loudly.

"Being shot," the voice grumbled, and disappeared back down the corridor.

"Fat chance," he murmured to himself, but deep down he knew it could happen at any time. When talking to Philip he had acted out of sheer instinct, not daring to think that the boy could have him killed. He knew their lives were in extreme danger, and time was beginning to run out.

Another set of footsteps entered his hearing range, and Joey walked in. "Sorry I'm late," he said jovially, but quickly turned sour at the sight of dried blood on his friends head.

"Where'd you go?"

"They thought it was best to separate us. Is your head alright?"

They were interrupted by the guard, who had remained in the cell. "You're wanted," he growled in his usual manner.

"I can't wait," Hayden said dryly. "By the way, was it you who hit me yesterday?"

Viper looked suspicious. "Why do you want to know?"

"I was going to send them a thank-you card," Hayden explained. "But of course, there's no shop."

Philip was again waiting for them in the library. "I know you won't have a good morning, nor do I wish you to have one, so I won't bother to say it."

"You could have just lied and saved yourself a speech," Hayden muttered.

"Do not interrupt," Philip said sternly.

"He's been taking teaching lessons," Joey murmured back, grim and defiant.

There was an awkward silence as Philip tried to impose his influence. "I'm surprised," the boy remarked coldly. "You actually listened. You've hardly shut up since you got here."

Joey stayed silent, but Hayden ploughed ahead. "We have nothing to say. You wanted to speak to us, otherwise we wouldn't be here."

Philip's expression never changed. "You still haven't asked me why you are here," he said, following every reaction with calculative eyes.

"Such a question is expected," Hayden returned briefly. He'd had enough of the games, and he just wanted to go home.

Philip paused. He was a good judge of character, but these two had kept him guessing for over two days. The inability was getting to him, and each session was becoming more of a period to endure.

Joey decided to cooperate. "Seeing as you brought it up, why are we here?"

"It is of no consequence."

"See," Hayden said shortly to Joey. "He'll consider ransom too amateur, so I'll imagine he's using us as bait for something. Or he's just mentally unstable and thought he'd kidnap two people to play with." He turned back to Philip. "Tell me, what's 'suitcase' in French?" he asked.

"Valise" Philip replied cautiously.

A light gleamed in Hayden's eyes. "Sorry mate," he grinned. "No idea where Italy came into the plan, because it went to America."

"What are you talking about?"

"The suitcases," Hayden repeated, waiting for it to sink in. "Valise"

"The guy on the plane said Valise," Joey said, suddenly realising where Hayden was going. "The same ones that Wright had?" he questioned.

"You remember those cases that the airport put our bags in," Hayden said to Joey. "They are the same ones that Wright nearly had stolen from his house."

"And the same as the photos the Italian police had," Joey pounced. "You mean we were right? The cases were important."

Hayden nodded sourly, the full weight of the realisation hitting him like a hammer. "He used us as a diversion, and judging by our current situation, I'd say it worked."

Joey stiffened. "If I ever meet him I'm going to throttle him," he declared angrily. "I knew he was a bad egg ever since we found him selling technology to Lapcon."

Philip stood up suddenly. "How do you know that?" he demanded. Fury was etched in his face.

"Internet," Hayden said tentatively, wondering why it was important.

"In Italy?"

Hayden nodded, and Philip leapt into a vigorous outburst in French, shouting orders at the guards. "Find whoever put Lapcon onto the websites and kill him," he roared. "If anyone else finds Lapcon dispose of them as well."

Joey put his hands over his ears before turning serious again. "You could simply have taken the suitcases from the plane instead of kidnapping us and killing civilians," he glared, focusing Philip in a deathly stare.

Philips eyes remained frozen. "There are at least five major terrorist organisations aware of those cases, and at least three that would dare an attempt to steal it," Philip replied icily. "I am not foolish enough to steal in England: the whole country would be shut off. I had to wait until it was out of the country."

"Unlucky for all of us I suppose," Hayden said glumly. "You don't have your package, and we're locked up like prisoners of war."

"Do you know what is in that suitcase?" Philip replied curiously.

"No idea. Wright said they were family heirlooms, although we think it's something military. Simple research maybe, but the man on the plane was shouting Valise at the pilot, and then you turned up in Italy for our luggage, taking us for insurance."

"But still," Joey insisted. "Why bother with us? They could have checked the suitcases in Italy and then gone."

"I guess we'll find that out when we learn the contents," Hayden said heavily. "You probably have to open it in liquid helium or something. Stop terrorists getting it. They didn't know if we knew anything."

"Something you won't find out," Philip interrupted.

"Does that mean we're surplus to requirements?" Hayden said glumly.

"I know when you're going to die," he replied nastily.

A surge of determination rose in Hayden's chest. "If we're going to die you will have no cooperation at all," he said squarely. "We are quite happy to mess up your life."

Philip laughed. "What exactly are you going to do?"

Hayden ignored him. "This is an expensive rug," he said expansively. "If you don't wish to get blood on it, I suggest you tell your men not to shoot us. We might anger them a bit."

"If this room is in anyway damaged, you will," he started.

"Will what?" Hayden interrupted. "Die?" he laughed. "We're already dead men." He picked up an ornament off the glass table and weighed it in his hand. "Value?" he asked, as Joey did the same.

"€4000," Philip said frostily, daring him to move.

"Any objections?" Hayden asked Joey.

Joey shrugged. "Might as well."

"Ok," Hayden said, and chucked the figurine at the window. It shattered, leaving a mass web of cracks with a neat hole in the centre.

Joey too released his catapult, hurling a glass paperweight into a fish tank. The water flooded the floor amid bits of plant, gravel and debris.

"Stop," Philip screamed sharply, rising to his feet.

Joey and Hayden froze in the act of picking up the table, as did the guards, now within feet of their prey, batons extended.

Philip lowered his hands. "Actions like that will get you killed," he said scathingly. "And I would have killed you already, if I had not previously decided your future."

Hayden bit his tongue, wondering whether to hurl insults back at the boy or to simply proclaim him as the mighty seer of a thousand seas.

"It so happens that in four days the Black Carbon Rally is coming through France," Philip continued, unaware of the internal battle going on before him. "The richest men in the world will be coming to visit us with their supercars."

Hayden and Joey both knew what the Black Carbon Rally was. The enigmatic drivers that raced through the country had caused a terrific accident a few years back, although it was never fully proven. The race was illegal and no records existed to convict anyone.

"Didn't the police ban it?"

"This year we've moved it from the roads to Magny-Cours race track," Philip acknowledged. "But the rules, or rather, lack of them, are still the same. No professional drivers, only road vehicles allowed, and if anyone gets shoved off the road, tough luck."

"That piece of information makes my life better how?" Hayden retorted.

"I thought it was obvious," Philip replied insanely. "You'll be entering."

Chapter 13

Later that evening Hayden was back with Joey, this time in a different cell, studying the details of an Aston Martin Vantage that Philip had given them to race in. They both knew a bit about cars, and considering the wealth of the competitors and underworld prestige that surrounded this race, he was sure that posse's of Mercedes SLRs, Ferrari's and Lamborghini's would turn up. Basically, it was a lost cause from the start. The Aston was nice, but the V8 was too slow in the heavy vehicle. It was primarily built for luxury at the lower end of the Aston range, and speed was only as an afterthought. The top speed was only 170mph. Pathetic when compared to the 252mph that sprouted from the exhaust of a Bugatti Veyron; the £1million price tag of which was about two hours work for all invited.

Hayden stared around the room and strained his mind for options. He noted the security camera hidden in the grill, and the steel door, undoubtedly locked. The PC in one corner was connected to the internet, but only a stock-car buying-and-selling site was accessible. Philip had left them £1000 in an online account, supposedly for jazzing up the car, but Hayden suspected it was only there to frustrate them. Joey had checked earlier, and they could only afford half a racing tire.

Hayden slumped back against the wall and closed his eyes, seemingly admitting defeat. Then suddenly he sat bolt upright, an idea charging crazily into his head.

He leaned over and whispered in Joey's ear. Joey raised his eyebrows slightly, unsure whether the plan would work. "Spectacular," he said finally, "but this is the stuff dreams are made of."

Hayden shrugged nonchalantly. Life wasn't a game, but if he was forced to play by Philip's rules, then he was going to cheat.

He turned to the PC and typed in a few keywords. Half an hour later and inexplicably £10,000 better off, he leant back on the chair and grinned.

Saturday morning dawned grey and dull, a feeling that mirrored the moods of Hayden and Joey. The odds were stacked against them, and their opponents were calling the shots.

Breakfast, brought to them by a hooded guard, was a silent affair, both brooding on the likelihood that Philip meant them to die on the track. They doubted that embarrassment from no driving skills and a rubbish car would be the only treatment they'd get.

Hayden sat on his bed, staring emotionless at the floor. His plan, which had seemed so confident yesterday, was now shrouded with uncertainty. Still, the look on Philip's face when he realised he'd been duped would be worth it. Suppressing a grin, he turned to Joey and said, "what do you think?"

Joey pulled a face, then changed his mind. There's no point in being miserable, he thought. "Fancy a press-up competition," he said casually.

"Sure, why not."

They eased slowly onto the floor, stretching before beginning to pump their muscles. To the man idly watching the camera, it looked like madness. He called his superior and within a few minutes, the whole control room was filled with laughing staff.

"Mental," one of them muttered.

Hayden and Joey sat up again, thankful for the exercise. Hayden caught onto Joey's drift and suggested a singing contest.

"Yeah ok." Joey paused, and then whispered, "lets find any bugs and shout at them."

Together they searched the cell, but found nothing. Hayden looked at the grill. The camera probably had a microphone somewhere, so he grinned manically into the lens and stepped back.

"Hit it," Hayden yelled, and Joey started bashing spoons against the beds and walls while Hayden belted out lyrics into the camera.

They stopped upon the entrance of the Viper-faced guard. "Sorry," said Joey nonchalantly, looking like he'd been caught raiding the sweet jar. "I was bored."

Viper pointed out with his hand, and they were led upstairs at gunpoint.

Philip was waiting for them on the drive. He smiled nastily. "I hope you enjoy your last day on earth. Just think, the last thing you'll see is a cloud of dust as cars go roaring past."

Hayden's eyes danced in the gloom, no longer the downbeat prisoner. Fireworks exploded in the back of his brain, which focused like twin streams of fire on Philip.

Joey too seemed to grow taller in the breeze: he stood aloof, his face hardened with confident determination. "Don't worry," he said brazenly. "You'll have your race. One that you won't forget."

The two teens turned their backs and walked off to the nearest car, but not before Hayden raised his hand in a casual salute.

Philip paused in the back of his limousine, his ears twitching as he thought. It seemed stupid, but it was as if they knew something he didn't. His ego diminished the idea as helped himself to a coke, and imagined the media outcry when two deaths were reported as English schoolboys.

As the racing circuit approached through the windows, Hayden couldn't figure how a place so full of life could fell so empty. Car mechanics and reporters covered the ground like ants, but they all seemed distant and disconnected. The cars he had discussed with Joey were already out of their lorries, showing off spotless glitz and glamour at every opportunity. It wasn't just a case of the best stats: big companies had splashed out money for their car to be driven. Others had gone for upgraded classics including some from the 1950s. Still, there was not one car that failed the 190mph mark.

Joey nudged Hayden and pointed to the last lorry in line, a faded cattle carrier with plastic bags stuffed in the gaps. Hayden grinned with satisfaction: the media were staying well clear of the pile of scrap.

The car stopped and the pair stepped out, followed by Viper and his companion. Both carried hidden weapons under their mechanic outfits.

Joey, as the older of the two, confirmed and chatted to the lorry driver, while Hayden entered the rear of the truck.

"Excellent," Joey said. He handed the man a slip of paper. "Thank your company for me."

The driver nodded and reached under his seat for a long thin package, which gave to Joey. The cover, embossed in angels with 'Merry Christmas' written on the side. "Sorry about the paper," the man said. "Its all we had."

"Pleasure," Joey returned.

Viper expressed a suspicious interest in the package, but before he could intervene, a throaty roar echoed out of the tailgate. Hayden exited, the throttle of a Caterham CSR beneath his foot.

The Caterham was a kit car built purely for fun: cartoon magazine was the first thought that entered anyone's mind. It had no roof, no windows, and absolutely no finesse. The interior console was virtually non-existent, and the front headlights looked like a bee's antennae, popping up between the body and the front wheels. The rear wheels were covered with thin aerofoils, but the engine had been squashed, narrowing as it neared the front of the car and leaving the front wheels exposed. Most of it was made of carbon fibre, making it, as Hayden put it, very, very light. The small engine could take it to 60mph in 3.7seconds, and it had a top speed of 150mph.

Viper's companion walked over to the sunshine-yellow vehicle and asked where the Aston was. "It makes no difference to me," he said nastily, knowing the hidden surprises his boss had in store for the English men, "but I was told you'd be driving an Aston Vantage."

"We sold it," Joey said lightly, examining the high-grade racing tires.

Viper raised his eyebrows.

"Yeah," Hayden said as he cut the ignition. "We found someone on the internet quite willing to pay £80,000 for it. After that went through, we got in touch with a car rental place, bought this beauty from Caterham, and a few mechanics did the rest."

"You'd never get this from a car rental place," Viper said sceptically, eying the advanced sport seats and rear wing.

"That was just the power," Hayden replied, as if discussing the weather. He lifted the bonnet, revealing a sparkling Ferrari engine. "We rented one out for £2,000, got a few mechanics to change the engines over, and we've got the same power, but half the weight, as that." He pointed down the line to a glistening Ferrari Enzo. "Of course," he continued, "we still had a bit of cash to spend after that, so we modified it."

Hayden switched the engine on again, taking enormous satisfaction in Viper's perplexed features. "I wouldn't like to be around your boss when you tell him we ripped him off," he said cheekily. "But I'm afraid our accommodation wasn't up to scratch."

"We don't expect mongooses to bring us food," Joey added brightly, climbing into the passenger seat.

Viper's face darkened, but before he could do anything, he was engulfed with eager reporters.

"Say sorry to the chief," Hayden yelled, "but it can only seat two people. See you later." He gunned the throttle and disappeared down the road before the startled guards could react.

Viper started after them, brutally pushing past the microphones shoved under his nose, and ran towards the main building. He elbowed through the crowd and sprinted up a staircase before grabbing a receptionist, demanding to know where Philip Morel was.

The frightened receptionist quailed under the furious stare Viper directed at her, and gestured towards the front gantry. "You'll need a pass," she protested, but the man had already gone.

Up in the gantry, Philip was piling a plate of crab sandwiches when Viper approached him. "What is it?" Philip said quietly.

"They disappeared," Viper spat, his ears reddening. "They simply got in the car and drove off," he explained as Philip's knuckles whitened. "We weren't expecting to escort them into the driver's compound."

Philip stiffened. "You'd better make sure you find them," he hissed, knowing his head of security could set up road blocks and call out helicopters if necessary. "Just keep it quiet." He turned back to the buffet as the Viper pushed his way back through the doors.

Chapter 14

Once Hayden and Joey were out of sight of the lorry, they turned into the driver's compound. Drivers normally entered with five minutes to go before the race: no mechanics or team members were allowed in, but the Caterham cruised in half an hour early. The press, who had by this time seen the car, were turned back at the barriers, allowing the pair a cool rest in the underground chamber.

Joey turned to an included mp3 player and selected some tracks, listening to the pounding bass – speakers were hidden behind the seats – while they changed into their clothes. Both had blue and yellow racing suits, but Joey zipped his up over grey work overalls.

Joey went off to the toilets to sort his package out, so Hayden sat back, propped his feet up, and promptly dozed off, totally unaware of the furious activity that began to surround him. He knew what he had to do, and that was all that mattered. The pair had no idea what to expect from Philip, but phase 1 of their own plan had already been completed. Phase 2 was underway, and phase 3 was yet to come.

Joey came back with a minute to go, turned the music off and tapped Hayden on the shoulder. He got into the passenger seat, keeping the package tucked under his arm.

The sun was now beating down outside, and the cars were getting ready to begin their warm up lap. Hayden hardly thought it necessary with the beautiful weather overhead, but it was ideal for show boating. The media would lap it up, and his car was open top, so he wasn't bothered. He pointed this out to Joey, finding it hilarious that the other drivers, sitting in their £millions worth of cars, couldn't wind their windows down. They'd be boiling, while Hayden and Joey sat in an open top tin can which only cost £31,000.

Smiling to himself, Hayden donned a pair of wind deflective sunglasses, chosen over a ski mask to keep cool, and imagined what 200mph would do to his hair.

The overhead lights, mounted above every car, turned green. He was furthest the exit, so followed the rest out, exhilarated by the noise.

The track lay at the end of the tunnel, and the crowd's shout could just be heard above the engines. One by one, stylish super-cars climbed the gentle slope to the tarmac, and sped off into the distance. All but one.

The last car to enter looked like a sunshine-yellow antique. The trapezium-shaped body resembled an advanced dune buggy, but the low suspension and boyish back wing kept it stuck to road racing. The two drivers sat relaxed behind the wheel, waving slowly to the crowd.

Hayden gently trundled off down the straight, almost hearing the cameras click and muffled laughter that followed them.

Once out of sight from the crowds, he switched his mp3 player back on, sat back in his seat and began to drive, stopping just past the second stand to let Joey off. His friend made his way into the undergrowth before heading towards the buildings.

Hayden came back to the start a full minute after everyone else, music still echoing from the speakers. The start had been modified to two lines, each following the same distance before entering the main track. Every car was on an equal stance, giving a mad rush into the first corner a mile distant. By this time, the Ferrari engine would be propelling the Caterham at nearly 250mph.

The lights went red, than orange, and then finally turned green. Thirty exhausts belched in fury, emitting clouds of invisible smoke as they spurted off down the track. None however, went faster than the Caterham.

The racing tires, low draft and light body enabled it to hit 60mph in three seconds, and then onto a 100, and then 150mph.

"Yehah!" Hayden exclaimed as he watched the speedometer fly upwards. His previous driving experience was limited to go-karts, but Caterham had removed the gear stick and changed the transmission into three gears, accessed by paddles in the steering wheel. They had also fitted an automatic clutch, meaning he only had to release the accelerator when he hit 5000 revs, and flick the switch.

"Philip needs to think twice before he enters people in a race," Joey muttered from his perch on top of the second stand. "Any twirp can push a pedal."

It was much more than pushing a pedal, Hayden realised, as the wind flew past, forcing him back into his seat. The forces were incredible, and he could barely force the rushing air into his lungs: it simply didn't stay in his mouth long enough for him to gulp it in. He hit 180mph, but from then on it was guesswork, as the technicians had left the old gauge on.

A sign came and went, and Hayden realised it must have been the 200 meter mark. He slammed the brakes on as 100 meters went past, and hoped he hadn't left it too late. He was lucky. The u-turn came up sharply and he swung the wheel. The Caterham nimbly responded, cutting in from the outside and crudely perfecting the turn. He thanked the times he had sat down and watched Formula 1, even though it had bored him.

Hayden mashed down the pedals again, but the engine groaned and shuddered. He realised he was still in top gear and quickly flicked down.

The mistake cost him three places. Quick acceleration saved him from a fourth car, an ugly Noble, slipping past, but he was stuck in competition, and now that speed wasn't an issue in the tight twists and turns, the driving became downright dirty.

Twice the Noble came perilously close the Caterham's rear wing and one car was pushed off the track, but Hayden stuck to the Merc in front of him and copied his every move. He followed inch by inch the rear bumper, feet poised over the brake and accelerator pedals whenever the other was in use, mirroring Merc's brake lights.

The second straight in the track came and went, and thrust them back into cornering. Hayden grimly hung on, trying not to breathe in the Merc's exhaust. Then they were out, onto a wide sweeping bank that opened up into the straight.

He shoved the lever into top gear and jammed his right foot to the floor. He broke out of the slipstream and hurtled round the outside corner at 180mph.

The Merc kept pace around the inside, but didn't turn and cut across the track, trying to block the Caterham's route. The move came too late; Hayden's superior speed eating up to space and sweeping through the start line in front.

Joey was lying down on the roof of the stand half way round the course. Wedging himself between two girders, he was almost impossible to spot. He put on surgical gloves before carefully opening his package, discarding the box. The first lap had almost finished when he was sure the rifle he held was ready, and put his eye to the scope. Quickly adjusting the focus, Joey watched the leading pack.

Hayden was concentrating hard. The Caterham was flying ahead in the straits but falling behind in the turns. He spun and hit the fence, but the expensive tires gripped the road and pulled him away.

The steering was extremely responsive, seeming to direct the car easily wherever Hayden willed it to go. It became stiffer at higher speeds, but that served to remind him to slow for the corners and helped prevent spinning. He raced round the circuit, becoming more and more confident. He realised he'd got through the first laps only by copying the Merc, but now his adrenaline-pumped brain was coming back, and he started to push.

Joey gazed through his scope, lined up his sights, and squeezed the trigger. The Barrett cracked, signalling the bullet was on its way. It reached its target, entering the wheel of a Porsche. The tire ruptured, and the car slowly drifted to a halt amid the curses of its driver.

Joey knew he couldn't take out many: the rifle would be heard by the crowd unless there was a car racing below. His window was small, but he watched in satisfaction as the cars behind the Porsche skidded to avoid it. "That'll slow them down," he murmured, choosing his next shot.

Hayden entered the 19th lap still in 3rd place, mainly due to Joey's exquisite shooting, and started hunting down the front runners. Two laps later he was within sight of the Lamborghini. The shining blue body was streaking away into the distance, advanced aerodynamics working to perfection, but Hayden was up for a challenge. He jammed the throttle to the stops and hurtled after it, gaining with every second.

21 attempts at the first 170 degree corner had perfected and honed Hayden's ability to a fine art. He braked late, throwing his left foot forward as he went past the 100 meter mark. Hayden shot into second, and was still breaking when he flung the wheel round. The tires screamed in protest, but carried the car round the curve, sliding the back wheels into the gravel. Clouds of dust billowed up as Hayden threw the car forward, deftly flicking through gears. The Lamborghini ploughed into

the dust and lost control, sliding off the track and into the barriers. One down, one to go.

Hayden managed to reach the first placed Koenigsegg with three laps to go. The cars surged around the bends and rocketed down the straits, fighting inch by inch for the lead. The driver in the Koenigsegg was dark skinned with black hair, and unusually cobalt eyes revealed him as Mark Swain. A former rally champion across Europe, he knew how to handle speed, and the CCR he had underfoot was astonishingly fast. He drove calmly with smooth precision, handling the power with controlled aggression, and took an increased liking to blocking the lighter Caterham.

Hayden fought back, using the CCR's slipstream to keep in touch, but he didn't have the skill or experience to go past.

Just as the final lap sign was being readied by the finish line, Hayden grew frustrated and cut in on the inside. The final corner before the sweeping bank veered up sharply as the cars raced side by side for the lead, but Hayden had the wrong line, away from the worn tracks other cars had left.

The Koenigsegg began edging closer to the Caterham's side, blocking the inside lane and forcing it to brake early. The other alternative as the viewers saw it, was that the

Caterham would be pushed off the road, but Hayden had none of these in mind.

It was a move he had learnt on the computer: instead of going from inside to outside round the bend, he used his opponent as a buffer and power-slid into it. The wheels kissed, but the momentum of the Caterham was greater and the CCR was shunted to the outside. It slid onto the grass, cutting a wide swath of destruction across the turf, while the Caterham used the touch as an emergency brake and stayed on the inside of the track.

Hayden recovered from the slight wobble and shot out down the track, the speed paralyzing him into his seat. Hayden let out a sigh of relief and didn't notice a sign held up as he entered his last lap. There were more important things on his mind as he realised that the Koenigsegg had impossibly caught him up.

The CCR drew level, the driver holding up a triumphant fist as he pointed to his back window. A badly painted banner hung there. "Eat my dust turkey," the man mouthed, echoing the words on his poster. He pushed a button on the steering wheel and went past, the smell of gas in the air.

"Cheek!" exclaimed Hayden indignantly. "He's got NO3." The gas, which boosts engine power, is only used for short bursts, but by the time it cut out, the CCR would be long gone. Hayden half considered cutting the first corner to regain the lead, but dismissed it as the CCR inexplicably lost control and crashed into a hedge. A detailed autopsy would reveal a small bullet hole through the rear axle.

"Eat mine," Hayden yelled, half out of the cockpit, but soon sat down as he saw the wall. It came out of nowhere: the temporary tire wall that used to be by the side, stretched across the track. Hayden swerved round the barrier, missing it by centimetres, and drove through the gap the wall had left. A sign read, 'new route for last lap'.

"Someone's not going to be very happy," Hayden muttered as he glanced in his mirrors.

He focused on the new track, going fast but leaving room to correct any mistakes. He had studied the map of the normal track on the internet, but he was in the dark here and knew nothing about the sharpness of the corners.

He had only covered 100 meters when a shot rang out. Not the deep crack of a rifle, but a whining barrage of automatic fire. Hayden ducked down behind the wheel, knowing that whoever was shooting wasn't good news. A Hummer, lying silently on the grass, suddenly started. The headlights flicked up and glared at the Caterham, temporarily blinding Hayden.

He hurled the wheel to one side, leaving tire marks as the car skidded to the other side of the track, quickly passing the Hummer. A window rolled down and out popped a face, the sharp nose and pointed eyes revealing him as Viper. A gun was clenched below his chin.

Two more bangs told Hayden his life was in danger and he hurtled into the distance, unaware of the second barrier. He reached it and stopped, knowing he'd been set up.

His heart thumping madly, Hayden turned the car around and roared back to meet the Hummer, grabbing his mp3 player as he did so.

"I hope this works," he murmured grimly. The stakes were set: he was outgunned and cornered. All he had now was the unexpected.

He entered the same section the Hummer, hand poised over the buttons, and then pressed play.

The track he had downloaded was a high pitched drone, loud enough to drive anyone mad. To most people, it was a noise, but to Hayden and the website that sold it, it was the note of C Major, a noise that would break glass. The speakers blasted out the manufactured shrieks, the frequency of which tore into the Hummer's windows.

They shattered, sending glass flying everywhere. The occupants all flinched, covering themselves from the shards. The Hummer veered sideways, and by the time it hit the side Hayden was gone, back in the race and hunting down the cars that had slipped past.

Hayden drove furiously, surprised the accelerator could withstand the punishment it was getting. He cut a corner and found himself behind a Noble. Recognising it as the one that had tried to take him out earlier, he had no qualms about dirty play, and again released the high pitched whine.

The Noble careened over to the side and stopped. Hayden swept past - the Caterham, having no glass, unscathed.

Half a mile later, another cut corner and two more cars out of commission, the lead pack entered Joey's line of fire. He didn't wait for them to slow at the corners, but lined up the sights and squeezed the trigger.

The front car went, as did the second, watching helplessly as they drifted to a halt, their hopes dashed.

The Ferrari was luckier. It had swerved to avoid the cars in front and Joey had missed, clipping the wheel trim. It spun but stayed on the track.

The driver reversed the car to the next corner before accelerating off again, but the slip had allowed the Caterham to close the gap. The race was on.

The last corner appeared and Hayden again darted inside, willing the Ferrari to make the same mistake as the Koenigsegg, but it stayed outside.

The man in the Enzo had no mean streak and let the Caterham go, getting ready to turn past the yellow vehicle when Hayden overshot.

Hayden felt the Ferrari fell back and knew he wasn't going to fall for it. He wondered whether he could take the corner without braking, but quickly dismissed the idea.

He shoved the brakes on and flew into a skid, knowing there was little he could do. He prepared to crash into the wall flying towards him, but struck by sudden inspiration, he pressed the accelerator lightly as he slid across the tarmac. The Caterham kicked forward, squirming for traction, and miraculously slid round the corner.

Hayden jammed his foot down again, sending the Caterham tearing round the bend, crossing the line in first.

Chapter 15

Joey was waiting for Hayden as he cruised on his victory lap. He'd dismantled the rifle and left parts in the most obscure places he could find, and quickly descended through the ambient crowd to the track. Dodging a jacketed-official, he sprinted onto the blazing tarmac and jumped in the car.

Hayden nodded a greeting as he accelerated away, a triumphant cunningness etched on his face.

"I thought we were given prizes on the podium," Joey asked breathlessly, holding up the gold plate he'd nearly sat on.

"I nicked them and drove off before anyone could stop me," Hayden replied calmly. "Strap yourself in. We're getting out of here."

Joey understood. They both knew that Philip wouldn't let them stand on a podium for very long before they were shot. "Where are we going," he asked.

"Did you get a map?"

"Yes." Joey pulled out a folded piece of paper he had lifted from a shop in the stand. Straightening it out, he read the front cover. "Welcome to Disneyland Paris," he said impressively. "It's all they had, but it does show where the ghost house is."

"Sounds like fun," Hayden replied dryly. He hadn't expected Joey to find a map of France, but the Mickey Mouse leaflet irritated him. "In that case, we're going this way. I hope you're not scared of the mummies." He nosed the Caterham into the driver's compound where they hurriedly stashed several cans of petrol into the tiny boot. Two more went in between Joey's legs, and then they were off.

The horn blasted it's was through the gate, which was hastily opened by race attendants. Hayden revved the throttle, grimly thinking they'd be lucky if the noise only told half of the spectators that they were leaving, and then raced down the road.

"All we have to worry about now is the police," Hayden said a few hours later. They were cruising along a quiet road somewhere in France, trying to stay away from populated areas. The car's sunshine-yellow paint didn't help them, but they had speed on their side.

"Do you speak French?" Joey asked.

"German is my game," Hayden replied. "Any idea where it is?"

Joey shrugged and pointed into the hedge. "Take us back onto a road and we'll find somewhere with a map."

Hayden complied, spurring the car forwards until he saw signs for an intersection. Two minutes later they descended a small hill onto a slip-way, a four-lane motorway streaking past.

"I'm getting a bit peckish too," Hayden added, joining the throng of speeding cars.

"I don't think they have Little Chef in these parts," Joey said dully.

"Who said anything about Little Chef," Hayden replied lightly, pointing ahead to a 'Services' sign. "There's a petrol station."

Joey groaned good naturedly. "So I'm sitting in tonnes of smelly cans, and you decide to take me to a petrol pump for my birthday," he grumbled.

"I'll get you a cake," Hayden promised.

They turned into the station, parking behind the shop. "Orders?" Hayden asked, getting out. "Jimmy's paying."

"Everything," Joey said. "But make sure its chocolate cake."

"Don't go away."

Despite Joey's protests, Hayden filled the car up before he went into the shop and joined the queue. He filled a basket with food; sandwiches, drinks and chocolate bars, before surveying the other customers. There was an English man at the back of the shop. He was in luck.

The young woman behind the till stared at Hayden's basket in disbelief. She muttered something in French, taking in the now half empty shelves.

Hayden nodded noncommittally. "J'ai mange," he said in limited French, playing the role of a dim-witted foreigner.

The woman passed everything through the till and stated a price. Hayden didn't have a clue what it was. He thought that quarante was something to do with 40, but he wasn't sure.

He turned around, whispering "mon père payer" to the assistant. He waved to the English man. "Hey, Jimmy," he called out. "Having a good time in France?"

The man wondered who he was talking to, but then realised he was the only English man in the queue. He waved back, not quite sure why this kid was talking to him.

Hayden walked over to the door and said, "She wants you to go to the front. I'll take these outside. Ok?"

The man was totally baffled now, but he nodded and went to the till. Hayden exited the building, shoved the bag into Joey's hands and quickly drove off.

By the time the shop assistant had realised what had happened, they were long gone.

"Where do you get these ridiculous ideas from?" Joey said in mock despair, still laughing five minutes after Hayden told him what had happened.

"I can't actually believe it came off," Hayden admitted, and then remembered the half-empty bottle behind the attendant. "I suppose the woman was half drunk, but still."

"And technically we didn't steal it," Joey decided. "The other man just didn't pay."

Hayden had also smuggled a map into the bag, so once they had eaten, they set off east.

"Why are we going to Germany again?" Joey asked. Dusk was falling, and the evening was beginning to turn cold. They were only a few miles from the border and hadn't rested since escaping from the racetrack.

"I don't reckon Philip has as much influence with the German police as he does with the French," Hayden said carefully. "And they have Autobahns in Germany."

Joey saw the trap but decided to play along anyway. "What's wrong with French roads?"

"The French are on it," Hayden joked. "You'll find out in a minute. We haven't got passports have we?"

"Ah." Joey screwed his face up. "No."

"We haven't really got much," Hayden stated cheerfully.

"No," Joey agreed. "We're stuck in France with no money, no passport, the police are looking for us, and we don't have any proper food," he grumbled.

"Have faith my friend," Hayden said slowly. "We'll work something out."

"Another of your master plans," Joey asked cheekily.

"I'll have you know," Hayden said in mock indignation, "the last time my master plan failed was four years ago."

Joey's face brightened. "I remember that," he said. "You couldn't show your face for a week without being laughed at."

Hayden shrugged indifferently. "You should have seen the other guy."

"They've got us," Joey said suddenly, noticing a pair of flashing lights following them along the road. "Ten miles out as well," he added, pointing to a sign nestled in the hedgerow.

Hayden glanced in his mirror and groaned at the police car, his mind quickly running through scenarios. "We have five options, and two possible outcomes," he said calmly. "One, the police catch us, and Philip has access to them, we've lost. Two, they are Philip's men, and they catch us, we've lost. Situation three and four, we run, and whoever they are, they catch us, and we've lost. Scenario five, we run, escape, and we win. Take your pick."

Joey looked at his friend in amazement. "You have an incredible knack for simplicity," he said wonderingly. "But you failed to mention the crash-into-a-tree scenario," he added cheekily.

Hayden rebuffed him. "I suggest we take number five," he said, only a slight hint of strain edging his voice. The driving was tiresome, and although Joey had spelled him for a few hours, he'd need all his wit and dare if he was to run from the cops. "I'm not going to risk stopping," Hayden continued seriously. "Or I'd make you drive."

Joey laughed. He had passed his driving test a year ago, but Hayden was more aggressive behind the wheel, frequently beating him in go-kart races. He'd also had the Magny-Cours experience: Joey had been eager to show his shooting prowess instead.

"When you're ready," Hayden said, taking a deep breath, but before he could do anything, a deep bullhorn rang out from behind them.

It was in French, but there was no doubt to the meaning. Pull over and stop.

"How do you say 'would you like to listen to some music' in French?" Hayden muttered, not stopping.

Joey shrugged. "Make it up."

"How come I have to do it all?" Hayden complained sarcastically, but soon all humour died as he noticed another police car coming up in front of them. He was sandwiched.

Hayden wearily pulled over to the side, but Joey pushed the gear into reverse, told Hayden to push the accelerator and twiddled the wheel, reversing back into the verge. The lights were now aiming at an angle to the other side of the road. It was probably pointless, Hayden thought, but it would be easier for an escape.

The two police cars converged. The car facing them sat still with its engine running, but a passenger door opened behind them and a man stepped out.

He was young, with smooth blond hair and a crisp uniform. Approaching the Caterham, his eyes widened in disbelief as he saw the age of the men behind the wheel.

"I don't think he'll buy the story about Pluto and the chicken's magic wand," Joey whispered.

The man said something in French.

Hayden and Joey just sat there, saying nothing.

The man repeated it. Still no reaction, so he pulled out his gun.

Hayden went limp. At first Joey thought he'd been shot, but Hayden shuddered and froze in his seat, staring at the gun with sheer fright. He tweaked Joey's trouser led with his left arm, out of sight of the policeman.

The policeman faltered, hastily holstering his gun. He'd had people scared at gunpoint before, but never this frightened.

Hayden collapsed over the steering wheel, using the movement to murmur, "play for time." Joey understood, and tried his hand at French.

"Excoisemoir," he spluttered. "Je ne nonn parlez an French. Je me suis parlez Engliche."

The man stared at this complete nonsense use of French and walked over to the other car He said something, and a woman got out and went back over to Joey.

"I speak English," she said. "He wants you to get out of the car and put your hands on the bonnet."

"Bummer." Joey gave her a devastating smile, but she failed to find amusement. Joey stayed in his seat, still grinning like a bulldog. "Are you going to believe our story about the rabbit that chased us down the road because we wouldn't give him any chocolate cake?"

The man said something else in French, and the woman pulled her handcuffs out. "This can be easy, or I can do it the hard way."

Hayden slowly sat up, the convulsing miraculously stopped. He looked her dead in the eye. "Basically, we stole this car plus about €40 worth of food and two tanks of petrol, have no driving license, no money, are probably reported missing in our own country by now, and have a mass murderer trying to find us," he said directly. "So therefore, we are not going to be arrested, because if we are, the man who wants us would offer to finance the French Police for the next decade if you turned us over to him, which your head office would rather like, and would probably accept." The sentence finished with stark finality, daring the woman to challenge it.

"In that case, seeing as we would rather fight than be arrested to die, we are going to drive off in five seconds," Joey added with emphasis, as if to a six year old. "And it's your job to stop us. Good luck."

Hayden threw the gear into forward and hit the pedals, flicking the headlights up as he did so. The policeman was blinded, and he held his gun to his face to shield the glare.

The Caterham darted past the first police car, and Hayden switched off the headlights, smothering them in darkness to prevent the police having anything to aim at.

"Houston, where's the nearest autobahn," Hayden said, deep in concentration.

"Turn right," Joey said, "and then forward for a couple of miles before we cross the border. Head for Saarbrücken. The autobahn goes around the outside of it."

The border came and went with no fuss. They had chosen a small road to attempt their cross, and it was deserted. A large sign declared the land as Germany as Hayden roared past, putting as much distance between them and the police as possible.

Ten minutes later they reached it, and Hayden pointed at the sign which hung above the entrance. "See," he laughed, the chase now over. "There's no speed limit. Mach 4 here we come."

Chapter 16

They drove well into the night, stopping only to refuel and stretch their legs. By sunrise they were nearing the middle of Germany, and Joey had taken over the wheel.

"Cheek!" Joey exclaimed as he nosed the car down the road. "This is easy. I had to pass my test in a Ford banger."

"See how fast you can push it," Hayden grinned.

Joey looked sideways at his partner and then again at the road. Their side was deserted, and the smooth tarmac beckoned. He smashed up a gear and sped off.

Hayden watched the speedometer rise with amusement. His friend was a good driver, but his aggression was for the battlefield. He usually had an indestructible tank under his foot, not a cardboard cut-out.

At 110mph the wind was streaming into their eyes, and by 150mph tears were forced out by the second. Still Joey pushed the car forward, squinting through the cold blast of air. He hit 180mph and clenched a fist in triumph, gradually coming down to a respectable speed.

"Gotcha," he smiled, when his lungs had recovered, checking Hayden's reaction.

"You should have worn your glasses," he replied, indicating the diagonal streaks from his irises.

"In this light," Joey said incredulously. "You wouldn't even be able to see the headlamps with your super-sunnies."

The brief interlude of speed had temporarily re-awakened their senses. Hours on the road had drained them, and the night was cold.

Hayden shrugged. "It'd be funny. How far is it to Fulda?"

"The last sign we went past said 20 kilometres."

"Good. Philip will have to be a lot smarter than we think to catch us now. Unless he's got the German police on our case we've got a home run."

"Fulda is in the middle of the mainline run from Dortmund to Frankfurt, via Kassel. We take the train north for 30 miles, then swap for the speed-train to Hamburg."

"The small solution to a big problem," Hayden agreed, referring to Fulda's size. "Trains are quicker to board which means we won't get stopped waiting at an airport, and we won't need to check in by names."

"My main fear is Hamburg. We need to get back to England."

"The safe way is to go further east. Boat is the best way to get into England. We should take the train to Russia and come back to Norway. The only problem with that is it'll take days, and we don't have Russian money."

"We don't have any money," Joey stated simply.

Hayden grimaced. "Well, no," he replied dourly, yawning. "We need to stop soon though," he said. "We're both exhausted, and I can't even remember any of the Spanish women we saw in Italy. We're in no shape to trek across Europe. We'll stand out like a fly in custard."

"We take our chances in Hamburg then," Joey said grimly. "And take whatever fate throws at us."

It dimly registered in Hayden's bedraggled mind. "I thought you didn't believe in fate?"

Joey shook his head. "That's what worries me."

15 minutes later Joey pulled over in a lay-by. "1 Kilometre," he said gladly, pointing to a sign. "Time for another of your disappearing acts."

Hayden groaned. "I'm not putting one of these in a tree. Drive it into the wood and leave it. We'll hike the last stretch to avoid being seen."

Stiff and worn, Hayden pulled the remaining food out of the car before Joey eased it through a gap in the trees. Then, laden with as much as they could comfortably carry, they set off slowly in the darkness.

"Did you get the mp3?" Hayden asked after a minute. The first few steps had been slow with exhaustion and cramp, but their muscles eventually warmed to the task, and they began to speed up.

"Yeah, but we've only got one set of headphones," Joey said, grateful for the movement.

"Remember when we used to go running?" Hayden asked amusedly.

"We could do a kilometre in three and a half minutes," Joey recollected with a smile.

"Still, one foot after the other," Hayden said. "No point in rushing if we have to wait six hours for the next train."

"And if the train before that leaves one minute before we get there?"

"Then we lose no matter what speed we go," Hayden grinned.

Joey pushed him, and then too collapsed on the verge, laughing.

"Honestly mate, the sugar has gone to my head," he muttered: the staple food of petrol stations being doughnuts and chocolate. "The sooner we get on the train the better."

"The lights are getting closer."

For a moment Joey thought his friend had lost the plot, but he saw the dim glow, casually hovering above a clump of trees not far away. "Fulda?" he questioned.

"As good a guess as any."

"I need a cup of tea. Pringles are fine, but when you've been outside for 17 hours solid, you need a warm cup of sludge."

"I'll settle for a burger," Hayden announced, depriving his normally healthy-eating mind of its usual scraps.

"We really are in a bad state," Joey said darkly, having a full knowledge of Hayden's diet.

"I see buildings," Hayden said thankfully, although his heart dreaded the prospect of entering a silent town. Out in the wild he could hide and survive for weeks if he was lucky, but in settlements it depended on the people he met, not on skill and his own strong mentality. On the face of it, he thought, I'm a silent person. I prefer to avoid and escape on my own, living close to nature, than mix with the business of city-life.

"Acknowledged." Joey held the same feelings as Hayden, but was secretly excited at the prospect of skirting through a town unseen.

They crept into Fulda, walking quickly but silently through the streets. The streetlights illuminated most of the roads, but others faded into secluded corners where they sat dark, hiding from the strangers. Overcrowded housing lined the paved roads, shut against the night.

"Which way?" Joey asked upon reaching a crossroads.

Hayden paused. "We'll find it eventually," he replied, and walked straight on.

Ten minutes later the first sign of shops began to appear, closed off from the night air to stand silent and foreboding. "We must be nearing the town centre," Joey said brightly, spotting a town plan. It was a tall, tree-like post with boards on its limbs, once the pride of the stone-flagged square. Neglect had left it ruined, and it bore streaks of paint presumably where vandals had attacked it.

Joey tripped over an empty beer can and sent it scuttling across the cobbles. He froze, checking if the noise had disturbed anything, but apart from a soft, wooden scrape stillness still dominated the urban landscape.

"Doesn't look like this place has tourists," Hayden said, eyeing the ripped paper and uncared-for frame.

"They don't have hotels," Joey confirmed, scanning the list of places. "The train station is left down there, and then the second right."

"I suggest we start moving then," Hayden said slowly, now staring silently at a house opposite them. "Unless you want to rob the supermarket."

"We could use some cash," Joey admitted, "but not from honest company. I'd swipe a thief anytime, but they aren't on the map."

"Is that an alarm?" Hayden nodded in the direction of the red flashing light he'd been watching.

"I would have thought so," Joey replied, puzzled.

"Weren't the other alarms blue?"

Joey frowned. There had been blue alarms all the way down the last three streets. "A different type?" he suggested.

"I think it's a camera," Hayden said quietly. "That scraping noise could easily have been a window."

Joey froze. The red light was blinking in the far corner of the square away from the streetlights, making it impossible to tell.

"Run or investigate?"

Joey paused. "Both." He picked up a chunk of wood that had been torn off the stand, and hurled it at the light. The light, or the person that was holding it, flinched.

"That's not mechanical," Hayden said lightly.

"Alarms don't make thumping noises either," Joey added, as the house seemed to come alive with vibrations.

"I think," Hayden said in mock exasperation, "that you've managed to stir up another hornet nest."

Joey followed his ears and found an open door, out of which shapes had begun to emerge. "This is the part where we run," he said.

Hayden raised his eyebrows. "And what if they're thieves? We could save someone their TV."

Joey paused and threw a second piece of wood into the crowd. A burst of curses filled the air as they group entered the outer ring of light, revealing several boys with anger written on their faces.

"They're smaller than me," Joey commented. "That's good."

Hayden sniffed. "Cocaine?"

Joey took a deep breath of air. "97% positive," he said, grinning. "That's even better than thieves."

The foremost man, who looked to be in his early twenties, stopped a few feet away from them and spoke viciously in rapid German.

"They want to know who we are and what we're doing here," Hayden murmured in translation.

"Is that translation the polite version?"

"Definitely."

The man spoke again, thundering out words like a bull on a rampage.

"They're going to beat us up," Hayden grinned. "We have 10 seconds."

Joey rolled his eyes. "Ok," he resigned, and dropped his bag. "When they move, we move."

"Back-to-back or split up?" He spoke calmly, but Joey knew his friend had measured every angle and knew there was a reasonable chance of success. He wouldn't fight to lose.

"Split up, because then I can turn them."

"Go." They both started forward, feet poised and fists raised.

They met head on with an onslaught of curses as the German boys realised the foreigners were prepared to fight. The leader began to kick but Joey felled him with a quick punch to the face. Hayden too had found his first man, a rounded fellow who tried to go behind him. He grabbed his t-shirt and yanked, pulling it tight round the neck before letting him sink to the floor.

The gang poured on, surrounding the English youths with a fierce hate spurned on by the cocaine, but Hayden and Joey were unrelenting, giving punch for punch, striking out whenever their opponent slipped. Hours cooped in a car had built a fierce energy that they had no qualms about releasing.

The number of bodies on the floor grew as Joey began exerting his army influence on the fight, beating his enemies with strength, agility and power. A crunching sound split the air: another broken nose to add to his collection, Hayden thought grimly.

The fight slowly dwindled until there were only three men left standing. Hayden and Joey stood side by side facing the last man in the gang. He looked from one man to the other, fear replacing the drug-induced hatred. He turned and ran.

"That was lucky," breathed Joey, massaging his arm.

"Let's take a look inside." Hayden stepped through the open doorway into a dingy hallway. The air was thick with smoke and dust, and a pungent aroma entered his nostrils. Stains marked the walls, and the lurid paint was shedding flakes under the stress.

He poked his head around the first doorway, pulling it back in disgust. The next door didn't exist: it had presumably turned into firewood at some point, judging by the ash littering the floor.

Joey stabbed a pencil at a packet of white powder lying on a table. "This has to be worth a few bob," he said.

"I doubt the ticket man will accept it," Hayden replied, rifling through a drawer. "Here we go." He straightened up, a wad of notes in his hand.

"How much is that?"

"Enough." He turned to leave, but Joey stopped him.

"Take a look at the floor," he said, a gleam in his eye.

Hayden surveyed the tiled kitchen. "Looks normal to me," he said, but trusted Joey's instinct. "What do you see?"

"The central tiles seem a bit worn around the edges."

"You're getting paranoid," Hayden chuckled, walking over and prising up the stone in question. He stopped still, and then turned back to his friend. "Looks like you took the wrong career path," he said seriously. "The drug police would love you." He stood back, revealing a horde of sealed bags buried beneath the floor.

Joey grinned. "That's Molly's Flying Circus for you. Take it and let's get out of here."

Hayden walked back outside, stepping over the motionless bodies and slipping back into the shadows as he left the square in the direction of the train station.

The station was still open – an overnight train due to pass through at any moment – and was manned by a sleepy-looking man in a grey hat. He hastily propped himself up against the side of the window and stared blearily at the two teens facing him.

Hayden gave the orders, handed over some money and collected his tickets, the place void of automatic machines. He paused, but declined the temptation to ask for an envelope addressed to the police. The drugs could come in handy somewhere along the line.

Joey was reading the leaflets on the platform. "What time does the train come?" he asked, when Hayden rejoined him.

"Earlier than I expected. It's for the unlucky guys who have to be in Frankfurt for a 7:00 office start. Just under two hours to kill."

"Who's going to stay awake?"

"I will," Hayden said wearily. "I'll go and see if they have anything worth doing in their shop."

Later that morning, Hayden awoke to find green hills rolling past his window. Joey was opposite him, still asleep. A note was in front of him, telling him the arrival time in Hamburg. He checked the time again and, finding they only had one hour to go, decided to stretch his legs.

He went towards the rear carriage and found a bar half way down. Pinpointing the barman, he asked for a newspaper.

"Sorry," the barman replied. "We started before they were printed, but we do have the news." He turned to a screen mounted on the wall and pressed a few buttons.

Hayden found a swivel chair and sat down, trying to struggle through the complex language that newsreaders seem to use. A small crowd was drawn to the bar to watch, but luckily the German media hadn't caught wind of the escape from the race circuit in France. Satisfied his tracks were covered, he returned to find Joey re-reading a magazine on American cruise ships with a stack of donuts on the table.

"It never ceases to amaze me how you manage to produce food at every single opportunity."

"Its all in the mind," grinned Joey between bites. "We're nearing the outskirts of Hamburg. Any idea how to catch a boat to England?"

"Worry about that when it happens," he replied airily. "How much money do we have left?"

"Enough to get us across, but the train tickets were completely over-priced. Any unexpected costs and we won't make it."

"What about a taxi?"

"Only if we manage cheap ferry tickets."

"Doesn't look like we have much choice."

Chapter 17

Once off the train onto the bustling platform, the pair headed straight for the exit. Hayden nearly managed to knock an old lady into a porter, but the curses that followed them soon died as they hurried away from the scene. Joey was in front, concentrating on weaving between passengers while Hayden followed behind: his job to look out for security. Any attention that came their way was unwelcome.

They reached the big glass doors: the entrance to a wide stretch of open pavement and a furious scramble for taxis. Save from the cabs and sporadic colourful coat, a grey expanse of concrete filled every angle. Tower blocks could be seen not too far away, dominating the skyline with broad shoulders and huge company embossing. Welcome to the city, Hayden thought grimly, staring at the small droplets of water that had begun to fall over Hamburg.

The queue for taxis intensified as the rain started to pour down, but Hayden and Joey stood side by side, their spirits lifted. They were used to the rain in England, and they felt at home in the wet as in the dry.

"Nothing like a free shower," Joey shouted over the pounding water, running a hand through his hair.

Hayden nodded in acknowledgement. The rain would disguise the fact that neither had washed since Italy, nearly a week ago, and provide cover for a dash to the docks. "Let's go to the back," he shouted back, turning to the incoming taxis.

The first cab to spot them was a rattling motor, looking like it belonged in a scrapyard as it honked and bounced over to the kerb. Hayden skipped it and waved to the car behind it: a new Mondeo.

"The dock," he shouted, climbing in the back.

The driver looked distastefully at the water dripping of the pair's clothes, but shrugged when he saw money come out of the pocket. It was a company car anyway, he reasoned, pulling back into the road.

A tunnel loomed up as the taxi faced a solid wall of corporate buildings, and when it emerged the roads were truly soaked.

"Fantastic weather," Joey said brightly. "Everyone's so obsessed with global warming; it's good to know we can still have a good old-fashioned downpour. The cops won't see us in this."

"Hiding from the police eh," the driver tutted, obviously having a decent command of the English language. "You don't want to go to the harbour then. One of their major bases is near there."

Hayden and Joey exchanged glances.

"I used to be a smuggler," the man explained, showing a toothless grin. "I was quite good at it in the early days, but I got turned in by my partner."

"Does that mean you know how to leave the country undetected?" Hayden asked, trying to sound casual.

"Sure," the man replied cheerfully. "What's your problem?"

"Money," Hayden replied, not certain he should be telling the man this.

"You don't have enough for the ferry?"

"If this costs over €15, no."

"Sorry mate, but its more than that." He thought for a while, letting the cab go silent while he negotiated his way through a set of traffic lights. "Ferry tickets are quite expensive aren't they?" he continued, making careful calculations in his head.

Hayden read the man like a book. "Care to offer us a better deal?"

"Taxi work isn't the best pay a man can ask for," the driver admitted. "If you stay in Hamburg for another few hours, I can get you out of the country."

"What's the catch?"

"My contacts are powerful people who enjoy money. You'd be asked to take some stuff over to England. I take it that's where you're going?"

Joey raised his eyebrows. "We're going to smuggle stuff into England?"

"If you say you're interested I'll outline the plan," the man replied quietly. "Don't expect it to be easy, but I can't tell you anything unless I have cooperation. Then again," he grinned. "I could be pulling your leg and making all this up."

Hayden looked at Joey, who nodded. He pulled the cocaine out of its bag and flicked some onto the front seat. "That's the first part of our payment."

The driver glanced down and whistled. "I was actually joking," he said smoothly. "But seeing as you're not, I'll ask no questions," he continued. "It's difficult for smugglers to bring others into the fold, and our numbers have dwindled since the new laws. Most of the smuggling now is done by millionaires who front fake companies to put on a show for officials. Under every tonne of Scandinavian wood is at least a dozen bags of class A drugs." He paused. "Seeing as we'll be together for a while, do you mind if I get some coffee?"

He pulled over to the side as Hayden and Joey shook their heads, and departed into a corner shop. Hayden immediately grabbed the door handle, ready to run if any trouble appeared.

"Relax mate," Joey said. "If he's turning us in, he'll phone the police now and then drive us into a trap."

"That's comforting," Hayden replied, watching the driver return with a steaming cup.

"Where was I?" the man said, sipping his coffee. "Ah yes. Small scale smugglers are much harder to come by, which where you come in."

"You mean we get the work no-one else wants?" Joey muttered dryly.

The man laughed. "Seeing as it involves taking a boat to England in this weather, that's a pretty accurate summary. I'll drop you off somewhere, and then you'll have to collect whatever they want smuggling and take it about a mile up the western beach near Cuxhaven. A small boat will have been dropped off and hidden in the bushes, which you'll have to inflate and paddle out to sea. The boat you'll cross the channel in will be moored somewhere offshore."

"No wonder you have trouble finding people to do it," Hayden said darkly.

A smile crossed the taut features and again revealed the missing teeth. "I'll drop you somewhere near where I think they'll get you to pick the merchandise up and call when it's arranged. You do have a phone?"

Joey shook his head. "It's in France."

The man shook his head and produced a mobile. "Take this, but don't lose it. Send it to me when you arrive in England," he said, writing his address on a piece of paper.

"So where we going now?"

"You're here," was the short reply. The taxi pulled over towards a bus station and stopped.

Hayden thanked him and climbed out, stepping back as it roared off with a splash. The pavements around were deserted: faces peered out of shop windows and huddled under doorways to avoid the shower. A few people were occasionally brave or desperate enough to tackle the onslaught, but they kept their heads down and didn't linger for long.

"At least the road cleaners will be happy," muttered Joey, wiping their latest game of noughts and crosses off the steamed-up window of the shelter. So far they had turned down several buses and taxis, desperate to take advantage of the weather by pocketing cash from soaking travellers, but received the opposite treatment from two other busses, which simply didn't bother stopping.

"What's the score?"

"21-18 to you," Joey replied, searching for another clean patch of condensation. "Honestly, I thought that guy was just messing around when he mentioned smuggling."

"So did I," Hayden admitted. "But it's too late now."

He was interrupted by a vibrating from within his jacket. He picked the phone up, connected the call, but stayed silent.

"Hello?" The voice on the other end came out smooth yet timid sounding. It was obviously a fake voice reserved for the telephone; the type that is forgotten instantly. Hayden knew he'd never be able to place the man in a police station.

"Address?" The taxi driver had told them to be sharp and get straight to the point. In this business, he had said, the less you know about everyone else the better.

"43 Keltenstrasse. Be there in 15 minutes." There was a click as the man disconnected.

"We've got it," Hayden announced. "43 Keltenstrasse."

Joey frowned. "Fat lot of good that is," he remarked. "We could get to the north pole before we find Keltenstrasse."

"All in good time," Hayden said. "Did you notice that all taxis seem to have satellite navigation in them?"

"We can't go in a taxi," Joey exclaimed.

"We can get dropped off two streets away," Hayden pointed out.

"You mean we pretend we can't remember the address of dear aunty Phyllis, but know it's near Keltenstrasse."

"Then pick a street off the screen when we get close," Hayden finished. "Let's go."

They hailed the next taxi that went past, this time a ludicrously painted Opel that was at least twice as big as any other cab. The driver, a smiling man from Trinidad, was playing indie-rock through loud, expensive looking speakers.

"If I'm spending eight hours a day in this beast," he said, nodding his head to the beat, "then I'm going to make it fun. I hope you don't mind?"

Joey, whose musical taste extended from punk to world and anything in between, shrugged and settled in the back.

"Somewhere near Keltenstrasse please," Hayden said, closing the door behind him.

The man turned a bald head to his screen and punched in a few keys. "This is a big city," he complained, as the screen went blank. "And it takes some getting used to." He yanked it forward and pushed the connector more securely into its slot. "We're off," he enthused, the screen blinking back into life.

Ten minutes later they were staring down a narrow road of old council houses. Litter was strewn about among the overgrown gardens, and a few boarded up windows could be seen decorating one residence.

They slowly set off down the street, avoiding the broken glass and empty bottles that the corner pub had provided. Number 43 was in better condition than most of its neighbours. The door looked like it had been recently painted, and the front hedge was neat in the parts where solid growth had occurred. A deflated football gave the reason for a few bent branches and shaken leaves, nestling in the grass by the door.

Hayden knocked while Joey stood back. A shape emerged in the glass, getting bigger as the person inside moved towards the door. The handle was pulled back to reveal a large lady wearing an embroidered cardigan.

"Hello." The voice might have been interpreted for sweet in England, but the heavy North-German accent covered the trace.

"Hello."

"You have lost your luggage?"

"Probably."

"Come inside." She led them indoors to a rear room that looked onto the back garden, but pulled the curtains shut anyway and switched on the light. The dusty bulb hung unprotected from the ceiling, casting a fake glow over the drab furniture. A worn dresser was the most recognisable piece despite numerous cigarette burns, and a broken lamp sat in the corner.

The woman left the pair for a moment, and returned with a hiking rucksack and a suitcase. "Instructions," she said shortly, pulling a piece of paper out from within a pocket. "You have five minutes to memorise." She tapped the pistol in her pocket and left for the other bags.

Hayden ripped the paper in half and grabbed a pencil. "I'm never going to remember that," he muttered in English, copying the notes onto the blank bit.

"If we get caught with that then there's no way out," Joey warned, but Hayden took the phone and pulled the rear casing off. Carefully folding the paper, he wedged it behind the battery before replacing the cover.

"I bet you smugglers cheat each other all the time," he replied, turning the phone back on.

"That's enough time. Out," the woman barked, dispensing of the sweetness. She threw the other bags at Hayden and ushered them out of the door, pulling off the wig to once they were out of sight. Panting slightly, the man slid out of the enormous body suit and went to make a phone call.

"Jamie speaking."

"The party has finished here. The parents came and took away the celebration. They're headed for your place right now, so I'd hide The Beer."

"I'll give them a nice welcome."

Jamie's place, which was actually a lone tree surrounded by bushes and sand dunes, was where Joey and Hayden were aiming for. The Beer, the name given to the inflatable boat, would be dropped off a good hour before they arrived. Unknown to Jamie, Joey had spent two weeks in the Pennines with twice as much weight as the drugs he was carrying, and Hayden had practised his two-mile race for sports day with his three-year old sister on his back. They were a fast team.

"I say we go from A to C and ignore B," Joey said, annoyed at all the check-points they were scheduled for. "I'm not waiting any longer than I have to." They were at the first of seven stops, presumably for someone to check they were still doing what they were meant to be doing.

"I'm off," Hayden said, starting across the road. The rain had lessened considerably, but puddles extended from one side of the city to the other, and conditions were precarious.

Joey called after his friend, taking a street map from a tourist information stand and marking on it the route they had been given.

"Right then," he said, eyes on fire. "Let's see how they like being messed around." He handed the map over so Hayden could check it.

"They've had us going round in circles!" Hayden exclaimed angrily. "Screw this. We should turn them in."

Joey shook his head. "I've got a better idea. If we cut that bit out we'll be there in half the time they expect us." Joey pointed to the map. "I say we take the shortcut, get the boat and turn it all in to the English police."

Hayden looked squarely at his friend. "I never really thought about this before, but this means we've got to find a boat in the open ocean and then sail it across to England. If it's anything bigger than a matchbox we'll be spotted on radar and caught by the Coast Guard. Not only that, but if we beat the authorities we then have to escape from a group of smugglers to hand the drugs over to the police. Do you realise what we're getting into?"

"It's win or lose," Joey said seriously. "But we don't have much of a choice. The guy 25 yards behind us has been following us ever since we passed the first checkpoint," he added in an undertone. "He got his mobile out as soon as we turned off the designated route."

Hayden turned to ice. "I've had enough of this," he blasted. "Everyone thinks they can take advantage of us, and I'm not taking any more. We're going to England." He stepped up the pace, striding through the grey labyrinth of passages as if the past few days were forgotten. He rarely got angry, but when he did, very few people encountered him and came off better.

The follower soon dropped behind, unable to break into a run because it would mean knowledge that he'd been noticed.

Chapter 18

Hayden arrived at the drop-off point still worked up. He'd been setting a furious pace ever since he'd learnt they were being followed, and hadn't let up until they were half a mile up the beach. Joey, who had the suitcase to lumber across the beach, was a few paces behind him.

"There's the tree," Hayden said shortly. He was covered in sweat, but he didn't care. He walked up to the trunk and kicked it, cursing silently as pain broke through his mental barrier.

"Hayden!" Joey yelled, watching in horror as a shadow loomed up behind him.

Hayden turned, feeling the heavy shape as it crashed into him, knocking him to the floor. He rolled over, sand sticking to his face, and struck out at his attacker, scratching and hitting at anything he could reach. The man stumbled and fell to the floor, bearing the full force of Hayden's cold fury.

Joey reached them and jumped on the pair, squashing the unknown man to the ground.

"Who are you?" Hayden panted, regaining his feet. "Where's the boat?"

The man stopped struggling and lay limp, Joey's body pressing him into the sand. He held him there while Hayden searched the surroundings, finally uncovering a black box. He undid the clasp to reveal a portable pump and a collapsed boat.

"The time?"

Hayden checked the phone. "11:50."

"40 minutes before we're meant to be here. He could be the delivery guy protecting his boat."

"Don't count on it," Hayden warned, instructing Joey to keep a firm grip. "I'll set this up and then we'll get out of here as soon as possible." He plugged the battery-powered adaptor into the hole and turned it on. A humming noise emanated from the machine as it plunged air into the rubber.

Two minutes later Hayden was splashing out to sea, desperately pulling the craft after him as he hurdled the waves. "Come on," he yelled, knowing Joey would be behind him in seconds.

The cold water bit his freezing skin like ice, but he laboured feverishly at the boat, pushing it in front of him as he went deeper. Joey reached him and added his weight behind the black tubes, shoving the boat mercilessly forward, but the swells that rose up were becoming harder to overcome.

"In," Hayden shouted; his feet leaving the seafloor in a particularly large wave. He gripped the handles and heaved himself up, swinging both legs over the side in a smooth circular motion before grabbing the paddles. Joey followed his friend out of the water, showering water everywhere as he tumbled into the boat.

"Move!" Joey roared, the piercing cold driving them to perilous depths. The low pressure that had brought the flash storm to northern Germany hadn't fully dissipated, and the choppy water was throwing them about like an overenthusiastic dog. Spray flew about as the wind threw up walls of water, but the inflatable was buoyant and bounced its way between them.

"Tie down the bags," Hayden roared, trying to be heard over the crashing water, keeping his paddle to steer them as best he could while Joey secured the luggage.

Joey retook his own paddle and drove it into the water, sending chunks of water in all directions as the craft was propelled forwards. The paddle was nearly torn from his grip as the ferocious sea attempted to squash the travellers in an unfair war, but he clung on and vainly tried to brush the water from his face. Salt stung his eyes and made navigating impossible. "At least there's nothing to crash into," he muttered, paddling blind with his head down.

Stroke by painful stroke they slowly gained on the current, moving forward out to sea. Land was already a shadow, blocked by the waves and low clouds that hid the sunlight. They were alone with the raging sea, and Hayden realised that now even if they wanted to turn back to Germany, they wouldn't be able to find it.

"Give it another minute," Joey grunted, the pain of endless effort taking its toll. A few more strokes and they would be into deeper water, the waves behind them. Swells rose up as they entered the next stage, threatening to take them of course but not slow their speed.

"Keep your eyes peeled," Hayden shouted from the front. His arms were beginning to ache, but he kept them moving strongly down the paddle. The skin was beginning to rub and blister, but he couldn't and wouldn't stop. The more water between here and Cuxhaven the better, he thought.

"Ease off," Joey said after another two minutes, and they slowed their paddle strokes. The water here was still aggressive, but apart from the largest of swells that still loomed menacingly, there was no danger of being overturned.

Hayden felt his heart throbbing in his chest, the beat singing loudly in his head. He shook his numb hands to try and get the circulation going again. "I can't see anything," he said.

"We'd better keep moving," Joey replied, working out some quick maths in his head. They couldn't have been going more than four miles an hour with the rough weather, which meant they should have been paddling for 15 minutes to reach the boat.

Hayden motioned for Joey to stop paddling and stood up, bracing himself for the oncoming swell. It pushed the boat up onto its crest, revealing a landscape of swirling hills that rose and fell with the current. "30 degrees right," he said, spotting a small white cruiser, groaning as it meant that he, paddling on the left hand side, would have to go faster than his friend to change direction.

They both dug deep into reserves of strength they never knew they had, and thrust the rubber craft forwards, driving over swells and into troughs. Plumes of water reared up from the crowd and sent shivering droplets over the desperate pair, accumulating shouts of annoyance in return.

"20 meters," Joey choked, spluttering as another wall of water found its way over the gunwales.

Hayden braved the saltwater to steal a look at the powerboat, watching with terror as it suddenly disappeared behind a wall of water. The wave, ten times bigger than the ones they had struggled through to get away from the beach, was bearing down on them at breakneck speed. There was only time for him to desperately reverse his paddle and spin the boat round, hiding the broadside from the wave.

Joey, realising Hayden had directed them away from the yacht back towards the beach, shouted to his friend. The noise died in his throat as the wave swept over them, completely submerging the boat.

Hayden clutched the side in a vice-grip and waited for the dogged inflatable to rise to the surface. For a gut-wrenching moment, he thought they were never going to make it, but his head broke the surface and he gasped in lungfuls of air. Joey was still there, looking bewildered as to why he wasn't on the bottom. It was quickly replaced by a unshakable determination, and he grabbed his paddle.

The wave hadn't taken them far off course: the long-reaching backwash had countered the forward motion and merely pummelled them from all sides, and soon a white bow that tailored into a sophisticated-looking superstructure was dimly visible through the spray. Hayden could just make out a rope ladder hanging from the railings, and the jets of spurning water that held the boat in position were pinpricks against a speckled background.

"Nice lines," Joey said admiringly, despite his exhaustion. He pushed his paddle deeper into the water, eager to get on board out of the cold.

Hayden grabbed the boat's stern rope and waited until the hulls kissed before jumping onto the ladder. He scrambled up, the rope clenched in his teeth as the ladder swayed and turned. Reaching the top he fell through the railings onto deck, and lashed the rope to the bars. The bow rope landed next to him thanks to Joey's throw, which he tied a few feet further along.

"Load the bags up," he yelled, lying on the deck with his arms and head over the side. Joey took two bags in one arm and held onto the ladder for support, before passing them up. Hayden seized the handles and swung them backwards over his head, landing them on his back. He crawled backwards and shook them off, throwing them in the wheelhouse to prevent them going overboard.

Joey passed up the next load, barely holding his balance as the sea sent huge swells to rock the boats. He pulled out a knife that had been attached to the inflatable side, but stopped at Hayden's call.

"Keep it," he shouted, despairing with orders to sink it. He reached down to help him climb the ladder, before attempting to hoist the boat out of the water. Joey, soaked to the bone and exhausted from the effort, put his weight in as well, but the boat failed to move.

"Leave it tied up," Hayden panted, dying to get out of the wind. "We'll get it later." They picked up the last bags together with the knife, and staggered into the wheelhouse.

"Computer," Hayden muttered, stumbling over to the monitors while Joey shut the door. "It would help if they had it in English," he frowned, his numb mind unable to register the mass of foreign letters. It was touch screen, so he pressed what he thought was the options button. It came up with a list, and Hayden managed to find a tab with 'Sprache' on it. He changed it to English and went back to the start screen. Fumbling his way through a list of options, he found a destination section and typed in 'Lowestoft.' The grid co-ordinates flashed up immediately, and Hayden confirmed his choice. There was an increase of vibrations as the engines kicked in, churning water out of the back as it moved towards its new target.

"Hey, wer sind Sie?" A thin man with grey hair had appeared in the door behind them. He looked nervous, but clenched a pipe in his hands.

Joey turned round. "Do you want the drugs?" he demanded in German. Soaked from head to foot and gaunt from hard physical effort, his dark brown eyes looked capable of murder.

"You have them," the man said uneasily, staring at the wraiths that had come aboard his boat. "Where is Madras?"

"What's that?"

"The man who took the boat with you."

Hayden and Joey exchanged glances.

"He knows about the drugs. Dispose of him," Hayden said in English.

"I'll show you." Joey gestured to the man, leading him outside. He pointed to where the inflatable was moored, waiting until the grey head was over the railings before knocking the pipe out of his hands. He shoved a lifejacket into the man's chest. "Germany is that way," he pointed, lifting the struggling body clean over the bars before throwing him into the sea.

"20 knots," Joey said disgustedly, coming back into the wheelhouse. He looked at the lever mounted next to the screen, labelled 'Drossel'. He translated it into 'throttle', and kicked it with his foot, sending the boat squirming through the water as it delivered a burst of power.

"I'm going to explore the boat," Hayden said, rising to his feet. "Stay here and fiddle." He picked up the knife and departed through a door.

The boat was relatively new. Although small and built for only three people, the interior was comfortably furnished with neat touches of elegance. The main deck space was on the bow and housed the central wheelhouse, unusually situated at the front. A small path led round the boat, offering another entrance on the stern. Hayden took two mugs of hot chocolate from the kitchen and went back up the wheelhouse, satisfied there was no one else on board.

"How far is it to Lowestoft?"

"About 320 miles," Joey replied, gratefully taking the hot drink. "At current speed we'll be there by tea time."

Hayden registered the information into his sleep-deprived mind, took a last gulp from his hot chocolate, and immediately fell asleep.

Chapter 19

It was nearly 5:30 when Hayden woke up. He stretched in the chair, looking bemusedly at the hot chocolate he had obviously spilt while falling asleep. The monitor read 4 miles to their destination, so he pulled back the throttle to zero and checked the message board. Luckily no-one had tried to contact them during their trip, evidenced by the green lights.

He walked out into the brisk North Sea air. It was warm to the skin and the sun had broken through since Hamburg, trying in vain to put a sparkle into the dull water. The inflatable was still attached, albeit by only one rope. Hayden spotted the other trailing in the water, seemingly having lost its knot and falling off the side.

He walked back into the wheelhouse, the only sounds being the calm brush of water against the hull and a faint seagull cry as it circled, looking for food. He woke Joey, who looked refreshed although still slightly worn from the morning's ordeal. He looked down in disappointment at his empty mug.

"I fancy a fry-up," Hayden declared, another arrow in his healthy eating hat. He went down to the kitchen and found a bottle of sunflower oil. Pouring it into a pan, he lit the stove and went to collect some of the leftover mars bars and bread.

"Smells nice," Joey said, sniffing at the melted chocolate and warm bread wafting through the door.

"Toss us a plate," Hayden said, cheerful once more. "Its time for Sheila's Confectionary Committee."

He dished the food onto the plates, and within minutes only a few crumbs remained. Not exactly 5 star, but it was well cooked and tasted good.

"Right then," said Joey, returning to the wheelhouse. "Where are we going?"

Hayden enlarged the map until the east coastline filled the screen. It was flanked by two large towns, Lowestoft and Yarmouth, with a wide stretch of beach filling the gap.

"Go in between the two towns," Hayden instructed. "Turn it onto manual and take the wheel." He started opening drawers and rummaging through the contents, until he stood up triumphant. "Binoculars."

He retrieved the stand and shut the drawer. "Speed up," he said, staring west through the binoculars. "Slow when we see land."

Joey complied. "When do we swap boats? Or do we keep this and plough up a river in it?"

Hayden checked the map. "The rivers are too close to buildings," he replied. "We can either paddle in from when we can first see land, or drive this beast as far as it will take us. Land," he said suddenly.

Joey stopped the boat.

"Keep us going forward," Hayden muttered, trying to discern the image through the binoculars. "We should be able to go where we can see the beach with a naked eye. People won't see this thing. It's too small."

Joey edged the powerboat forward until he could see sand dunes in the distance. He checked his position on the GPS screen.

"Three, maybe four families," Hayden said, using the magnification of the binoculars. "Pick up speed until I can get a number count."

Joey pressed the throttle for ten seconds and then dropped off.

"Perfect," Hayden grinned. "I have seven people spread out in two miles of coastline. If we ram this thing forward we'd be extremely unlucky to be spotted by all of them. Take us in and stop 30 meters from the sand."

Joey nodded calmly and sent swirls of water kicking out of the back as the powerboat thrashed through the foot-high swells towards land. "We'll be there in one minute," Joey called, as Hayden swept up the bags and piled them behind a small box on the deck. The paddles were put there too.

Hayden held onto the box, the wind rippling through his hair and sending sprays of water over the boat. The beach drew closer, enlarging as the distance lessened. As far as he could tell no one had seen them, but the movement of the boat blurred his vision.

Joey, who had the benefit of glass between the air and his eyes, had a better view. The images grew sharper as they closed in, and he could see an excited toddler pointing in his direction.

"We've been spotted," he yelled, but the beach was already close enough to swim to. He pulled back on the throttle and slowed the swath of moving water he left in his wake.

"Man overboard!" Hayden dropped the bags into the inflatable and jumped down. Joey took one last look around the cabin and followed, diving over the side into the sea.

Stiff muscles, still damp from a sleep in wet clothes, pulled together for one last stretch of water. Joey stayed in the sea, pushing the back while kicking his legs, so

Hayden wielded both paddles, over-lapping them to give himself a bigger area.

Joey stumbled onto the sandy bottom, letting the soft waves wash over his back as Hayden jumped out for the tow to dry land.

Mark Andrews wasn't having a very nice day. Sitting on Gorleston beach, the sun had failed to live up to his expectations, his car had a flat tyre, and he'd run out of beer. Playing with his two-year-old son was the last thing he wanted to do. Grumpily he turned over and tried to ignore the pleas.

"Daddy," the toddler said, pulling his shorts. "There's a boat."

"Very good," Mark said, still glued to his sand-covered towel.

"Its going to crash," the boy insisted.

Mark half wondered whether his son was telling the truth, but then there was no harm in looking. He sat up and briefly looked out to sea, straightening out in shock at what he saw.

A white yacht was hurtling towards the beach. He couldn't see anyone on board, but it must have been going at close to 40 miles an hour. He started to gather up his things, then realised he didn't have time and hurriedly picked up his son.

The toddler, who thought it was part of a game as his dad ran across the sand to the cliffs, laughed and gurgled. He kicked out, thinking his dad was playing an evil man who was kidnapping him, but his dad merely panted up the hill.

The sound was audible now; a throaty roar that echoed across the water. Mark turned in time to see it slow and stop scant meters from the beach, and two men jumped off the side and started for the shore in a dingy.

He breathed a sigh of relief and put his struggling son down, who had forgotten the game and was staring at the boat.

He watched in amazement at the two men, now pulling the black inflatable across the sand. He could see them clearly now: the first with a mop of blonde hair and a handsome face, the second with brown. Both managed a cheerful nod and smile as they passed the amazed Mark, leaving the white yacht and disappearing over the hill.

Hayden and Joey paused for breath in the shallow forests behind the small sand dunes. From here on the territory was rough ground full of gorse, light dry foliage and ferns. They dropped the boat a few trees in, wrestling it out of sight as much as possible. Hayden took a swig from the bottles he had filled up on the boat, and hoisted a rucksack onto his back. "7 miles to Yarmouth," he grunted, strapping the bag tightly. Now they were back in England, it was dangerous. Not only was Philip still looking for them, but a gang of smugglers had been drawn into the mix.

"We should leave some of the bags here," Joey suggested. "There's no point in lugging this all the way to Yarmouth."

"Good idea," Hayden said, stashing a bag and suitcase in the inflatable. He was uncomfortable enough with wet clothes and sand, let alone two hiking bags. "We never found out what was in them."

Joey looked around him carefully before pulling out the knife and slashing through the rucksack. A trickle of white powder fell out of the gap, blocked in part by a clear plastic bag full of paper. Joey paused and probed further, revealing sacks of £20 notes. He fished one out of its packet and held it up to the light.

"It's genuine," he muttered. "We'd better get this to the police as soon as possible." He stuffed it back in the bag, covered it with loose fern and set off towards Yarmouth.

"Stay in the undergrowth," Joey said, sliding his way through the trees. He had done stealth training for the army and excelled at moving unnoticed, especially when off the paths.

A clearing came up, with no cover for several meters. Joey crouched on the edge, quickly scanning the area ahead. "Now!"

He jumped over the barrier of gorse and sprinted to the next set of trees, flattening against a trunk and checking round to see if they had been spotted. Hayden arrived a second later. "Perfect," Joey grinned, moving off again.

They reached the outskirts of Yarmouth an hour later, having spent a fair amount of time on the run. They were fairly sure that few people if any had seen them, but the trees thinned out and eventually disappeared altogether, turning into a maze of car parks and footpaths.

They stuck to the coastline, moving often at a run along the edges of the beach. There were more tourists here, eating ice creams and the traditional fish & chips, seated along the benches by wooden holiday huts.

"Where's the police station?"

Joey shrugged. "I don't have a clue. Shall we ask someone?"

"Nah, they'll run away. Have you seen the amount of weird looks we've had since we got here?"

"That old granny was looking at everyone like that," Joey protested.

"We could always leave it to a respectable citizen to do it," Hayden grinned, almost tripping over his feet at his hair-brained scheme.

"You mean threaten them, give them the bags and leg it?"

"Something along those lines."

"Pick your target."

"We need community support. I've got one," he said, pointing to an old man sitting peacefully at a bus stop.

"That's a better idea," Joey said brightening. "Leave them on a bus."

"In that case, you'd better run. Its nearly there."

Hayden and Joey sprinted up towards the road that followed the beach, full of betting shops, game shows and the amusement arcades all coastal tourist towns should have. Hayden skipped the path and hurdled a line of railings, coming down on a flowerbed before realising he was faced with a tall crazy golf fence, shutting him off. He sprang onto it, aware of the extra weight on his back, and climbed to the top. Avoiding the spikes, he jumped onto the roof of the ticket office and sprinted along the slate, throwing himself off the other end and onto the golf course. He ignored the angry calls and raced to the far side, taking a running leap off a ramp and clipping his feet on the way over the hedge.

He rolled onto the bag, softening his fall, and was straight on his feet running for the bus.

He caught it and looked around for Joey. His friend had stuck to the path and taken the long way round, now running the last 20 meters to catch up.

"How much for two bags to the police station?"

The driver looked at him like he was crazy. "What?"

"These bags are full of drugs and probably stolen money. Please tell the police that there are two more hidden in a black inflatable boat in the trees near Gorleston." Hayden dropped the bags on the bus and ran off, leaving the man open-mouthed and angry.

"What do we do about the other boat?" Hayden asked, running deeper into central Yarmouth.

Joey stopped. "We either leave it, or go back now and take it."

"Much as I'd love to deep-six a gang of smugglers, that's a 7 mile journey on strength we don't have. We need to get away from the coast."

"Where to then?"

"Home?"

"Philip will have been watching them," Joey said. "And hotels are out of the question, so unless you want to sleep rough, the only option left is a campsite."

Hayden smelled a rat. "It may seem a silly question, but I thought we needed a tent to sleep in a campsite," he said, falling into the trap.

Joey gave him one of his all-knowing winks. "I know just the place," he said, leading Hayden over a bridge that separated the brick from fields. "Fancy a walk in the country?"

Chapter 20

They arrived at Cutlass Camping & Caravan Park covered in yellow pollen – the result of a trek through a field of rape seed oil – dragging sore feet across the hard, crusted mud that was the driveway. The loss of the bags had been a blessing, and despite the weariness, the trek had accompanied much talking and laughing.

"Sam!" Joey erupted joyfully, locating his old high school friend walking across the campsite.

Sam Wiggins, a short fellow with strong legs and a slight paunch, looked up from under his array of multi-coloured hair. "Joey," he said, clapping his friend on the back. "What brings you to Cutlass?"

"We need a favour I'm afraid. We're not begging, but we need a place to stay."

Sam looked carefully at him, his hazel eyes covering the matted hair, rumpled clothes and exhausted faces. "You're in a bad way," he said simply.

Joey shrugged unwittingly. "I'll survive."

"Kingfisher is free for the next two nights. It's the furthest caravan up next to the stream. You can stay there, but only if you tell me what's going on."

Hayden raised his eyebrows. "How long have you got?" he said, limping after Joey in the direction of the caravan park.

Sam, whose dad owned Cutlass Camping & Caravan, went over to Kingfisher an hour later. The campsite was well laid out with sections for tents, temporary and fixed caravans. It was surrounded almost entirely by fields apart from a small section of wood, around which a small country road weaved to reach the site. People paid good money to stay here: it offered good attractions within easy distances and had a wide variety of walks and paths through the surrounding landscape, although, correctly judging by the yellow clothes, Sam assumed the pair hadn't used them.

He knocked on the door and let himself in with the spare key. The sound of running water came through the bathroom door with a cranky version of *You Never Miss The Water Until Its Gone*. Joey was in the kitchen the salt out of his shirt.

"A bad day at the beach then?" he asked, sitting on the counter.

Joey laughed. "Put a plural in that," he said.

"On days or beaches?"

"Both. Listen mate," Joey said seriously, laying his shirt on the rack. "Thanks for doing this."

"No problem. Are your parents out?"

"No, but it's a long walk home."

"10 miles should be a walk in the park for you."

"15," Joey corrected. "We'd have to go the long way round because there's a river we'd have to avoid."

"Only take you four hours," Sam grinned.

"After what we've been through," Joey muttered, thinking back to the last two days of cat and mouse through Europe. "We haven't just been to Yarmouth beach," he said. "We got stranded in Germany."

"Germany? How did you get out?"

"The taxi driver said he knew some people who would give us a boat."

"There were a few conditions," Hayden added, coming out of the shower with a towel wrapped round his waist.

Sam looked sceptical. "How many times have you rehearsed this?"

Joey threw a small bag of powder at him. "What do you think that is?"

Sam looked, confused, at the bag. "That's not salt," he said finally. "You're not on drugs are you?"

It was Hayden's turn to laugh. "If we were there'd be a lot more than this. We met a bunch of smugglers who lent us a boat stuffed with cocaine."

"Really?" If it was anyone else he would have laughed it off as a test of his gullibility, but he knew Joey too well to know when he was joking.

Joey nodded. "Check the news tomorrow. It'll be about a boy with blonde hair," he said, indicating Hayden, "who dropped £millions of cocaine on a bus and gave police locations of another load. There might also be an abandoned powerboat that nearly rammed into Gorleston beach." He recounted the story, omitting the Caterham and putting it across as a holiday in Germany.

Sam shook his head in bewilderment. "You're telling me that you tried to mess up German smugglers because you didn't have enough money to pay for ferry tickets."

"One more amazing feat in the extraordinary life of Hayden McGuire," Hayden said easily. "And now we're going for an encore."

Joey looked quizzically at him.

"I want to talk to Dr Wright," Hayden clarified.

"The military scientist?" Sam butted in.

"You know him?" Hayden asked, surprised.

"He was on the news this afternoon. He was sacked and is on police bail until the government can get him into court."

Hayden looked shocked. "Why?"

"It's all under wraps at the moment because of the legal implications. But there was a big bust up with the PM. They were shouting at each other across the street."

Joey chuckled, imagining the Prime Minister letting rip across the streets of London. That's a million votes lost, he thought.

"But it is very confusing," Sam added, furrowing his brow. "There has been nothing from any other parties. You'd have thought they would have jumped on the PM's back after that, but they seem to have disappeared. Their aides told the BBC that they weren't going to comment."

"Sounds like a crisis," Hayden said frankly. "Something bad has happened. We have to see Dr Wright as soon as possible."

"How? He's not going to let two random teenagers waltz into his house, and you have to get there first."

"Getting there shouldn't be a problem," Hayden said. "It's whether we can get there fast enough."

"Where does he live?"

"Essex."

Sam screwed his face up. "Trains are out," he said. "They're completely booked up with people going to London. We had three cancellations last week with people who couldn't get tickets and still have one family waiting for a space to go home."

"And that is going to stop me, as you put it, waltzing onto a train?" Hayden asked.

"No, but you can't get tickets, and they'll kick you off at the first station when you haven't got one."

"Only if they find us," Joey said casually, catching Hayden's drift.

"You're not going to swipe one off someone are you?"

Joey glanced at Hayden. "I doubt that's what you had in mind?"

Hayden shook his head. "Have you noticed that a ticket conductor always starts from one end and works towards the other? If you manage to get past him, you're free."

"Yeah," Sam said slowly. "But that still leaves you with one problem. How do you get past?"

Hayden and Joey arrived at Norwich station early the next morning. The incoming train that was making the reverse trip to London was a minute out, so they bought a chocolate bar and shared it sitting on the platform. Even though the station was a main entrance into their home county, Joey didn't imagine Philip would have it covered.

They'd have to get into England before attempting home, so the channel would have the main scrutiny.

"Let's go," Hayden said, the train pulling into the station. They chose folding seats in the middle as a hoard of people stormed up behind them, eager to get a space with tables.

"Out of a few hundred, someone isn't going to turn up," Hayden had said, turning down a plan to hide on the roof.

Whistles blew as the last few people dashed onto the train, coats flying and mothers urging children to hurry up. One man spilt his coffee and shouted in anger as it stained his jumper.

The train blustered out a honk of its horn and spun its wheels, moving slowly across the track before picking up speed.

"Action stations," Hayden said, eager to get underway.

"Let's go to the back." Joey turned and headed towards the rear of the train. A few people tried to tell him there were no seats further up, but he merely smiled and walked on.

He reached the last set of toilets and waited in the doorway for the queue to disappear, before slapping a sticker on the door and slipping inside. Hayden followed when no-one was looking. Soon after, the sound of raised voices could be heard just outside the door.

"Nothing works these days," a woman exclaimed, staring at the out-of-order sign. "All this technology and everything keeps breaking down." She marched off in search of another toilet, leaving Hayden and Joey trying to stifle their laughter inside.

Having spent over an hour in the cramped cubicle, they left the train at Cambridge to go south-east towards Colchester. They nearly forgot their out-of-order poster, but the oversized male figure hanging above a door in WHSmith reminded Hayden, who dashed back for it.

Repeating their trick, Hayden and Joey arrived in Colchester by mid-morning. They caught a bus with their remaining change, and spent the trip looking longingly out of the window. The sun-drenched landscape bathed bright colours where settlement was absent, and there was no wind factor that beaches had to deal with.

"Do you know if there is a bike hire place near here?" Hayden asked, before getting off at his stop.

The driver shrugged. "If there is the post office will know," he said, pointing down the road to a small cottage. A few advertisements sat outside on the pavement, and a newly-painted post box was by the corner.

"Thanks," Hayden smiled, jogging to catch up with Joey.

They approached the white-washed cottage and pushed open the door, hearing a jangle as overhead bells clanged together. A small lady entered through a curtain of beads and stood behind the counter.

"Can I help you," she squawked. She was old but bright eyed and eager to help, with a hat to cover what was left of her grey hair.

"Yes," Hayden replied. "We're looking for bikes to hire."

"There was one once," she said softly, delving into old memories with misty eyes. "But it closed down about 20 years ago. We do have one for sale though," she added, getting down from her box behind the counter to reveal her short height. She padded across the floor in lavender slippers and took a piece of paper from the window.

Hayden looked at the sheet. There was no picture, but for £20 it probably wasn't much cop. He turned to find the woman sitting in an armchair, sipping a cup of tea.

"It's dreadful you know," she said sadly. "Everyone moves off to the big cities, and no one here can make a living."

"You seem to be doing alright," Hayden offered.

"Ohh no," the woman chuckled. "I barely make a profit. My husband's pension keeps us alive. I only do this to help the other villagers."

Hayden glanced round. The woman was right. The interior of the shop was more of a living room than a shop. Two shelves lined the walls, surrounded by chairs, old pictures, half-finished knitting, and even a kettle stood on a table, ready to whistle up another pot.

"Well, I suppose we'd better go on foot," Hayden said, pinning the sheet back up.

"Where are you going?"

Hayden thought for a moment, realising the dotty old woman probably knew everything that went on. "The big mansion a few miles out of the village."

"Friends are you?" she said curiously.

"We've got a few things to sort out," Joey agreed. "Its north of here isn't it?"

"It's an awfully long way," the woman said, nodding. "I can lend you some bikes if you want?" She seemed genuine enough, so Joey accepted and watched as she disappeared through a curtain of frills.

Hayden glanced at Joey, wondering what was going to happen next.

The woman returned nodding her head. "You can use my husband's bike," she announced. "It's a little rusty, but it works." She sat down again. "Would you like a cup of tea before you go?"

Joey could probably have drunk several cups, but realised that they'd still be there at midnight listening to the entire history of Essex. "Sorry, but we have to go. Maybe another time?"

"That would be lovely," the woman chattered. "You must have one when you bring the bikes back. It's not everyday that two handsome young men walk into my shop."

Hayden thanked her for her time and went back outside. Two bicycles awaited them, put there by a seasoned man who had obviously taken advantage of the weather.

"Hop on," Joey grinned, pouncing on the male bike before Hayden could react, who shrugged and got on the female version, grimacing at the fat saddle and wicker shopping basket. Cranking it into second gear he wobbled off the pavement and started up the road.

Dr Wright's house looked the same as before, the long sweeping driveway the only gap in the wall of hedges, whose recent trimming coincided, Hayden noticed, with the removal of the lower tree branches. Upon approaching the gates however, it was clear that it was a very different place. Gone was the sense of splendour and sunshine, replaced by an aura of silence and hostility. Even the air felt like it was about to break.

Joey studied the padlock on the gates. "It'll take a tank to get through that," he said. He called out, but the hidden guards didn't reply. He sighed. "If the wolf doesn't come to the meat, take the meat to the wolf."

He put his foot on the gate and reached up for a handhold, and this time the guards moved. Springing to their feet one quickly covered the ground while his partner provided back-up.

Joey dropped back to the floor. "I knew you'd fall for that one," he grinned. "If I'd gone over you'd have had to unlock the gate to let me back out."

"This is private property," the guard said curtly. "You have no business here."

"I would have thought they'd have given you better guns considering what's at stake," Hayden said, ignoring the guard and eyeing his holstered pistol. "You do know what is at stake don't you?"

"I know that it is of no concern to you."

"Prove it."

The guard slowly reached for a radio and spoke into it. A few minutes later it crackled again.

"Sorry," the guard replied, not bothering to hide his pleasure. "The owner doesn't want to see anyone."

Hayden stared coldly at him, watching the man redden slightly as his the fierce green gaze overcame the military solidity. "See you later," he said. He sat back on his bike and slowly rolled down the hill towards the village.

"Plan b?" Joey asked.

"We go in late evening and force our way through."

Joey groaned. "Does that mean we have to go and listen to the old woman for seven hours?"

"Unfortunately, but I'm betting she might have a few more tricks to help us."

Chapter 21

When evening fell Hayden and Joey made their way back to Dr Wright's fortress. Buffered by a seemingly endless supply of biscuits, scones and tea, they dropped the bikes off as soon as they were within sight of the house, and carried on by foot.

Joey led the way, keeping to the grassy bank to prevent echoing footsteps that the roads were keen to offer. Hayden stayed behind, carrying a rope and a packet of chewing gum.

They reached the outer fence and lay still for a minute, silently scoping out any sound from within. Satisfied that if cameras existed by the hedge, they weren't trained at their spot, Joey lofted the rope into the sky, watching as it glided successfully over a branch. He made a mental note to spend more time with old ladies as he hoisted himself up; talking had been forbidden and communication was now made through hand-signals.

Hayden joined him and gradually pulled the rope up before loosely tying it to a branch. Joey was already on the floor, ear to the ground to catch any foot vibrations.

Slowly moving between the hedges, they made for the house. It was still too light for infra-red cameras, the power of which would have made easier to break in by daylight, but dusk was just beginning to creep in at the edges.

Joey paused at the last corner: Hayden had told him that cameras were at every corner on the house. Peering round, he found the camera fixed in another direction. He breathed a sigh of relief, noticing the window was open. Turning back to Hayden he gave the thumbs up sign, checked one last time for any hidden menace, and sprinted towards the window.

Hayden followed quickly, crouching down by the window ledge. The curtains were shut, but no sound floated through. Easing the window further open, he carefully climbed inside and nudged the curtains apart. The room was empty.

He dropped to the floor and dived behind the sofa as the door suddenly opened, but it was too late.

"I can hardly say welcome and offer you a drink if you're breaking into my house," Dr Wright said.

Hayden stood up. Dr Wright stood by the fireplace, a glass of whiskey in his hand. A uniformed guard stood in the doorway, a SUF rifle in his hands.

"An upgrade, like you suggested," Dr Wright said, nodding at the weapon. "Why don't you ask your friend to join us so we can talk? It would be a waste of effort for you to have come all this way and not find what you are looking for."

Joey stepped out from behind the curtain. "How long have you been watching us?"

"Since you ditched the bikes," Dr Wright said casually. "I have movement sensors covering a mile outside my house. There is also a high-tech Defence satellite that I am logged into. It picked you up like a goat in a rosebush."

"And I suppose the window was conveniently opened?"

Dr Wright nodded, pleased with his catch. He sat down. "So what did you want to talk about?"

"I thought that was obvious," Hayden replied. "What's so important that you nearly had us killed?"

Dr Wright blinked in surprise, looking puzzled. "I nearly had you killed?"

"What's in the suitcases, and why do at least two terrorist organisations want it?" Hayden replied starkly.

Dr Wright chuckled, visibly easing. "The men who tried to break into my house were not terrorists. They were merely seeking to make a profit. When news of this erm, device, leaked onto the black market, we knew we'd encounter some tough opponents, and some weaker ones. I'm sad to say that in terms of world terrorism, they would hardly register."

"They nearly managed it," Joey pointed out.

"They had an insider," Dr Wright said, almost disappointed with himself for not finding out. "The suitcases were under the guard of the most sophisticated security system I could lay my hands on. Unfortunately my security man decided to make a break with them and called in his friends. I should have known that several billion on the black market would be a lot more tempting than £2000 a day."

"What is so important?" Hayden asked. "If it's worth so much then why isn't it at a military base?"

"A long tale of bluffing and double-bluffing anyone who was watching us," Wright explained wearily. "We were transporting the cases to America but because of what's in them, flying above 500 feet would be a death wish. Cargo planes would be unsuitable for that height and jets are subject to too much pressure. Ship was the best option."

"Yet you sent out decoys," Joey stated wrathfully, focusing on Dr Wright with a furious glare.

Wright looked heavily at the floor. "You were the third," he said quietly. "A military convoy went to the HMS Ark Royal under heavy guard. The real stuff was here. It rook 10 years of scientific genius to recreate unanuminium."

"Unanuminium," Hayden mumbled, but Dr Wright cut across him.

"First, tell me what you know about Chernobyl?" he asked, his eyes curious.

Joey frowned, smelling a set-up. "Russian nuclear power station that blew up in the 1980's."

"The site is present day Ukraine, but yes," Dr Wright answered slowly. "But what was the cause?"

Joeys frown deepened. "They missed out a safety test and the reactor exploded."

"You know your history," Wright said, impressed, "or at least, you think you do."

Joey raised his eyebrows questioningly. "You mean the reactor didn't fail?" he asked narrowly.

"It didn't," Wright confirmed, letting the reality sink in. "The world's worst nuclear accident was a scam."

"You blew it up?" Joey blurted.

Dr Wright laughed. "Don't be ridiculous. Especially not with the government we had then. Let me tell you." He paused and took a slow sip of whisky. "There are very few people who know about unanuminium, and very few of those know where it was discovered. In 1986 a two-man research team was surveying a lonesome mountain only a few miles from Chernobyl. They were looking for shelter when they came across a well-disguised cave at the base, hidden behind a grove of trees. Unfortunately, not knowing that this was the only place on earth where unanuminium resides, they entered, lit some torches, and blew the whole place to pieces."

Hayden and Joey exchanged raised glances.

"This is some sort of joke right?" Hayden asked, not sure whether to believe him or not.

Wright shook his head sourly. "Unanuminium is the most radioactive and diverse element that we've ever found. The theory is that it somehow came upon the earth during the big bang, but to be honest, we don't have a clue. All we know is that it's the most toxic substance on the Defence databases."

"You mean that this rogue element blew up Chernobyl?" Joey asked sceptically.

"Satellite pictures showed the source to come from inside the mountain where the research team disappeared. Chernobyl might have missed out safety checks, but it wasn't their fault the station blew up," Wright finished.

"Where does this lead us?" Hayden asked slowly. "You can't have found more of this stuff?"

"Luckily it's too sensitive in the wild," Dr Wright confirmed. "What's left will have buried itself deep in the earth, hopefully near Iraq."

It was Hayden's turn to frown. "Then if unanuminium is what the fuss is all about," he murmured hollowly, thinking back to the impregnable suitcases and Wright's position as a scientist of destruction. "You copied the molecular formula and come up with your own version."

Dr Wright nodded slowly.

"You recreated an element?" Joey said dubiously. "That's impossible."

"We modified existing particles, not invented them," Wright corrected.

"You changed the substances that make up the existence of our world," Joey said curiously. "That's disproportionate," he said, realising the implications. "This world is made up of certain things, and if you change these things you change the world."

"I know," Dr Wright said heavily.

"You've got one massive problem," he said starkly. "Just how deadly is this gas?"

"One particle per billion will kill a human."

"What's the antidote?"

"There isn't one."

Hayden stared at him. "Where are the suitcases?"

"America."

"Then I suppose you have them under control."

"I personally drove them onto HMS Montrose, who delivered them safely into the hands of General Morson whilst in the protection of two nuclear submarines."

"When was this?"

"Five days ago. Look, do not concern yourselves with the safety of the weapon," Dr Wright said, getting irritated. "You're talking more like politicians than teenagers. The best that the British and Americans can offer is behind this."

"I don't doubt the British Security Forces," Joey said quietly. "But I do think there is something that you should know. It is obvious to me that this gas is proving too much of a temptation for many people that should be left undisturbed, and things are very soon going to get out of hand. What if we said you your main threat was from France?"

Dr Wright looked momentarily taken aback, but quickly regained his composure. "Do you mean the government?"

"I mean Philip Morel."

"Never heard of him. Listen, all terrorist organisations have been fully scrutinised by the best security analysts in the world. We know who and what we're up against."

"Like your security man," Hayden said sarcastically.

Wright glared at him.

"And if we said that we spent the last week in a cellar underneath his mansion in France, faced by armed guards and high-voltage doors?"

"I would say you made the entire affair up," Wright said calmly.

Hayden fixed him with a deathly stare. The stakes had been set.

"Ok," Joey butted in harshly. "Thank you for a nice evening, but in case you haven't heard from your brother recently, he had a little disagreement with a few mercenaries in Italy. At least two people were killed, and there may be CCTV footage of a helicopter lying around somewhere. That helicopter went to France with our suitcases."

Wright froze.

"Is there anything else we might need to know in case the gas turns up on our doorstep. Such as how to open it safely?"

Wright looked angrily at him. "The substance is only stable in a vacuum with a special mixture of scandium and soap."

"Soap?"

"Yes, soap," he retorted. "In case you ever study university chemistry, soap has one of the most complicated formulas known to man."

"Well done you," Hayden said sarcastically. "Did you spin that when the government started investigating whether you were working for Lapcon Industries? Try and impress officials with the divineness of chemistry?"

"Who are Lapcon Industries?" Wright said incredulously. "You're pulling story after story. I think its time you left."

"I'm going happily," Hayden answered, throwing back the curtains.

Joey paused and turned with one foot on the window ledge. "One more thing," he said quietly. "What happened with the PM?"

Dr Wright glared at him with disgust. "When the government investigated me it was on the whims of some political idiot trying to make a name for himself. That idiot is now the PM."

"So if you deny knowledge of Lapcon, why were they investigating you?"

"We were massively over budget," Wright said exasperatedly, still not having the faintest idea who Lapcon were. "Now get out."

"Catch you later," Joey smiled sardonically, following Hayden out of the window.

He jogged to catch up with Hayden: his friend had ignored the hedge and marched instead to the main gate, taking a sarcastic pleasure in making the guards open it for him. They found their bikes exactly where they'd left them, damp from dew.

"What do you think?" Joey's voice broke through the rhythmic squeaking pattern of rusty bike chains.

Hayden was too dazed by the seriousness of their discussion to answer. Normally he would have laughed it off, but their experience in France weighed heavily on his mind. "Why was he fired in the first place? He said the gas was in a military base in America?"

Joey shrugged. "Beats me. Do you think he was telling the truth?"

"About unanuminium?" Hayden took a long breath of air. "Yes," he said finally. "Philip pretty much proved there was something strange going on. All Wright did was tell us what."

Joey looked at him. A mask of quiet seriousness was brewing in the back of his friend's mind, and Joey let it simmer for a moment. "So where do we go from here?" he asked eventually.

"I don't know," Hayden replied heavily. "I need some sleep, and a good English breakfast. We'll figure something out after then."

Chapter 22

In France, Philip Morel was pacing his study. Aldo was attempting to talk to him, but the length of the room meant he was only in earshot for a few seconds.

"I trust I find you in good health. Your hard work has been extremely valuable to us."

Philip ignored him. "Did you understand the document I sent you?"

"I got the gist," Aldo replied, annoyed at the display of ignorance Philip was demonstrating. "Your development has met a setback and you can't continue."

"Nothing is impossible," Philip retorted, "but I won't deny I need several items to speed up the process."

"Namely?"

"Plutonium."

Aldo raised his eyebrows. "I thought we had already discussed the futility of that path. Surely carbon is as effective."

"That will set us back two weeks," Philip said angrily. "The army used a very complicated process to concentrate the stuff."

"We can copy it," Aldo offered. Despite being a methodical and cold-heartedly ruthless man, he knew better than to antagonise Philip. The young scientist was valuable.

"I can do better than that," Philip said, though under the tension his cleverness was failing to excite him. "They made two major mistakes that will save us three days and £millions in equipment."

"I'm glad for you," Aldo replied dryly.

"Plutonium is the closest we can get without modifying the atom," Philip lectured.

"As soon as the atom breaks it's the same with every element," Aldo argued. "The slight advantage of plutonium over carbon doesn't justify the risk of getting it."

"Have faith," Philip grinned. "The similarities between plutonium and unanuminium will make the final stages easier. Plus, I don't posses an army of dead volunteers for nothing." He paused for a moment. "Lapcon Industries have headquarters near the Civaux nuclear plant. I will arrange for them to pick some plutonium up next time they drive past."

"You're cutting it thin," Aldo warned.

"How?"

"The British gas has left the Pentagon test labs. Armoured trucks left the compound and registered signs of radioactivity."

"That could be anything," Philip snapped.

"The US Air Force has just been ordered to stand-by, and two nuclear submarines that were on patrol have turned towards Chesapeake Bay," Aldo interrupted, secretly pleased that Philip had guessed wrongly.

"They're using the same tactics as before then," Philip smirked. "Don't they know who they're dealing with?"

Aldo smiled wryly at Philips statement. The British were cunning in their secrecy, and second-guessing their moves was proving tougher than he had anticipated. "We did collect the scandium though," he said, dropping a bundle on the desk. "We found Lucio and offered him a deal."

Philip grinned. "They might have the gas, but they can't control it," he said, turning his attention to the scandium.

"And soon they won't have that either," Aldo added. "One of our Arab friends has loaned us a few hundred English citizens. They've all decided to go and sunbathe in Portsmouth for their holidays."

Philip narrowed his eyes. "You're having a few hundred men face a military convoy? Isn't that a death mission?"

"Those are my orders," Aldo replied simply. "A few lives lost will mean nothing to our cause. Anyway, I doubt there will be massive bloodshed: Ashal-Ruhi will be leading them."

Ashal-Ruhi was a tough customer. Methodical in his planning and ruthless in execution, both men knew the capabilities of the cold-hearted Iraqi. Aldo had little doubt that Ashal would succeed.

"How powerful is the spread of gas?" Aldo asked.

"The particles stick together in a dense molecular structure," Philip said slowly. "They have a positive charge of over a thousand percent, which would make them spread like wildfire but for the carefully calculated weight, which is strong enough to keep it moving below 30mph. Think of it as an expanding barrier that will never stop until the particles are as far away from each other as they can be."

"And that won't that affect us here?"

Philip smiled. "Let's just say the British shot themselves in the foot when they decided to create a gas that breaks apart itself after 48 hours. By then it will only have reached southern Greece if weather is favourable."

"Plenty of time for an escape. By the way, have you had any news on the renegade teenagers?"

"They managed to escape the French police," Philip replied disgustedly. "All airports and ferries are being watched, but if they do manage to get back to England, I have a man near Dr Wright's house. When they go there, we'll have them."

Aldo failed to have the same sense of optimism, but said nothing. The English boys had already wormed through situations far beyond their control, and a sense of unease settled over his normally calm mind. Brushing it off, he left Philip with instructions to make contact at the merest whimper, and made his way back to the helipad. The gas had the potential to kill everyone on earth, and he wasn't going to let Philip's lack of concern allow the opportunity to pass.

Hayden and Joey eventually gave up on the sleep after deciding to travel back to Norfolk. They had nothing with them, and needed to restock. Once they could access their bank accounts they could travel honestly, going undercover as far as Philip pushed them.

Hayden slid down the banister onto Colchester station and checked for trains. There was nothing for several hours, so they decided to walk to the next stop a few miles down the road.

It was dark out of the city: the lights that emitted a dim glow were behind them and the clouds were fully formed, protecting the moon. It was chilly, so they were glad to get moving. "Those seats were disgusting," Joey said, referring back to Colchester platform.

"I wouldn't sit on them for five minutes," Hayden agreed, half-wishing for food but the taste of fruit scones still sick in his mouth.

"The next station better be along this road," Joey muttered. "I'm not walking for hours to find that I have to go back."

"Have faith my friend," Hayden replied. "How about a morale-boosting song?"

To the silent tracker hunting at night, loud prey can be a blessing or a curse. The victims can give away their position or draw unwanted attention. To two separate stalkers, the sound of singing brought different circumstances. An owl hooted its disappointment as the chosen field mouse hurried into a hole, while a black tourist caught the voices and hurried on. In his bag was a handgun, and his mission was to kill.

"What's next?" Hayden wondered, watching the birds flutter into sky at his crude rendition of *Eat the Word*.

Joey didn't answer. A loud blast reverberated through the air as a .7mm bullet tore through his arm. He fell to the ground instantly, a mass of blood pooling at his side.

Hayden dived into the bushes, acting from pure instinct, and lay there gasping. He looked desperately around for a weapon as a shape hurried up to Joey's body and shook it. There was no response.

The man turned and faced the bushes, revealing a taut, eager face shrouded by darkness. He fired several shots into the hedge, looking for the other target. Nothing. His gun clicked empty, and he scurried off up the lane.

Hayden flew back onto the road, his ripped shirt already in his hands. He wrapped the crude bandage around Joey's sodden clothes and hoisted his friend onto his back. A slight contraction told him the body wasn't dead yet, but he soon would be if he didn't hurry.

Hayden neared the outskirts of the city at a run, his back sore from carrying his partner, but didn't let up for a moment. Joey had gone limp; a sign of unconsciousness, but Hayden didn't bother to check. The first car he saw was a red SUV pulling into a driveway. He ran towards it yelling. "Bullet wound," he gasped, barely noticing the shocked look on the drivers face. "Take him to hospital."

They manhandled Joey carefully onto the backseat and ran to the front. The late hour meant that the roads were deserted, and Hayden urged the car over 70mph.

"I'll pay for it," Hayden said, watching a speed camera flash as they go past. "How far is the hospital?"

"Call an ambulance," the driver said, pointing to the side of his seat. He was a balding man in his early 50's, and his face fairly shone with sweat.

Hayden pulled the phone out and dialled 999. "Where do they want to meet us?"

"At Bluetown crossroads."

Hayden gave the information and a minute later, sirens could be heard pulling out of the hospital.

They made the switch; the medics immediately placing Joey under anaesthetic with an oxygen mask, and roared back to the hospital. The man stood watching the entire affair in a mild shock, and then returned to his car.

He glanced at his backseat and groaned at sight of bloodstains on the newly-padded leather. On a good note though, he noticed Hayden had been good enough to leave the mobile.

Knowing that the adrenaline he'd pumped round his veins wasn't going to let him sleep in the next hour, he wearily turned his car around and headed towards the police station to explain his speeding.

Chapter 23

Hayden stayed in the hospital all night. There was nowhere else he could have gone. The police stationed a guard outside Joey's room, but Hayden refused to go to the station for questioning. It was done instead in the coroner's office: the owner not having a night-shift counterpart. Not that there was much to say: the shot had been in the dark and he had no idea they were being followed. After finishing his story he merely asked the police to phone Dr Wright to fill him in, and then returned to wait outside Joey's room. Hurried surgery was underway, but it didn't appear serious.

"He's lucky," the doctor said, an hour after the operation. "It looks bad and it's tricky work, but the bullet only nicked the skin. He'll be back to normal within two days."

Hayden counted in his head. Their story was becoming more believable by the moment, and three days was ample time for Philip to find out the events and come gunning. He had to get Joey out.

His thoughts were interrupted by brisk footsteps. Dr Wright marched up the corridor, focusing on the stretched-out figure lying on a bench.

"Will you tell me what you're playing at?" Dr Wright said angrily. "You come up here telling me all sorts of rubbish and demanding answers, and now your friend's in hospital with a bullet through his arm."

"Check your security," Hayden said emptily. "If we were being targeted before we met you then we'd both have been dead a long time ago. The tail came from your house."

"What makes you sure it was meant to be you?"

"How about the man emptying his gun into the bushes when I tried to hide," Hayden said sarcastically.

"We can do without the humour," Wright said seriously. "Why did you phone me?"

"To prove to you the dangers we're facing," Hayden answered testily. "There are people in England that you can't catch simply because you are not aware of them. Get onto the intelligence agencies and get them onto Philip Morel."

Wright sat down. "I really have messed this up," he muttered dejectedly.

Hayden took in Wright's features, noting the tense shoulders and off-centred tie. The increased mass of lines on his forehead and dark circles under tired eyes gave signs of a stressed man.

Wright thumped the wall in frustration and turned back to Hayden. "I feel terrible about your friend. I should have seen it coming, but this damn gas business is going to murder a lot of people if we don't solve it, and I guess I just didn't take you seriously enough. If there is anything that I can do, just name it."

Hayden grinned. "The last time you said that, I ended up being chased across the continent by a bunch of terrorists."

Wright let a small chuckle cross his lips, but was more embarrassed by the reminder of his obvious double-crossing. "I mean it this time. I can arrange safe-houses for you, and get you out of harms way while the intelligence services investigate Philip Morel. I can't promise anything, but I'll talk to the Prime Minister personally."

"We don't want a safe-house," Hayden replied shiftily, having already talked this through with Joey. "We need a bigger favour."

Wright looked carefully at him: his past encounters with the teenager enough for him to expect the unexpected. His gaze met with silent, purposeful, determined eyes.

"I can't promise anything," he repeated, but his voice sounded optimistic.

"All we need is your influence in the army," Hayden said swiftly, little by little injecting his guile into the conversation.

"I can't give you that. I lost all respect when the scandium went missing. I was fired."

Hayden ignored him. "You can still bluff your way past the bureaucratic tape and gain the immediate release of a special task force."

"What for?"

"As soon as Joey is out, we're going into France. If you can help, contact ATR Winchester and get me some papers for a release team. If not, the wish us luck."

"That's a bit rash," Dr Wright said harshly, but quickly wilted under the furious stare of the teenager.

"Tell me how successful you think the British Intelligence Service is?" Hayden asked, softening.

Wright closed his eyes in desperation. "The PM has taken control of the operation," he revealed sourly. "As much as I hate to admit it, he isn't going to listen to me."

"Then trust me," Hayden said quietly. "All I'm asking for is time. What does your future hold if this gas blows up? Nothing, apart from guilt and worldwide condemnation. Let us go, and we can prevent this."

Wright resigned. "I'm not going to be able to stop you am I?"

Hayden shook his head. "You've got nothing to lose."

The silence that followed was almost unbearable, but eventually Wright turned and studied Hayden's face. There was a dark seriousness there; a confident determination in what he could do. He remembered the video of him fighting, and a glimmer of hope began to emerge.

"The unexpected is always the best option when there are no options left," he quoted. Then he grinned. "The army back-channels are well-oiled," he said. "I will have a team released immediately."

Hayden handed him the sheet of names Joey had provided him. Wright scanned it and nodded, business-like once more. "This is the most serious mission I have ever been involved with," he said starkly.

"I'll count on it," Hayden grinned.

"ATR Winchester, 94th Unit," a voice said.

"This is Colonel Jessop," Joey replied. "I need to speak to Niklas Fairclough immediately." There was total conviction and authority in his voice. *That's what you need for a good scam*, he mused.

He was patched through to the main assault room where another recruit picked up the phone.

"What can I do for you sir," the recruit said curtly. Joey could almost imagine him standing to attention by the phone, desperate to make a good impression. If only he knew, Joey thought, I hold as much weight in the army as the General's cat.

"Good morning," Joey said quietly. He knew that if his voice rose it would be easier to tell his age. "I need to speak to Niklas Fairclough immediately."

The recruit hesitated. "I'm afraid that's impossible sir," he said apologetically. "He is in the middle of an intensive training program which cannot be interrupted."

"Tell me," Joey said smoothly. "Who is in charge there? And are those his orders?"

"Yes they are Sergeant O'Neill's orders." He was uncertain now. He had no problem obeying the order; but was fearful of the Sergeants wrath. O'Neill had left him in no doubt as to the fact that he didn't want anyone interrupting. He gripped the phone and prepared for the onslaught that was about to come.

It didn't. Instead, Joey replied calmly, "Do you know when the last person in my position said immediately? It was the beginning of the Iraq war," his voice hardening. "Now give the phone to recruit Fairclough."

The recruit recovered. "Yes sir. He may be a minute sir; he is in the middle of the spiders net assault course."

"In that case, can you ready a landing crew," Joey replied briskly. "My associate will be landing shortly."

"Yes sir." The recruit waited until the sweating Nik arrived, and then hurried off to ready the helipad.

"Good morning sir. Niklas Fairclough speaking," the voice came over the line.

Joey laughed. "Hello Nik."

"Oh hi. You had me freaked out there," Nik said wiping his face. "The other guy said it was a colonel. What did you do, bug the man's line or something?"

"Honestly Nik," Joey replied sarcastically. "You need more respect for your superiors. I am the colonel."

"You what?"

"We can talk later. I need your help," said Joey, abruptly turning serious.

"What going on?" Nik said.

"Would you and the guys consider taking a bit of time out of the army? I could do with some hired muscle."

"What is it?"

"Some idiot put a bullet in my back and we've traced it to central Europe. I'm going to sort them out when I've recovered. Interested?"

"Definitely."

By this time the sergeant had noticed and had come over. Silently he pressed the speaker phone button so the voice was amplified around the room.

"When shall I report in sir?" Nik hoped that Joey would catch on as his role of colonel again.

"My guy will be there in 12 minutes. You'll need weapons and supplies for just under a week. Meet him at the helipad."

"Excuse me," Sergeant O'Neill interjected smoothly. "I have no idea who you are, but this man is on an intensive training program which cannot and will not be interrupted. Nor will he leave this compound while he is on this course. You are breaking regiment rules and I will have to terminate this call."

"Then please inform the sergeant that there is more to life in the army than his pompous training procedures," Joey replied calmly. By now, half the people in the room were listening.

"I can hear you perfectly well," O' Neill spat. "You need to watch your mouth."

"This is Colonel Jessop, and if you think you can scare me with your cocky, non-existent rules made up to scare the public away from you precious regime, then you've got another thing coming."

Everyone froze. No one, even his superiors, had dared down-talk the sergeant before. He gave as good as he got.

"Colonel or not, you have no authorisation to use the helipad," he retorted icily. "Despite your rank you still have to go through the proper channels and no one has been notified. Therefore we cannot permit you to use it."

"Just face the facts man. My man is landing in ten minutes and if you don't like it then I'll have you assigned to toilet duty," Joey said exasperatedly.

"The helipad is covered." He couldn't hide the smugness in his voice. "And seeing as your visit is unauthorised, I see no reason to order a landing crew."

"Too little, too late. I've already ordered one."

"You have no authorization," fumed O'Neill. "I command the landing crew. Not even a general could land without notifying me first."

"Oh yeah, I forgot to mention that," Joey replied sarcastically. "By the way, is your first name Piers?"

Brainless idiot, thought Sergeant O'Neill. He's enjoying this. "What's that got to do with anything," he snapped.

"You sound like that sort of guy," came the reply cheekily before the buzzing that told them he had hung up.

"Peters," barked O'Neill. "Get the army records and check for a Colonel Jessop. That guy has a death wish."

"Sir, there is no record of Colonel Jessop, in the army files," Peters said after a brief check.

"Damn," spat O'Neill. "You lot, get your weapons and follow me."

The helicopter was just touching down when they arrived. They spread out, weapons raised, waiting for the rotor blades to stop. Sergeant O'Neill recognized the vehicle as a Hawk Attack helicopter. Where in the world did he get one of those?

A man stepped out, almost at unawares to the guns aimed at his chest. He wore dark green combat trousers, a white tank top and expensive running shoes.

An alarm bell rang in the back of the sergeant's mind. He's too casual, he thought. He was an accurate judge of character; but this man puzzled him. Dark sunglasses obscured his eyes making it impossible to size him up, immediately putting him at an advantage. The jaw was set, although O'Neill suspected it could break into a smile and lighten up a party in an instant; and the dark blonde hair was swept back. The thing that most startled him though was his apparent carelessness. He stood utterly at ease as if waiting for a bus, his eyes probably roving around the men.

"Colonel Jessop, I presume," he sneered.

The man shook his head calmly. "His delivery guy, but I did listen to the call."

"Then you know the (he let out a torrent of abuse) I'm looking for," he continued heatedly. "You have no authorisation for anything, are guilty of wasting army time and impersonating a colonel. You're both going to jail."

"If you're referring to the landing crew, I'm not even in the army so how was I supposed to know?" Hayden replied coolly.

"Yeah whatever," O'Neill snorted. "If you can get this far into the army without being stopped then you'll know the rules."

Hayden shrugged indifferently. "I'm only 16; you can't expect me to know everything." He took his sunglasses off, revealing young, light-green eyes that sparkled in the light.

O'Neill was in shock.

"Yeah, I'm 16, and if you don't like it, then you can take a hike!" Hayden said roughly, his voice suddenly rising.

"Do you know how long they'll lock you away for this," O'Neill whispered coldly. "At least 8 years, and that's just for the impersonation and deception of a colonel."

"Oh, but I do have what you don't want to see" he replied, his eyes twinkling.

O'Neill didn't like it. The man obviously knew something the he didn't. It was as if the man knew he could get away with anything.

"And you're dead meat," Hayden continued. He began moving his hand behind his back when a shout filled the air.

"Freeze!" One of the soldiers that had accompanied Sergeant O'Neill brought his rifle to bear.

Hayden froze, wondering what was going on; then, to O'Neill's amazement, burst out laughing. "I'm unarmed," he said, turning around so that his back faced the audience. Slowly with one hand clearly in view he pulled his wallet out of his back pocket.

"Your guys sharp. I'll give you that," Hayden said mischievously.

"Yeah, I trained him," O'Neill snarled.

Hayden ignored him. "My name is Hayden McGuire," he said seriously, showing his ID. "The man I represent is an officer for the SAS and is currently in an investigation involving MI5 and CIA. I need Nik and," he paused, reading out a list of names, "to come with me. I might also add that chief military scientist Dr Wright has approved."

O'Neill was not to be outdone. "Surely there are more suitable people? These men haven't even finished training and the way I see it, if this task force is ordered by the top, you could get anyone you wanted."

"My man has reported that these men already have the skills needed for the army. This camp is merely to prove them. I trust you won't get in our way sergeant."

O'Neill snatched the papers Hayden had given him, studying them fastidiously before resigning. "Ok, you've got your unit. Fairclough," he barked. "Round up these men and report here with needed equipment in five minutes."

"Thank you sergeant."

Hayden climbed back into the chopper and called Joey to report mission success.

"The documents hold up ok?"

"Thankfully," said Hayden. "We owe Wright on this one."

"Just make sure you deliver," Wright said grimly, listening in on the call. "If this fails and men die as a result, they'll bring back capital punishment."

Chapter 24

Richard Marsh was struggling to keep his eyes open. His superiors, after going endlessly through satellite photos involving the cargo from America, had retired home, leaving him to sift through the less important business. His office was small and boring, but it housed a water cooler and a coffee pot, the latter of which he went to now. It tasted like chemical-filled water, but at least it would keep him awake. His position in the British Intelligence network didn't normally keep him late, and his wife was wondering what was happening.

He returned to his desk and nearly spat out his coffee. Some prankster had landed him the job of trying to find an 18th Century mansion in the vastness of the French Alps. He shrugged and jerked his computer awake. He began accessing data from the European MS satellite, a super-focused magician in the sky. It could tell how many layers of ham he had in his sandwich, in any weather and with any lighting conditions. The power still managed to amaze him after two years of its benefits.

He found several possibilities in a matter of minutes, but none of them had the trees that were supposed to surround it. He carried on relentlessly, grateful for the double pay he earned when working overtime. Wearily pushing his octagonal glasses further up his nose, he turned on a heat detector.

The heat detector is a marvellous tool. Easily adjusted, it can pick up minute traces of temperature difference and program the results through a computer, which automatically consults temperature charts for that region, showing its results with luminous colours.

Marsh saw what he expected, scrolling across his the Alps on his screen, observing the dots of red that were human forms. He paused once when small cluster appeared in a forest, but quickly discovered the mystery as a campfire. Three men with dogs appeared with firewood, so Marsh moved on.

Two hours later he received a call from his wife. He glanced at the clock, only just realising it was now early morning. "I'll be home soon," he reassured her, propping his head on his elbow. "In five more minutes I'll be in the car." He hung up and hurriedly tried to finish the last section of his search grid. There was no snow on this part, and the hills could not exactly be called mountains, but there was no harm in looking.

The computer discharged a sharp buzz, alerting Marsh that something wasn't right. He switched off the temperature gauge and twiddled with the night-vision equipment. A lorry was making its way down the mountains. Marsh moved his cursor over the vehicle and the computer refined its noise. Interested, Marsh switched the irritating sound off, using the flashing purple light on the screen as notification, and followed the lorry through the valley. The computer clearly didn't like something, and Marsh decided to find out what it was.

He turned on every sensor he could find, and stared at the results in horror. Quickly grabbing his phone, he dialled the emergency switchboard. "Get me someone important," he said tersely, watching the scanner that read radioactive material.

"I understand your predicament, but I can't order troops into the area." The Director of the French Secret Service sat up in bed, trying to fight off the urge to yawn.

"I don't think you understand the situation," replied the British Foreign Secretary, getting exasperated. "I hate getting yanked out of bed, but the fact remains that some nutter is driving a lorry with radioactive weapons through

France. If we find it links to British Security, which there is a distinct possibility of, we will come in and neutralise the threat ourselves."

"Are you blackmailing me?" the director said incredulously.

"This is serious Trevor." The use of first names was unusual, but neither noticed under the situation.

"If we go charging in because of a hitch on your computer the fallout will be catastrophic," he argued. "You know more than me the tensions we are having with our peace talks in the middle-east. If the media get news of a nuclear panic in the Alps, it'll blow all we have."

"I'm not asking the world Trevor, but I am asking that you investigate the possibility of terrorist activity in your own backyard."

"Ok ok, I'll check it out," the man grumbled wearily. "Fax the details to my office and men will be out first thing tomorrow morning. Only to investigate mind you; I am not ordering an alert and all proceedings with be done with minimum fuss. How did your satellites find the plutonium by the way?"

"Good night," the Foreign Secretary said. He hung up and dialled head of security. "How did we find out about this?" he demanded.

"Our MS Defence Satellite can pick up radioactive gamma rays on the earth's surface," the man replied.

"I'm not bothered with the science," he interrupted brutally. "Who gave us the tip-off?"

The man consulted his notes. "A man called Dr Wright asked us to investigate an old mansion in the Alps. We were searching the area when we came across the lorry, which then proceeded to what we believe is the house he was asking for."

"Have you contacted him?"

"Not yet sir."

The Foreign Secretary grabbed another phone. "I'm calling him now. Stay next to this phone where I can reach you."

"Who's this?" Dr Wright grumbled, not pleased at being woken.

"Why don't you answer your phone man?"

"Its downstairs," Wright said, becoming more awake. "I'm not normally in the habit of being woken up by idiots in the middle of the night."

"The idiot you're referring to is the Foreign Secretary," he snapped. "What on earth did you mean by requesting satellite photos of a house in the Alps?"

Wright started. It wasn't everyday a cabinet minister rang in at 2am for answers to a simple request. "What's happened?"

"A lorry with radioactive material has been spotted going into a building that matches your description. I'm sending a fax now for you to confirm this was the place you meant."

"I didn't give the description," Wright said hurriedly. "It was given to me by," he faltered, wondering what to say. His mind was numbed with shock as the sudden complication in Hayden's plan hit him. Nuclear material was the last thing he wanted news of, and he immediately realised the possible implications.

"Pull yourself together," the minister roared. "Who gave you the description?"

"Two men," Wright said, not wanting to give more than was necessary, but quickly realised the Secretary could do more than Hayden and Joey could. "They've gone to France. I was to send them photos of the place when I got them from British Intelligence."

"Tell them to get back here now. The French are investigating, but it's limited. They're scared of international fall-out with Iran if the press get news of enriched uranium and plutonium in central France. We can't have tourists messing the place up. Tell them if they are not on English soil by midday they can expect a call from the SAS."

"You're sending troops into France?" Wright said incredulously.

"By tomorrow night at the latest."

Wright sighed as he hung up and checked Hayden's mobile number. His old phone had been taken with the rest of his luggage in France, so Wright had reluctantly signed the bill for a new one. Right at this moment the team would be on the Eurostar heading for Paris. He hoped they would be either side of the tunnel.

He was lucky. Hayden had arrived in France five minutes before his phone rang.

"Hello."

"You've got a problem," Wright said, wasting no time.

Hayden froze. "What is it?" He dreaded the prospect of being caught, and hoped they hadn't bitten off more than they could chew.

"Nothing that concerns you directly, but the satellites picked up traces of uranium going to a settlement in the Alps. I can't say whether it was the place you're looking for, but the Foreign Secretary is going mad. He wants you back over here now and is considering sending the SAS in."

"What did you tell him about Philip?"

"Only what I told British Intelligence. They don't think anyone could be trying to duplicate the gas but this has shocked a lot of people."

"Philip has the capability, if not the patience," Hayden said carefully. "This is going to get desperate."

"I suggest you pull out," Wright said. "This is coming from the top. You've done your part; now get out before it starts getting dangerous."

Hayden paused for a minute. "I can't speak for the others, but I'm going to the Alps. Life isn't a game you can win, but you can choose how you play."

"Listen," Wright said harshly. "We acted because no one else would. Now they are. You have what you wanted. You proved to us that Philip was dangerous, and now we're acting on it."

"If Philip has the ingredients, he has a purpose for them," Hayden argued. "He's got magnetic trapping devices in an underground lab, and I'm betting he's found a way to duplicate your process."

"That's impossible. It took years for us to reach that stage."

"And that's coming from a man who needed a bullet to realise that his enemy existed," Hayden retorted. "I'm not taking any chances."

"And what happens when the SAS come in and find British soldiers dead because of an ill-conceived plan? The best men in the British infantry are preparing for action and you're attempting to block them."

"You owe this to us," Hayden said, ignoring the question. "Don't let us down."

Wright sighed. "The SAS will arrive tomorrow night. I can't order you back, but I'm telling you to question your actions." He warned. "I'll send the photos to the British Embassy anyway. Call me from there and tell me what your plan is."

"I will do." He hung up.

"What was that?" Joey asked.

"The satellite picked up uranium going into Philip's place in the Alps. Wright has basically been ordered by the Foreign Secretary to pull us out."

Joey whistled. "That's serious."

"I thought we should carry to Paris and find out what to do from there. I intend to get close and see what happens."

"What are they doing about it in England?"

Hayden grimaced. "The SAS are going in tomorrow evening if nothing is resolved, but they have to wait for the French to investigate."

"I'd better tell the lads," Joey said with a rueful smile.

Back in England, Dr Wright switched on the news. He realised he'd be under a barrage of pressure as soon as London woke up for the morning, and decided to stay awake. He resisted the temptation to open a bottle of whiskey, and settled on the sofa.

He sighed and listened to the newsreader waffling on about taxes and a policeman in Cheshire, and then sat bolt upright, staring at the screen.

"An electronics company in Berlin has been fined millions of pounds today for hacking," the newswoman said, her solemn expression never changing whilst on screen. "Lapcon Industries faces closure as all major employees look ready to fight jail sentences, it has been revealed by German police. It was uncovered that countless crimes of hacking since 1997 have remained hidden from law officials, and the company is thought to have collected several million from anonymous companies as a result of lifted information. This outbreak has caused wild speculation after a French nuclear energy company claimed its network had been hacked into by Lapcon. All reports of missing uranium have been denied."

Wright froze. Lapcon Industries again. The teenagers had mentioned them. He leaned back and stared at his ceiling, wondering why they had accused him of siding with them. His mind travelled to their tale through France and tried to put himself in Philip Morel's place. He assumed that was where they had picked the information up, but couldn't figure why Philip would want the pair connecting him with an illegal computer company.

Getting frustrated as his brain swept round in circles, he logged onto his laptop and typed Lapcon into a search engine. He found nothing: just the main storyline repeated everywhere. He was about to give up when he spotted a side story in the corner of a newspaper site. He scrolled over and downloaded it. The story told of a widow – her husband's body found days after a finished job in the Alps – who had been sent some papers by her solicitor. In a long and heartfelt letter, the dead man spilled out words only to be read after his passing. As well as words of comfort to his wife, he'd included details of his latest assignment, to be published if anything happened to him. Dr Wright's eyes widened, reading that the man, a renegade internet-publisher, regularly copied work to his own website, the address of which was also in the letter.

Sensing light at the end of the tunnel, he typed the address in, eagerly looking at the webpage that flashed up before him. It was part of an Al-Jazeera page, connecting his picture with a headline about Lapcon. The pieces beginning to fall into place, he entered Al-Jazeera into his computer, found their real site, and found no trace of the page. Heart thumping furiously in his mouth, he realised that Hayden and Joey had been set up from the start. He picked up the phone and dialled British Intelligence.

Richard Marsh picked up the phone. "Good morning."

"Richard, I need you to check out Lapcon Industries."

"Lapcon," Richard mused. The name sounded familiar, but he couldn't place it. Perhaps it was because he hadn't slept in 20 hours. He keyed it into his computer and waited for it to come up with a match. He didn't have to wait long. Lapcon Industries was the company logo that was depicted on the roof of the uranium-carrying lorry.

"Lapcon Industries own the company who took the uranium to the Alps," he said swiftly. "Was there anything specific that you wanted?"

"Find out who owns Lapcon," Wright replied tersely.

"I'm on it," Richard said instantly.

There was a pause as Richards fingers flew over the keyboard, accessing files and encrypted government records. "I've got a parent company," he said. "No wait. Two parent companies with equal shares. Both legitimate traders."

"Doing what?"

"Clothes manufacture and atomic research. Do you want me to look into them?"

"Do the atomic company first," Wright replied stiffly. Lapcon tied with atomic research was too like unanuminium to be coincidence.

"Another parent company specialising in dive equipment, which is owned by Alex Bauchet," Richard said. "The clothes manufacturer is owned by," he paused, waiting for his computer to display the next screen, and then whistled. "Alex Bauchet."

"Find out who that is," Wright snapped. The tension was beginning to get to him.

"Accessing French birth records," Richard muttered. "Bauchet's a French name. We've got two under that heading. One was born in 1897 and the other in 1962."

"The latter might be the best option."

Marsh opened a new window and typed Bauchet into the search engine. "Strange," he murmured.

"What?"

"There is no Alex Bauchet in any of our records," Marsh replied, at loss as to his blank screen.

"Try someone else's records then," Wright said flippantly.

"We're logged into every major database in the world," Richard protested. "Banks, insurance, shop records, credit cars, holiday outlets, passports, schools. He just doesn't exist."

"Where does he live?"

"His registered home is a tenancy in the French Alps."

"Can you be more specific?"

Marsh brought up his satellite images. "Looks like we've stirred up a hornets nest here," he said slowly, confirming Dr Wright's suspicions. "The same place the plutonium went to."

"Who's the owner?"

"Of Bauchet's residence? A Mr Philip Morel."

Wright sucked in his breath. "Bauchet doesn't exist," he said seriously. "He's a front. Tell me who else lives on his patch."

Marsh pressed a few buttons, and didn't see Dr Wright close his eyes in horror as he read off the names. The actual syllables meant little: it was the sheer number of the 200 non-existent, company-owning people that shocked him the most.

Philip Morel's arm was stronger than he had ever expected.

Aldo had also been watching the news. The closure of Lapcon had shocked him badly, and he knew it was only a matter of time before someone traced it to Philips door. He cursed the Frenchman and picked up the phone. "Philip," he demanded.

"It's worth it," Philip replied calmly.

"They could trace this to your door."

"Too little too late," Philip interjected smoothly. "I've completed the process. The second batch of French unanuminium will be packaged and sealed in the next hour."

Aldo froze. "You're not serious?"

"Welcome to the new world order," Philip replied smugly. For the first time in his life, he felt like he'd achieved something. The amount of deaths, stolen information, and the fact that he had merely adjusted the work the army had already done never occurred to him. He would eventually have got the same results by patience and hard-work, but despite his cleverness, these were never gifts granted to him.

"Absolutely magnificent," Aldo whispered, all anger completely evaporating. "Then we can dispose of the British gas?"

"Correct. Our team is in position?"

"They moved into Portsmouth yesterday."

Philip let a small glint enter his eyes. "Our painful conquest is nearly complete."

Aldo nodded. "I'll order the attack." He disconnected and turned to his other line. "Ashal?"

"Here."

"You heard?"

"Every word."

"Then you know your timetable."

Ashal-Ruhi smiled. He was a meticulous and efficient assassin, and all of his hundred-man force was primed and ready for action. "We changed the plan a little," he said quietly. "Part of the Portsmouth industrial estate came up for lease, so we've moved operations there."

"Any problems?"

"The roof leaks, but it's close to the road. We've got over 2000 square feet of floor for the vans, and plenty of space for weapons."

"Then I can expect a stable victory?"

Ashal looked around him at his operation. Numerous vans, intriguing steel girders attached to their sides, lay waiting alongside a wall. Guns were stockpiled, and his men were either sleeping on floor-mats or constructing bombs at a long workstation. The warehouse was only 20 meters away from the intersection on Southampton Road, and there he would place his attack. His plan was simple, bordering on the mundane even, but he had the numbers and the doggedness to pull it off. "Definitely."

Chapter 25

Hayden and Joey collected the satellite photos at the Embassy, much to Hayden's relief. It seemed Dr Wright hadn't given up on them just yet. There were also train tickets to Lyon and then onto Chambéry, the nearest major town to that section of the Alps. They could hire a rental car and complete the last stretch of journey from there.

Hayden rang Dr Wright to thank him. "We weren't sure if you were turning us in," he grinned.

We know more than you do over here," Wright replied, sounding stressed. "The situation is getting urgent. A team of accountants uncovered Philip's scheme this morning." He recounted the Frenchman's arrangement of businesses, not omitting the fact that three genetic foundations were uncovered. He also mentioned Lapcon Industries.

"It looks like Philip was following us from the beginning," Hayden said gravely, recollecting the hacker to Wrights system. "Although what he gained from switching internet sites I don't know."

"Confusion I'd guess. Unsettle the opposition. Anyway, seeing as you're already over there I didn't think it necessary to pull you back," he carried on. "It's more urgent than we supposed. Philip reaches all over the globe."

"How do you know that Philip controls all of the people staying at his house?"

"We checked with the French. They were all legitimate people at one point, but everyone involved had two names with birth registration. It seems the genuine humans died a long time ago and Philip managed to change the date on the birth certificates. The oldest would now be over 100 years old."

"How much is he worth then?"

"Billions. Its still being looked into now, but you'd better be careful. He has weapons and a security outfit under his leash."

"We'll hit him where he least expects it," Hayden said determinedly. "Does anyone apart from you know we're here?"

"Not yet. I was planning on keeping it a secret for as long as I can, but once you come within ten miles the Defence satellites will have you. From there, you're on your own."

"Are the SAS still coming in?"

"They've doubled their force and moved the timetable up 12 hours. You have until midday tomorrow before they arrive."

Hayden glanced at his watch. A little over 24 hours. "We'll act if we have to," he replied. "If not, we'll block off the exits while the SAS do what they were trained for." He hung up and rejoined the group.

There were 11 of them, all primed and eager for a fight. Not one of them had actually shot real bullets before – blanks were used at the training ground – but there was an assured confidence and trust between them.

Joey acknowledged the news, spreading the satellite photos on the table. They had the luxury of first class carriages to Lyon: Hayden had wanted privacy as they planned their attack.

"The boundaries are here," Joey said, outlining the map with a pen. "Our main objective was to reach the central building and take Philip Morel hostage. That has been complicated by the uranium delivery, but judging by the labyrinth of underground passages I encountered with Hayden, it could be anywhere. I suggest we still concentrate on Philip, and let the SAS deal with uranium."

"The trees give us good cover until we get inside the compound," said a particularly muscled fellow. "Although once we're in we become sitting ducks to any guard who retreats to the forest. We need a clear escape route."

"Is this man to be assassinated or taken hostage?" Nik asked.

Hayden paused. "If possible, take him alive. He shouldn't put up much of a fight: it's his guards that we need to eliminate."

"How many do you reckon there are?"

Mike, the thinnest member of the team, leaned over and stared at the photos. His eagle-like eyes could tell man from tree without hesitation, and he scorned a magnifying glass. "There are about 30 men around the outer defences," he said, "including the hidden bunkers that the specialists managed to spot. We don't know about inside."

"It's a large area though," one man pointed out. "If we go over the mountain and come in from behind we'll have more miles to cover, but snipers will have a better aim and be up against more limited defences."

"And once we get inside there's less distance to the buildings," Joey added, checking the map.

"How do we shut off power supplies?" Hayden asked.

"He'll have back-up units," Joey warned.

"They will only last for about four hours," Mike said. "These external units burn up more fuel than a rocket with a bladder problem."

"That'll be more than enough time for them to find the sabotage and put them on full alert," Joey reminded them.

"We don't need sabotage," Hayden said loftily. "I'll get Dr Wright to shut the power stations down," he grinned.

By the time the team reached Chambéry a comprehensive plan was underway. Mike organised some rental cars and they headed up for the mountains. Joey, knowing that the MS Defence Satellite was soon going to be zooming down on them, wrote a note on the cars instruction manual and held it above his head, informing the army specialists of their intentions. When the note was passed onto General Anderson and then to London, a furious Foreign Secretary grilled Dr Wright to the bones before letting him speak. Eventually ATR Winchester was called and the Foreign Secretary began to realise that 11 of their recruits had been snatched for a potential suicide mission.

"None of us listened when they were taken captive and nearly starved to death. They then managed to escape, outfoxing a gang of German smugglers and putting a major drug dealer basically on the streets, and then turned up at my house knowing more than anyone outside the Official Secrets Act should ever be told," Wright lamented.

"They are no ordinary teenagers and England has let them down. I'm sorry Foreign Secretary, but there is nothing you can do about it."

Ten minutes later the SAS were on their way to France.

Joey jumped out of the car, picked up his gear and leapt into the trees. They were on a small road that weaved its way up the mountain behind Philips lair. It would mean extra hours on foot, but would give them a key tactical advantage over their adversary.

The two drivers waited until everyone was out, and then drove off the road, parking as neatly as they could in the undergrowth.

Gathering a little way in, Hayden shivered slightly against the chilly temperature. There was no snow, but even in summer the air surrounding the high Alps was thin, and frost was beginning to seep in around the edges of the forest.

"Eight miles until we can get a visual on this place," Joey whispered. He inserted an earpiece and set the frequency channel to 867, watching as the team did the same. "Lets go."

They started across the mountain, the occasional crunch the only sound to punctuate the silent forest.

"No pep talk," Hayden enquired mischievously, stifling his laughter at the strict running technique the army employed.

"No such luck," Joey returned with a slight grin, also noticing the men in front were striding forward in a carbon copy of each other. He was at the back with Hayden, moving swiftly over the hard ground in a single line.

"They like trees over here don't they," Joey muttered, annoyed at the constant weaving in and out.

Hayden said nothing in reply: concentrating instead on the frozen earth. The minutes passed in silence, and only the increasingly laboured breath told them the miles were passing: the scenery remained as bleak and dark as ever.

The navigator slowed to a brisk march to conserve strength, announcing the completion of six miles. Walking would also give them more time to spot any traps.

Nearer they drew, checking and re-checking their weapons, until the first signs of human activity entered their sights. A ring of razor sharp wire was spread across the ground, curling up until it reached head height before dropping again in vicious circles of pain. Nik pulled a set of wire cutters from his pack, but Hayden put his hand on the man's arm.

"The wire's triggered," he whispered, pointing to several posts set in the middle of the wire. A small black object was perched on top, a tell-tale red light glowing softly on the side.

"Motion sensors," Nik cursed. "How do we get past them?"

Joey and Hayden grinned in unison, both nodding at the canopy above them. "How are you with heights," Hayden teased.

"All in a days work," Joey retorted, slinging a rope around his shoulder. He climbed the tree, tied one end to a branch, and jumped over the fence. Catching hold of the tree on the other side of the wire, he lashed it to the trunk, making a rope bridge between the two trees.

Hayden followed his friend over, dropping lightly to the ground once they were sure there were no further cameras. Instead the back of a small hut arose, barely visible behind a trunk; a small red flag perched forlornly on top.

Joey motioned for the rest of the team to advance, watching as the marines tested his rope bridge. It held. All assembled, Joey led a wide route around the hut before circling and coming back at it.

"Movement," Nik whispered, and Joey flattened himself against the floor. Studying the landscape through a pair of binoculars, Nik slipped to the front and stared in the direction of the hut. He felt a trace of warmth, and guessed the hut was occupied.

Hayden joined him. "What is it?"

"That shed is guarded. I don't know who it is or what they are doing, but they could be a problem."

Hayden looked through his own binoculars. The front of the hut was furnished with steel, and two swivelling cameras were perched on the top. A man could be seen inside, reading a magazine and occasionally looking over his shoulder at some screens behind him.

"An outpost?" Joey asked, not liking the sight of more cameras.

"Looks like it," Hayden concluded. He visualised going further and further towards Philip while the net closed in from the outside. "We're going to have to take care of him," he told Joey.

Joey stood up, ordering the others to spread out and keep a look-out while they formulated a plan. "Gap between camera turns?" he asked.

"About 3 seconds," Nik replied.

"We've done harder in training," Joey said, glad he didn't have to render the cameras inoperable and then dodge an enquiry into their failure.

"How do we get his attention?"

"Throw something at his window," Joey suggested, but Hayden grinned and outlined his own plan.

Chapter 26

Captain Robert Blyth peered calmly at the weather charts pinned up on the wall. They were two hours from the port of Portsmouth, sailing quietly underneath smooth seas in the *HMS Gladiator*. The captain turned, happy with the forecast, and buzzed through to the engine room.

"Bring us up to full speed," he said. "We've got clean sailing weather for the trip in."

"Are we surfacing?"

"Orders are to stay below," Blyth replied. Despite the fact that aircraft carrier *Seagull* was floating above them, he preferred the dark murky waters under the Atlantic. The *Gladiator* carried the latest in anti-surveillance equipment, and could creep unseen through any ocean in the world. Down in the depths, she was invisible.

Robert returned to his cabin, hearing the clang of metal as his boots struck a rhythm on the gangway.

Pausing to look at his reflection in the mirror, he changed into his official uniform and called two officers to the bridge.

"Bring the cargo up from the holds," he ordered, joining them. "And keep an armed escort with them at all times."

The men nodded and departed, their professional minds not able to prevent them wondering about the special cargo they were carrying.

Rob hailed the *Seagull.* "Any issues?" he asked.

Admiral Mason came on the line. "We should have a visual on Portsmouth in ten minutes," he replied gruffly. "The land convoy has reported in and is awaiting our landing."

"Good."

Captain Blyth walked over to the navigation tables. The journey had been smooth and uncomplicated as expected. Precision navy techniques and smooth discipline had been ruled into his mind for the past 15 years, and he wasn't about to let a trip across the Atlantic ruin his image as the finest submarine captain the navy employed.

He looked up at a screen, watching the submarines GPS position as it turned to avoid a stretch of uplifted sand. With a bit of luck promotion might come his way in the following days, he thought, allowing his mind a brief wander. Shrugging, he mentally guided the ship through the coming passages, and satisfied that the route held no problems, sounded the landing alarm.

Unlike the loud sirens that are commonly associated with submarines, all notices are fed out through light signals. Noise is easily picked up underwater, so pulsating green beams swept the ship instead, creating a flurry of activity.

Captain Blyth monitored it all on the bridge; the suitcases and an armed guard beside him, and gave the order to proceed into the docking tunnels.

The submarine wove its way silently under the water, leaving no mark. The aircraft carrier remained in deeper water, leaving the *Gladiator* to pierce the shallows on its own.

Unknown to the *Gladiator*s inhabitants, the water surface above them grew darker as the sub passed under a covered hangar, the heavy steel doors clanging shut behind them.

The light beams changed to blue, signalling an ascent, and the *Gladiator* finally burst upwards in a shower of water.

Captain Blyth hurried topside and greeted Admiral Mason, who had been taken ashore by the smaller coast guard boats. The escort came with him: eight men, eight machine guns and four suitcases.

A Jeep rode up the quayside and rushed the suitcases in, peeling away to join the convoy as Captain Blyth's attentions turned to the maintenance of the *Gladiator*.

Behind him, containing three tanks, an extra two jeeps and an armoured cross country vehicle with mounted machine guns, the convoy set off into Portsmouth, leaving the safety of the navy compound behind.

Heads turned as the green-and-black tanks barrelled down the M275. Though the 2-mile motorway was accustomed to a daily pattern of navy vehicles, the deadly hulks of metal screeching past on caterpillar tires was a new sight for most.

The lead tank commander furrowed his brow as they neared 50 miles an hour: top speed for the 68-tonne animal. The sun, hidden above the metal canopy, shone brightly and warmed the interior.

He swivelled his lithe body in the cockpit and stared at the screens mounted on one wall, showing images from cameras mounted on the outside. He would have laughed at mention of an attack on English soil, but the General had ordered him to be extra vigilant on this trip, and if truth be told, he was bored.

The convoy rolled of to the left as the M275 split in two, and followed the road as it curved and then passed over the M27. The traffic was being extremely lenient about giving them room today, the commander noted. Perhaps it was because he had a tank under his foot, not an ordinary office car.

He grinned inwardly as a van tried to squeeze itself past on the slipway. He kept going and forced it onto the hard shoulder, giving a sharp blast of his whistle as he did so.

Paulsgrove Roundabout appeared on his screen, and he braked, glancing at the Industrial Estate on his left. The edges were shrouded with trees, and a lone man was walking his dog on the grass beneath, talking into a phone.

The lights changed, and he turned west onto Southampton Road, making sure that the convoy had enough time to stay together. A few civilians had to stop in order to let the 6-vehicle train pass unhindered.

The radio beeped in the tank commander's cabin. "Tank 3 to tank 1."

"Receiving."

"Making you aware of three heavy-duty vans behind us." The report was mandatory: all troops had to be aware of any possible threat, no matter how slight.

"How so?" the commander replied.

"They took advantage of the lapse in civilian movement at the roundabout to cut in behind us."

"Roger that." They were now in the middle of the Industrial Estate. Flourishing businesses were bundled onto one side of Southampton Road, but the other side was still a prime Greenfield site. Two red vans coughed into life as the navy convoy rolled past and edged their way across the flat field.

The commander glanced at them and then ahead to the next set of lights. Three more vans were waiting at the junction, and another truck lay on the opposite side of the road.

A sudden sense of foreboding swept his head, and he yelled into his microphone. "Under attack," he screamed, hearing rather than feeling the cartridge that bounced off the tanks armour.

The last two jeeps slammed their brakes on and yanked the wheels round, but already a hail of bullets began peppering the street. A burst of retaliatory fire spewed out from the tanks, but it was a futile gesture. To the lead tank commander watching through his cameras mounted on the exterior, it was like walking into a nightmare.

The seemingly innocuous vans stretched across the roads and formed barricades and cover for the men that spewed out of the back, clutching shotguns and rifles in eager anticipation. They formed lines and began peppering the hapless jeeps.

The tank commander jammed his breaks on and activated the formidable firepower housed in the OT64. 14.5mm and 7.62mm calibres opened fire into the midriff of the van blockade, ripping through metal and puncturing rubber.

Still the ambush continued, bravely defying the roar of devastation coming from the tanks. Reckless individuals attempted to cross the chasm in front of the wrecked rental vans, and the mass of men together poured single shots that formed clouds of bullets.

The armoured cross country vehicle closed its hatch and attempted to back out, thrashing its engine over the pavement and through the hedge to cross the Greenfield site. It reached the other side and lumbered back onto tarmac road before turning through several back-roads to approach the onslaught from behind.

Carnage was reigning supreme when the cross country vehicle arrived back on Southampton Road. Massively outnumbered and unaware if there was any civilian life nearby, the tanks were caught in a barrage of shotgun fire. The fortified machines withheld the onslaught with vigour, but the air was too thick to launch an effective fight-back.

The commander paused while his men hurriedly re-loaded the guns, and picked up the radio. "Request authority to blow this town to pieces," he yelled. If this wasn't a British town, he would have let loose a dozen grenades and reduced the surrounding buildings to rubble.

"You have it," Admiral Mason shouted angrily. He was watching from a helicopter, one of the first to have been scrambled after the emergency call had gone out.

The tank captain acknowledged the confirmation and patted his gunman on the arm. "Get us out of here," he said roughly.

Two rounds of high explosives burst from the tank, erupting in a ball of flame as they cannoned into the vans in front of them. The tank surged forwards, belching smoke as it climbed over the burning wreckage.

The second tank followed, and finally two of the battered jeeps shot through the barrier. The other lay in a smouldering wreckage of dust and death.

The tank's inhabitants didn't even think about celebrating: their freedom was short lived. More faces appeared in stolen cars, anger etched on their faces to show their intentions.

"Get on the motorway," Admiral Mason ordered sharply.

"What's the situation?" the tank captain replied, his breath laboured.

"Back-up forces are on their way from base," the Admiral said tersely. "Turn around at the next junction and we'll catch these convicts between the hammer and nail."

The tanks responded, surging forward under the relative safety of the tunnel beneath the M27. The commander looked uneasily at his co-driver as they entered the subway. If this falls down, he thought, there's going to be hell to pay.

Ashal-Ruhi watched the tanks pile through the vans and grinned at them leaving. He hurried forward to the savaged jeep, his heart fairly thumping in his mouth. He leapt into the air at the sight of four steel canisters nestling in the boot: their only successful target wielding the greatest prize.

Ashal grabbed the cases from the back of a jeep and held them aloft. He had no idea how many of his countrymen had died in the ferocious assault, but he knew it would be well worth it.

A small cheer went up, and Ashal settled the cases on the ground. "Blowing the cases will cause an explosion instead of releasing the gas," he said. "Portsmouth would be obliterated, but our lives may be spared for other duties if we achieve a slow release." He grinned: the thought of Britain suffering from their own gas too much for his discipline.

A small blue car raced through the wreckage and stopped inches from Ashal's right foot. Several men jumped out with the scandium mixture. It was carefully applied to the suitcase handles, and the men sat back to wait. There was nothing that could stop them now.

The tank commander pulled his tank around in Port Way T-junction and shunted one of the chasing cars to the side. Tortured metal screamed as the hideously exposed Renault span across the pavement and lodged itself under a tree.

The other tanks copied the manoeuvre and stood three-abreast, straddling the road. Only a short distance separated them from the tunnel underneath the M27. The terrorists lay around the corner.

"There is only one way to end this," Admiral Mason said calmly over the microphone. "And that solution lies in front of you. Bravery, skill, efficiency, and a dogged phlegmatic spirit is where the navy finds pride in its employees. Stand strong. None of you are destined to die today."

"Calm down boss," the commander said jokily, breaking the tension, but the Admiral's words were not lost on the men's ears. Confidence renewed by a stolid determination flooded back across the shaky crews, and they roared off down the road.

"All units slow," the commander ordered suddenly, braking just before dim lights on the tunnel walls enveloped his tank. "Tank 3 stop and wait at the entrance. Tank 2 follow me." He grinned at his hair-brained scheme. "We're going over the motorway."

He gunned the throttle and edged the powerful machine off the road, climbing the banks to the motorway. They crashed through the safety barriers and spun onto tarmac. Traffic had already been halted by the navy helicopter.

"Guns primed," the commander said eagerly, ploughing through the second safety barrier and down the embankment on the other side. "Unleash!"

A volley of smoking missiles exploded from the twin turrets, sending up clouds of dust where they erupted. Chunks of tarmac flew into the surrounding men and flattened trees with debris.

The terrorist forces split in panic: each running for their lives as shells pounded the road. Most of the group headed in the only direction available to them, and fled into the tunnel.

"They've gone under the motorway," the commander yelled. "Repeat, they've gone under the motorway." His mouth tightened grimly: the other tank was waiting at the other end. It would be a bloodbath.

He spun the turrets and fired at the side of the bridge, throwing a cloud of dust and smoke into the bedraggled men. A few attempted to fight back, but were quickly overwhelmed.

"Suicide bombers," Admiral Mason yelled, having a clear view from the chopper.

The commander watched in horror as a vague figure approached his tank and dove onto the shell. The cameras disappeared in a ball of flame.

"Request uplink to chopper camera," the commander shouted, letting off a hiss of gas in response.

"Use infra-red and get your shields up," Mason replied. He whispered a few words to the pilot, and a minute later an enormous smoke bomb covered the road.

The leading tank raised its protective shield. The commander pulled on infra-red goggles and stared through the exposed windshield. "Suitcases 90 degrees," he said brusquely. "I'm going out."

He leapt through the hatch and jumped off the tank, quickly covering the distance and hauling the suitcases back to safety.

"Get out of there," Mason ordered. "Infantry are half a minute out." He sighed as he watched the tanks roar off into the distance. He still couldn't grasp how an attack like that hadn't been spotted. Shaking his head, he called Dr Wright. "You're one lucky man," he said, recounting the battle. "But the cargo, the fake cargo, is now on it's way."

Wright gasped as he hung up. He knew he'd been wise to have launched the scandium as a decoy, but to have terrorists actually attempt it was unbelievable. It was beyond anything he could ever have envisioned, and he'd nearly paid with the lives of millions of people.

He thought back to Mason's words. *The cargo is on its way.* It was obvious that Philip Morel must have had a reason for the attack, and there was only one conclusion: he'd copied the army and no longer needed their gas. He thrust his head in his hands, knowing that the world's only hope lay with two teenagers, somewhere in France.

Chapter 27

The security guard adjusted his chair and glanced at the computer on the wall. He had often wondered who would encounter his fortified hut in countless square miles of freezing forest, but had a good stock of books and DVDs to keep him entertained. The rifle leaning by the door was oiled and well maintained, but had soon become merely a symbol of force in the wilderness: the last bullet to leave its barrel had been in Africa several years ago.

He scratched his head and turned a page, when a loud thumping sound echoed through the cabin. He swept round to look at the camera network that sent images to his computer, watching a replay of a large tree crashing to the floor.

He pulled on his gloves and opened the door, grabbing his rifle moments before a carefully placed tranquilizer dart shot into his neck.

Nik admired his handiwork before switching his rifle back to automatic and getting to his feet. He waited for the camera to swing to the end of its loop, and then sprinted forwards with three others. They reached the hut, hauled the inert body inside and waited for the rest of the team to follow.

Hayden arrived, and spotted the camera screens in the corner, still replaying the falling tree. "Hayden the Magnificent strikes again," he grinned.

Joey saved the scene onto a disk and handed it to Hayden. "For your collection," he said, before turning his attention to the stairs in the corner. Mike had been guarding it since he arrived: a downwards spiral staircase that opened to a dimly lit passageway once underground.

Joey glanced at Hayden, the memory of their stay all too familiar, and gingerly descended. A solid door blocked the way, but there was no camera recognition. Instead, a hand scanner hung on the wall.

Mike studied it before taking out a screwdriver. "Piece of cake," he said, fiddling with the wires. Sure enough, the door clicked as Mike put his hand on the adjusted plate.

The team donned masks and gently pushed the door open, rushing into the room in hit squad formation. It was empty apart from a man at a desk, who was unconscious before he could blink. A few filing cabinets sat in the corner with a lamp, and a set of windows lined one wall. It looked desolate and sparse, as though still in the 1950s. Faded paint and murky bulbs flickered off the walls. Hayden switched the lamp off, using the light that was streaming in through the windows.

He walked over, looking out into an expansive cavern. Arced lights hung from the ceiling, casting a cruel white glare over the contents of the cave. It looked like a storehouse: piles of furniture lay forgotten under sheets, and amongst them was an assortment of junk and rubbish. Computer monitors were littered along the floor, and bits of glass collected in the corner.

Joey called him over and flicked through a book. "Records," he said, pointing. "It seems that when Philip needs some new equipment, he dumps the old stuff in here."

"You mean that whenever something goes out of date he carts the old stuff down here and buys whatever is new."

"It'd make sense if he's dealing in atom reconstruction," Joey admitted. "Selling this stuff would only lead to questions."

"I won't grudge it against him though," Hayden said. "It's our way into his castle." He nodded towards the door.

Joey signalled for the team to follow him and, guns primed, they advanced onto the main floor. Spreading out in pairs, the remaining area was efficiently made secure.

"Two men down with tranquilizers," Nik said lightly, walking back into the middle of the cavern.

"Our side was clean," Joey replied, reporting that they had the area under control. The only exit was a single tunnel that provided Philip with access to the cave, blocked with a secure circular door.

Hayden joined them with the remaining force. "Any cameras?"

Mike shook his head. "None."

"What about the door?"

"Nothing a bit of dynamite can't solve," grinned Joey. "But we need to be careful in those tunnels."

"We can borrow their golf carts," Hayden said, pointing to a booth near the entrance of a small tunnel. He walked over and examined the dials. "Nice of them to leave the keys in the ignition," he commented, pushing the power button. A smooth electric purr filled the room, and Hayden backed the vehicle up.

"Split into three teams," Joey advised, starting another cart. "If we reach a fork we'll split up. It'll take too long to go if we stick together."

Hayden laughed. "I hate to point out the obvious, but look at the roof."

Joey arched his eyebrows before flicking them up to the green cover. "Well forgive me if I don't think like a French person," he said sarcastically. He took Mike's screwdriver and unscrewed the map from the roof, setting the hard plastic on the passenger's seat.

Nik chuckled to himself and examined the door. Not wanting to blow through it – the resulting noise would be amplified throughout the whole underground network – he put his shoulder to it and pushed. The hinges creaked faintly.

"Bring the spare golf cart," he grinned. "And give the wheel to Steve."

Steve, the group daredevil, lined up the door and hurtled into it as fast as the cart would let him. The door bounced slightly, throwing Steve from his seat. He stopped himself before he went over the steering wheel, and returned to have another shot.

This time the door cracked at the hinges, and Nik was able to push the rest out of the way.

Joey climbed into the lead cart, glancing determinedly at his friend behind the wheel, and gave the order to enter the gloom.

Hayden took a deep breath, feathering the pedals as he wove the golf cart around the broken door, and crept down the small tubular network. Light came from dim bulbs hanging on dusty wires from the ceiling, reflecting off the carts and throwing eerie shadows on the wall.

"Intersection coming up," Joey whispered, staring at the map. "Take the left fork."

The turning was sharper than Hayden expected, and a small bump revealed the vehicle would be leaving some paint behind.

"Can't you learn to drive properly?" Joey complained easily, breaking the tension.

"Not my fault the wheels are made of cardboard," Hayden muttered. He was referring to the tyres beneath the plastic body, which, although silent, had a habit of steering on their own.

"How are they at high speeds?" Joey knew that escape plans hadn't been made, as they didn't know how events would turn out. For all they knew Philip might have hidden himself underground, where he could hide for years.

"Risky, but I can manage," Hayden replied confidently. "If not we can blow them to block the tunnel and run."

Joey nodded and warned of another fork. "Slow down," he muttered.

Hayden looked at him quizzically: their speed hardly warranting a decrease, but slowed to a walk anyway. The light grew brighter as they drew near, spilling out of one of the passages.

Hayden stopped his cart while Nik clambered out of the back and sprinted to the opening, peering cautiously into the left channel. He walked back and reported that the light was merely a boosted light bulb with more power than its tunnel cousins.

Hayden turned the corner and found the boosted light bulb was in fact a floodlight. Its function was to overlook the bay of golf carts, and shielded a door carved into the wall.

Hayden paused again, staying in the darker part of the opening and allowing his eyes time to acclimatise before he planned to try the door. It looked secure, but rust was dotted in places to suggest weakness.

"There's a camera behind that light," Nik whispered, staring seemingly at the light. The powerful glare was an ideal place to hide a camera behind: it could remain virtually invisible while getting the best view of the well-lit enclosure.

Hayden and Joey immediately backed up until their legs felt the cold front of the golf cart. "Sniper sights won't block the light out," Joey said, thinking of a way to get a clean shot at the camera.

"This leads into the main house?" asked Hayden.

Joey nodded.

"If we want to take the camera out we might as well douse the light," Hayden reasoned. "If they're going to investigate a failed camera then we might as well double their work."

Joey nodded again, pulling out a compact handgun. He gripped the butt in two hands and refaced the light before it disappeared at the second bullet.

Nik, with his back to the light to protect his eyes from temporary light-blindness, sensed the drop in brightness and turned to face the camera. It was dead before Nik's mind registered the shot.

Mike stepped forward, unwrapping a bottle of clear fluid from his pack and applying it to the hinges of the door. Within a few minutes the sound of rusting iron could be heard as the cold acid ate its way into the frame.

Mike crept forward to top up the potion, but froze when he heard the scraping sound of the lock. He flattened himself behind the door as a burly guard stepped out, barely escaping being crushed as the metal frame swung open.

Gripping the remaining acid in his right hand, Mike pulled his handgun out of his waistband, waiting to pounce the minute the guard closed the door.

Nik crouched in the shadows with Joey and Hayden. He'd pulled them back as soon as he'd detected Mike's pause, and his vision now held a torch-wielding guard.

He held his hand flat, delaying the decision to fire despite the dozen guns trained on the hulking body. He doubted the single guards appearance. He was dressed casually in blue camouflage gear; a black beret perched loftily atop the short black hair. Nik breathed a sigh of relief at the lack of body armour.

The first guard paid scant attention to the broken light, instead focusing on the tunnels that spewed off to the right and left. He investigated a few lengths down each, but found nothing amiss.

Nik held his weapon steady as he retreated back into the subway, staying out of sight of the torch beam. He knew the rest of the team, lodged in the other fork, would follow suit, and pursued the lonely guard as he stopped and returned to the depot.

Sure enough, the man spoke into the open door, bringing out a further three men with his words.

"Fire," Nik barked, stealth no longer an issue. Muffled claps instantly rang out before the guards could pinpoint the location of the shout.

Mike emerged from behind the door, still clutching the bottle of acid. He stared at the dents in the metal before grinning at the materializing team. "You still can't shoot straight," he grumbled, poking his finger in one of the cavities.

Chapter 28

Nik joined his team emerging from the other tunnel and poured through the door into Philips complex. The hole revealed a lift, and all 11 men squashed in, guns pointing towards the ceiling. A soft whirring told them that they were on their ascent.

The lift began to slow and Hayden readied himself for the entrance, but it suddenly sped up again and resumed its journey towards the sky.

The doors opened onto a thickly carpeted corridor. Paintings graced on the walls, punctuated by carved doors that led into various rooms. The silence hung over the men like a vice after the lift.

"Directions?" Nik asked. They hadn't been able to get hold of the building blueprints and were trusting to blind luck.

Hayden sniffed. "Left," he said impassively.

Nik raised his eyebrows.

Hayden broke into a grin and retracted his last statement. "It's as good a guess as any. Which way is north?"

Joey pointed towards the wall.

Hayden glanced at the length of the corridor. "Philip had south-facing windows. We're in a separate building."

Mike glanced hurriedly at the satellite map. "It could be that one," he offered, pointing a long rectangular building nestled under a short cliff. Philips house lay a short distance to the right.

"Then we head straight on," Hayden said, glancing out of a window and realising they were above ground level. "We need to find some stairs."

They traversed the whole length of the building without encountering anyone, but a lack of stairs jabbed the fortune.

"Check the rooms," Hayden ordered. He was beginning to get a bad feeling about the stillness that clouded the mist-like air.

Adrenaline surged through his veins as he ran into the first side room, suddenly feeling an urge of haste. It was an office, spartanly furnished with a filing cabinet and metal chair. No-one occupied the space behind the desk. Hayden ran his finger along the surface and left a deep swipe in the dust that lay inch-thick on the table. It had obviously been deserted a long time ago, he thought, his sense of unease growing. He glanced at the double-layered, bullet-proof glass in the windows, and returned to the corridor. Reports told the same dilapidated state in every room.

Joey came out of a far office and sprinted back down the corridor. "Philips network," he panted. "The people that supposedly live here and own multi-national corporations. These are their offices."

"You mean this whole building is a façade?" Hayden asked.

Joey nodded. "I found the desk with Lapcon Industries on it. Looks like he set this place up to deter any investigations."

"Apparently no one has," Hayden said, still not settled with the environment. "Let's take the lift back down."

No sooner than the words left his mouth the lift began its rotational whirring.

Hayden closed his eyes in anguish. "It's a trap," he said quietly.

Joey stared at him and then quickly realised his friend was right. The jerk of the lift must have been the override button that had carried them up. Now they were faced with one exit that Philip was in control of. "Far room," he said, tossing a chunk of putty on the floor.

Nik crowded his team into the furthest rooms from the lift. The desks were upturned and placed across the corridor as a makeshift barrier, while Hayden studied the windows. All the offices had the same impenetrable glass. "I hope you can get through this," he said to Joey, as the first bullets began to whistle along the corridor.

Joey looked at him. "You're kidding."

"How else are we going to get out?" he asked simply, choosing to ignore the drop to ground that would follow.

"Our explosives are lined up along the corridor," Joey said sickeningly.

"Looks like it's the filing cabinet then," Hayden grinned.

Any argument from Joey was quickly quelled, and they manhandled the filling cabinet sideways onto the floor. It was too heavy to carry fully laden, yet taking the fake documents out would weaken the impact.

"Damn," Joey exclaimed. "The carpet's too thick to slide on."

A real sense of dread followed as the noise outside increased. Nik pulled one of his men inside and hastily bandaged up a wounded arm. "I wouldn't mind a ride out of here," he shouted, strain in his usually calm voice.

Hayden looked at Joey. "If you don't like the carpet, file a complaint," he grinned. "Although the Nice Housing

Committee might want some evidence." He moved to the wall and stuck a knife along the skirting, pulling up the red material.

"What are you doing," Nik yelled in bewilderment.

Joey looked up. "We don't like the decorating," he explained, adding his efforts into ripping up the flooring.

Hayden piled up the carpeting in the corner, choking out some of the dust. "Got any lubricant?" he asked, eyeing the rough wooden floor beneath.

Joey called Mike over the radio, who quickly appeared with another bottle of his special lotion. "It's my last one," he grimaced.

Hayden thanked him and asked if Steve was still in a fit shape. The bullets were now coming thick and fast and the noise was deafening, but Nik bravely held his gun out the door and emptied several magazines back through the smoke, shouting for Steve.

Steve tumbled through the door and immediately grasped the situation. "You need some muscle?"

"Our guest would like to take a trip downstairs," Hayden buzzed. Any thought of failure was instantly brushed from his mind as he tried to calculate their chances. He gave up and turned to Joey. "Is this going to work?"

"Doubt it," Joey said confidently.

"Worth a try," Steve said jovially, flexing his arms.

All three men got behind the filing cabinet and rammed it forward. It slid easily over the liquid and crashed into the glass. It cannoned back, knocking them off their feet.

Joey crawled over and inspected the wall-high window. "Not even a dent," he said sourly.

Steve rubbed his shoulders and looked forlornly at the filing cabinet. "We need more men," he cursed.

"Can we afford it?" Joey yelled. The blasts outside were getting louder.

"We have to afford it," Hayden replied seriously. "Have they set off the explosives yet?"

Steve shook his head.

"Then get as many men as we can fit in here and tell Nik to blow the fuse," Hayden said angrily.

Nik sent four men in to help: he was waiting until the last moment to blow the corridor and needed as many guns as he could wield. Space permitting, he would have had Hayden and Joey flourishing their own guns alongside him.

Joey levered two of the chair legs off the metal seat and wedged them through the roof of the filing cabinet. The smaller contact force would channel the impact. Then he stood back and admired his rough handiwork with a grim smile on his face.

The seven men crowded round the squashed filing cabinet. Steve was directly behind it, tensed against the wall like a coiled spring. Silence, and then "FIRE!"

Once again the filing cabinet rushed forwards, pushed by the fate of 11 lives. This time it stopped upon smacking the glass, its front end embedded in the window. A hiss of air escaped from between the two panes. Hayden's heart leapt. Without the compressed air as a buffer the glass strength waned, and they were able to kick out the remaining fragments with a salvo of bullets.

"I sure hope they haven't realised what we're doing?" Hayden muttered, staring down at the earth below.

"Why?" Joey shouted back.

Hayden pointed at the landscape. "We can either run for the trees or face a 200 yard dash across open ground to Philips house."

"We came here to do a job," Joey said determinedly, leaving no doubt as to their next more. He signalled for Nik to blow the explosives and turned grinning back to Hayden. "Do you need me to catch you?"

Hayden smiled off the sarcastic remark, amused that Joey could still find humour in the dire situation. "Go," he nodded, leaping down as a huge blast rocked the building.

Within seconds he was sprinting towards the white-walled mansion, a consignment of armed men running behind him.

The four swift-moving shadows blurred the strong lines of the mountainous Alp. A trained eye would identify them as 532 Cougar Helicopters, proudly displaying the British Army ensign. A top speed of 203mph made it the fastest military chopper capable of carrying a crack SAS team, kept in a constant state of readiness should the need arise.

"I wonder what the French will do when they realise we're flying covertly through their airspace," their leader said. A short but tough man with the traditional crew-cut hairstyle, he had served in Bosnia and Iraq during his stint with the SAS. His nickname of Johnson had grown out of the latter part of his service, which amused him somewhat as he had no idea why, but he knew from experience that humour was a good force on the strained battlefield, and so Johnson he remained.

Johnson turned and surveyed his team: they were silently checking their weapons. Two dozen men, silent, purposeful and deadly. He'd never seen such dedication and loyalty anywhere; these were men he'd trust his life with. "How much further?"

"10 minutes 30 seconds," his pilot replied automatically, lifting the cyclic to gain height over a snow-covered peak.

The remaining minutes were spent watching the landscape fly by. The pilot announced a visual sighting of the target, and banked the Cougar on a sharp turn before dropping out of the sky to land.

Johnson looked out and saw the white structure sitting proudly in the middle of a grassy expanse. Fences and walls were strung around the borders like string, and he could see that it was clearly manned. He spotted a dark blotch on top of the white roof, and shouted a warning as his eyes discerned the gunner.

A burst of automatic fire rang out, forcing the pilot to veer violently to one side. The armoured fuselage took a few dents, but the rotor blades escaped unhurt.

Johnson held onto a support strap as the manoeuvre threatened to fling him across the hold. "Keep two choppers manned and in the air," he rasped. "Pull back until we can find a place to land."

The cockpit acknowledged his order and forwarded it to the other aircraft. They swung broadside to the mansion and opened their cargo doors, revealing rows of muzzles to the determined defenders.

"Wake up lads," the pilot murmured. "Reinforcements have arrived."

Chapter 29

Nik heard the deep rumble of rotary engines and looked up as he ran, recognising the Cougar helicopter. A gun was waving out of the cockpit, and Nik reached for his radio. "Damn it's good to hear from the SAS," he gasped over open frequencies.

There was a pause, and then the gunship replied. "You're the British Marine Corps from Winchester?"

"Sure am. Get the sentries off our backs, and we'll meet for martinis in Paris."

The person handling the radio didn't sound too pleased. "Get out of here," the voice said tersely. "We'll tear this place apart."

"We're taking Philip and heading for the exit now," Hayden replied, listening in on his headset. He swept round the first corner, feet powering forward despite heaving lungs from the effort. He found what he was looking for: the floor-to-ceiling windows that belonged to Philips study.

Joey caught up with his calorie-burning friend, releasing a spray of bullets that cut the glass in half. How ironic, he thought, that Philips own house lacked the protection that he gave a block of unused offices.

Philip looked up, startled at the sight of a dozen armed men tumbling through his windows. "Who are you?" he choked in French.

"You don't recognise me," Hayden grinned, still flushed with adrenaline. "What a shame!"

Philips eyes widened in shock as Hayden's face shone through the dust and grime, stuck moss-like to his skin with sweat. "Impossible!" he whispered.

"You don't know how glad I am to prove you wrong," Hayden said, his eyes glinting. "I never got a chance to thank you for your hospitality, so I thought I'd offer you mine."

Two marines stepped forward and hoisted the boy into the air.

A stray bullet whined into the study. Hayden ducked and glanced back out to the garden. "Looks like we're leaving," he said, gesturing at the guards who had caught up.

"Back to the tunnels," Joey yelled, surging forward down the horribly-familiar passageway.

"Are you sure you can remember the way?" Nik bellowed from behind.

"If I get to something I don't recognise, we've gone the wrong way," Joey shouted back.

Running down a staircase to avoid the lift, Joey burst through a door. It was similar to the one they'd destroyed earlier, but no rank of electric cars lay waiting for them. He checked his compass to get a vague direction, and led the team at a fast jog into the dimness.

The echoing footsteps sounded hollow and loud to Joey's ears. He knew the network of underground tunnels was vast, and hopefully that would discourage their pursuers, but he couldn't shake off the feeling that, if found, they would face a certain death.

He had set a blistering pace after crudely blocking the entrance to the tunnel, and several of the men were suffering from cramp pains. Philip had been passed like a rag-doll from man to man to conserve strength, and had gradually fallen silent during the ordeal.

Much against his instincts, Joey slowed to a brisk walk. He was confident no one would catch them on foot, but the golf carts were another matter.

Hayden joined him up front. "How much further?" he asked. The stale air was demoralising, and the notion of being lost underground was far from pleasant.

Joey shook his head. "I don't know," he said heavily.

They trekked on, cautious of the time. Hayden put his hand on Joeys shoulder, motioning for him to stop. A faint squeak of rubber on stone could be heard in the distance.

"Douse the lights," Joey hissed, dropping to the floor.

Gradually the overhead lights disappeared with a quiet ping as Nik displaced them with darts from his gun. The corner in front provided the only light: Nik couldn't see the bulb to get a clear shot.

"Keep your silencer on," Hayden whispered, watching Nik unscrew it. "We're going to need it."

A minute later, the golf cart Hayden had heard rounded the corner. The driver paused at the lack of light, but it was too late.

To Nik, the light behind the cart backlit the scene and gave every outline. He filled his sights with the man controlling the cart and quickly neutralised him.

Hayden ran up to the cart and peered in. The unconscious man had a small dart in his temple and leaned to one side as the dead weight squashed his spine. He hefted the man out and shook his head in amusement: there was no way they would fit 11 men on the tiny cart.

"Looks like we need volunteers," he grunted, but Joey brushed him aside.

"We can easily manage," he said broadly. "But it will mean driving properly." He threw a sideways glance at Hayden.

"You fit us on and I won't shake anyone off," his friend retorted, climbing behind the wheel.

Hayden watched with trepidation as Joey wedged five soldiers on the roof. The rest piled into the four-seat ground floor, and with a wince at the straining engine, his foot pushed the pedal towards the floor.

Joey looked fleetingly at the roof above. He'd chosen the lightest bodies to burden the frail sheet of plastic, but wasn't entirely sure whether it would hold. The map was providing vital stiffness, and he had to crane his neck to navigate.

He breathed a sigh of relief. "We're nearly out," he said, realising where they were. "About another 5 minutes."

The news was greeted with silence: the atmosphere had become too tense to hold a normal conversation. Philip twisted uncomfortably, unable to shake the grip of the impassive marine.

"You will never get out," he muttered.

"Shut up," Joey said, yawning.

The growing light indicated they were nearing the cavern, and Hayden shot over the broken door, nearly sending Mike tumbling off the roof.

Mike managed to hold on, but slipped off as soon as the cart stopped, leading the way at a run up the stairs. Everything was as they had left it: Philip's eyes numbing as he found that there was already a way out.

Hayden overtook Mike and surged out into the stinging wind. He searched for and found their exit tree and lifted himself into the lower branches. The rope – suspended between his tree and an oak the other side of the barbed wire – had partly frozen, allowing tiny icicles to grace its underbelly.

He slipped once, grazing his hands, but quickly scrambled on, and soon all 11 men were escorting Philip across the cold Alp steppes, the cold booming of SAS guns fading behind them.

Chapter 30

Hayden and Joey saluted the SAS choppers as they circled ahead. The craft had emptied their personnel onto Philips complex, and were free to roam the skies. Two had stayed to support with air-to-surface missiles, but the others were shadowing the marines from Winchester, who were now heading back down the mountain in their rented cars.

"I wonder what our illustrious Home Secretary will make of this," Hayden said, grinning at the portly figure his mind conjured up.

"He probably won't leave us alone," Joey replied dryly. "Politicians use anything to bolster their career."

Hayden stayed silent, wondering what would happen now. Everything seemed over, and strangely, he felt bored, as if there was nothing left to do. A buzzing vibrated on his hip, and he unclasped the phone from a stiff belt. "Hello."

Dr Wright's smooth voice filled his ear. "We have you on satellite."

Hayden raised one hand and waved wearily at the sky. "Nice to know you kept an eye on us."

"All part of the job," Wright reassured. "I managed to cajole the French Air Force into lending us a jet. It's scheduled to land at Pointery Air Field in about 20 minutes to whisk you straight back to Stansted."

"Who takes care of Philip?"

"The French will. A division of their people will arrive on the plane." He sounded a little peeved. "I'm not too happy about it, but seeing as he has never actually been to England we never really had a claim."

Hayden held the phone to his chest and leaned across the seat, notifying the driver of change in destination. He thanked Dr Wright and hung up.

Upon descending the rocky Alps to Pointery Airfield, an ungainly craft lay waiting, squat on the tarmac. Mike, a military book-fanatic, identified it as a Breguet Atlantique. A propeller-driven patrol plane, it was ideally suited for reconnaissance due to its 5000 mile range, but its designers had managed to fit a solid array of weapons into the corpulent jet.

A formal-looking soldier marched up, and Hayden stood back while Nik breezed through the formalities. He scrutinised the surrounding landscape: the airfield was no more than a dreary field among the nestle of steep mountainside. The sun still shone faintly in the sky, although lower now as dusk began to creep in round the edges.

Nik presented Philip, who was roughly bundled into a van by two silent-faced marines. Salutes were exchanged, and Hayden was gestured in the direction of the Breguet. Exhaustion lingered somewhere in the back of his mind, slowly fighting its way forwards, and he collapsed on a seat.

Joey joined him as the plane started its take-off. The force slammed him back into his chair, but he enjoyed the sense of power that held him there.

The Breguet clawed its way heavenwards, leaving the frozen mountains drifting under its belly as it struggled for altitude. Soreness eventually blossoming into life, Hayden closed his eyes and quickly fell asleep.

Joey shook Hayden awake when the Breguet touched down at Stansted, the wheels screaming their customary howl of protest as they torched onto the runway in a flame of smoke.

Hayden glared out of the window, warily watching the unused hangar they were heading to. A blue car was waiting to greet them, looking surprisingly resplendent with a shimmering new coat of paint.

He approached the man leaning on the bonnet. Dr Wright turned easily, his grey eyes gleaming under the wisps of thinning hair. "I suppose I'm glad to see you again," he said, smiling slightly.

"I hope we haven't pulled you out of your way," Joey replied jovially.

"Not at all. The Home Secretary was about to court-martial me after learning that I'd sent you to France, so I took your return as a chance to escape," he said airily.

"So what's the schedule now?"

Dr Wright paused and looked uncomfortably at his fingernails. "Have you heard about Portsmouth?"

"What about it?"

Wright bit his lip. "We brought the gas back from America in a submarine, and an armoured convoy was supposed to take it from there to Greenham Air Base."

"What happened?" Joey said anxiously.

"We were ambushed. Over 400 men took over part of the industrial estate and blocked the roads off."

Joeys mouth dropped. "400 men attacked a British town?" he whispered, flabbergasted.

"I know," Wright said sourly. "The tanks managed to blow their way through with the gas, and the last I heard was the army were whittling them down."

"Maybe our Home Secretary won't be too pleased after all," Joey told Hayden.

"He looks capable of murder," Wright agreed.

"Get the army to broadcast pictures of Philips capture," Hayden suggested. "Those terrorists have no chance of surviving this, but I don't like unnecessary loss of life."

"We tried that," Wright said, suddenly looking puzzled. "They didn't respond at all. One report said they didn't even look French."

Hayden frowned. "So which nation did he say they were from?"

"Middle-east," Wright replied. "But no terrorist over there has this amount of power and guile. We're positive about that."

Hayden raised his eyebrows, earning a don't-try-that-with-me look from Wright.

"We're confident about this one," Wright said.

Joey looked at Hayden. "I know there are some burning questions buried in your tangled mess of a mind," he teased softly.

Hayden gave him a light punch. "Two things," he lectured slowly, still rifling through a dozen ideas. "If its true that there are terrorists from the middle-east, but there are no middle-east organizations with the means of achieving it, we can only have two possible conclusions. Scenario one; they have been ordered from people outside the middle-east, or two, which is that your man was wrong in his observations."

Wright shook his head. "I doubt that."

"Then we must ask who is capable of persuading men to die," Hayden stated simply. "And if they don't know anything about Philip, we either have one big problem, or two pieces of string that don't connect."

Dr Wright looked baffled.

"Philip and Portsmouth are either two separate events with two different groups," Joey explained, catching Hayden's drift, "or, if the terrorists don't recognise Philip, we're looking at a big corporation with powerful men all over the globe. Philip was a scientist in essence. It would make sense if he was only one of a dozen that hatched this plan. I'm guessing that there has been no Arab response to this gas until now."

Dr Wright nodded. "How did you know that?"

"They took us in under Philip, just in the odd chance that if he was discovered, it wouldn't foil their plans. Then when the ball starts rolling, they send in Arab men to make it look like a revenge attack for our involvement in Iraq."

"That would make sense with what I've picked up," Wright said, the reality suddenly dawning on him. "I think you may be right on this one."

"That just leaves us with one question," Hayden said, the blazing fire in his eyes gleaming as the disappearing sun waved a final goodbye. He looked at Joey and grinned. "I bet I can catch them before you can."

And with that, he and Joey turned and walked back towards the waiting Breguet.

About the Author

Toby Limbach is a 16-year-old author and has just left high-school. Despite his young age he has already written two books proving to be "highly creative" with his writing, and has had his work read on radio as well as gaining first place in several writing competitions during his short career. He has also been praised for a close attention to detail that complements a distinct narrative fliar. His first published book, Innocent Escape, began life when Toby was 15 and under the pressures of GCSE preparation, although he had the benefit of including part of his story in English coursework for full marks. Now enrolled at college studying English Literature, Toby feels free with his writing, taking pleasure in bringing possible but unlikely situations to life in "intriguing original fiction", as commented by one review. His unique and engaging style has been influenced by several major bestsellers including Clive Cussler, JK Rowling, Anthony Horrowitz and JRR Tolkien.